SAVAGE ENEMY

CRUEL KINGS

SAVAGE ENEMY

KELLIANN NELSON

978-1-958110-22-5
Published by Black Hearts Press LLC
hello@blackheartspress.com
Cover design by Damonza

CONTENT INFO

Some scenes and dark themes in this book may not be suitable for all readers. Visit kelliannnelson.com/content-info for specific content notes.

*For the girls who know
some enemies are worth the risk.*

ONE

VAL

I wondered about the corpse in my wedding gown while I watched my father's black sedan teetering over the edge of the bridge. Her name. Where she came from.

How did she really die?

Who had loved her?

For what felt like an eternity, the damn car didn't fall into the river. But it would—because it had to.

My freedom depended on it. My life depended on it.

"Drop, for God's sake," I whispered.

For mine.

At the last moment, the car tipped forward and plunged into the blue-green water, stunning the crowd into silence.

I let out the lung-burning breath I'd been holding.

The wake rocked the ferry beneath my feet, and the woman beside me let out a piercing shriek.

We both grabbed the guardrail.

The water settled. It was over.

Emergency sirens wailed through the streets.

In the days that followed, headlines would read, "Valentina Moscatelli, 18, Drowns in Chicago River on Wedding Day."

I doubted my fiancé would mourn—or pretend to—for even a minute. He would have a new bride within a week.

Friends and family would believe I drowned in my wedding dress, trapped in the submerged car, surrounded by floating layers of white lace.

All of them. All but my *nonna*.

After learning my father had sold me to Chicago's infamous forty-something Russian sociopath, Nonna planned my escape, managing every detail. She gave me a fighting chance to stay alive and to have the kind of life my mother never had before my father killed her.

Nonna saved me from the Mafia before Vladimir Klimov could marry me and imprison me in Bratva territory, where I would have disappeared forever. The sick bastard killed his wives when he got tired of them, usually within the first year.

My father knew this as well as anyone, but he never loved me enough to care whether I lived or died.

Only the business deal I could secure for him mattered.

Calling me his little princess didn't fool anyone.

"This is Valentina, *mia piccola principessa*," he would say whenever introducing me to potential business partners.

Most people saw through his motives and his false affection for me. His cold expressions and the way he never looked at me or touched me gave him away.

I was property.

My father believed he owned me. Like a rancher selling his prized heifer to the highest bidder seeking prime breeding stock.

Thanks to Nonna, I had a chance to escape the cruel,

depraved bastard. The life she'd planned for me offered a chance to live outside the Mafia. And maybe even marry a good, honest man with a steady job.

It didn't matter if my future husband and I lived on modest salaries. I only ever wanted a safe home with someone who wouldn't hurt me, and a warm house filled with the laughter of our children.

Nonna had arranged for a friend from the old country to put me up in her place in Brooklyn. The woman had promised Nonna she would love me like a granddaughter and help me start my new life as Valerie Salera.

Clouds drifted past the skyline, and sunlight warmed my cheeks, my shoulders, my arms, and my soul, burning away the shadows of my former life.

I tilted my face toward the sky and sighed.

As far as anyone knew, I was dead.

A soon-to-be distant memory.

The clock had started ticking the moment the paid truck driver crashed into my father's car. I had to move fast, stay on track, getting out of Chicago before my family found me. My father had connections everywhere. Associates in every corner of the world, so it seemed.

All except one.

New York.

A formal treaty between Chicago and New York kept the families from crossing into each other's territory.

No business. No bloodshed.

No visits to say hello or fuck you.

Those who broke the treaty faced severe punishments—if they even made it back alive.

Valentina Moscatelli could be taken captive in New York,

enslaved, or sent back to her father, but Valerie Salera? She was no one. Just a poor Italian girl trying to put food on her table and a roof over her head.

I slid my hand into my bag and gripped the train ticket until my knuckles turned white. A one-way ticket from Union Station to Penn Station in Manhattan.

Sunlight slipped through the bag's opening and bounced off the pistol I'd stolen from my big brother Marco's closet.

The ferry's arrival whistle blew, startling me, and I slammed my bag shut to hide the gun.

With my head down beneath a dark blue Cubs cap and my hair falling like a curtain around my face, I stepped onto the dock with the crowd and headed west toward the train station.

Sweat trickled down my back, and my pulse pounded in my ears. I watched over my shoulder during the entire thirty-five minute walk, expecting to see my father's men trailing me.

Or worse. My twin brother Aris.

If he found me, I wouldn't go back. I'd throw myself in front of a bus before I let that sadist touch me again.

His bruises and scars marked my body, a testament to years of cruelty. I could only imagine what he would do now that I'd jeopardized the family's multimillion dollar deal with the Russians.

I had no doubt. Aris would hurt me.

And our father would let him.

The evil bastard wouldn't just beat me. He would force our little brother Santo to watch. A sweet nine-year-old boy, still untouched by the realities of our life. Aris would kill Santo's soul in front of me, because he knew how much I loved my baby brother.

I stepped into Chicago's iconic train station.

With my head down and my eyes up, I scanned the great hall and found a spot to press my back against the cool marble wall and watch for familiar faces while keeping mine hidden.

A man nearby sat on a bench, talking into his phone.

"Such a shame," he said. "Pretty young thing. But her father's a monster. Everyone knows Moscatelli's no better than a common criminal. Lives in that mansion on the Gold Coast, pretending he's legit. I swear, the city would be better off without him. He's probably the reason there are so many guns on the street."

The stranger wasn't wrong.

If anything, he underestimated my father.

Saul "The Pianist" Moscatelli ran a lot more than guns. He profited from half of the heroin in Chicago, and he had no problem dealing death. He also had city officials on his payroll or in his debt—including the mayor and the police chief.

The mayor might have meant to be a good man. He campaigned on taking down the city's crime lords. But then my family got their hands on his daughter. My father let Aris do unspeakable things, and threatened worse, including releasing a video. My father took what he wanted by force.

God help anyone who got in his way. Friend, family, enemy.

The stranger on the bench suddenly let out an awkward laugh and scanned the area, his eyes flitting past me, then back again. His brows lowered like he was trying to place me.

I didn't move. Didn't dare breathe.

I ducked my head and let my hair fall forward.

And I prayed.

The man jumped up and grabbed his briefcase.

Boarding for his train must've been announced.

Fuck. He headed for the same track as mine.

My heart pounded as I raced to the sleeper car and hurried down the narrow corridor to my private room.

I slammed the door and yanked the curtain shut.

Peeking out through a small slit, I watched the man pass.

Had he recognized me?

Was he following me? Looking for me?

Fuck. Fuck. Fuck.

I didn't know what to do.

I checked the lock, unlocking it and re-locking it three times to satisfy my paranoia.

Then, for the next twenty and a half hours, curled up on the worn faux-leather two-seater instead of on the bed, I stared at that stupid metal door with the dirty red curtain.

I didn't sleep.

I refused food and drink every time the attendant knocked.

When the train finally pulled into New York's Penn Station, I closed my eyes for just a minute.

I took in a long, deep breath.

My first real breath as the free girl who'd escaped a brutal death by faking her death.

I had escaped the Mafia.

And the Bratva.

God, I hoped it would last.

TWO

VAL

NOW

arco Moscatelli's voice carried up the stairs to my son's bedroom, sending a chill down my spine.

"Open the fucking door, Vignali. Give us the girl."

My brother's voice hadn't changed much over the years, his low timbre and thick Chicago accent still crystal clear.

It took Marco only one day to track me down after the press ran Stefano's engagement announcement.

It wouldn't be easy to get away now, but I had to try.

For Enzo's sake. For Stefano's.

My father would kill them both.

Stefano had me caged in his arms, my back pressed against the wall. Fear paralyzed me, making it easier for him to hold me there, fully under his control.

The hurt in his eyes sent a shock wave of pain through my chest. I wanted to rip my heart out.

But I had to hurt him, so my boys could live.

I pulled his mouth to mine and kissed him.

The taste of whiskey and sweet citrus from his beloved old fashioned still lingered on his lips.

His addictive scent and the heat radiating from his body pressing against mine paralyzed me further. So safe. So warm. I didn't want to let go. I could hardly pull away from his mouth.

Could he take on my family and keep us alive?

I wanted nothing more than that, but the price of finding out if he could take on my father was too high to risk.

No. We couldn't take that chance with our son's life.

"I'm so sorry, Ace," I whispered.

His dark eyes narrowed in confusion, he tilted his head, and his grip on my chin softened.

"I'll take care of you, Angel. Whatever you've done, I don't care. I'll make it go away—whatever it takes."

His words broke me. I closed my eyes for a moment.

There was no other option. Enzo and I had to leave.

So, like the lying snake of a bitch I'd become, I used Stefano's tenderness to duck beneath his arm and sprint down the hall to my room.

Stefano had moved our son's room farther from mine.

I slammed the door and locked it before he caught me. Just as expected, he pounded on it and threatened to break it down.

"Val, goddamn it, open this door right fucking now or I'll tear the motherfucker apart!"

He would. That much I knew. I had to hurry.

After I quickly pulled on jeans and a sweater, I slung my emergency escape bag over my shoulder and opened the door. I brushed past him, catching him off guard, ducking beneath his arm before he could grab either of mine.

I avoided the gallery overlooking the foyer, making sure Marco couldn't see me.

Trying to avoid Marco was stupid as fuck, though. I couldn't hide anymore, not now that he'd come for me. Not even in this massive house.

Once he saw me, it would be over.

An icy chill rushed through me.

My brother wouldn't leave without me, even if he had to kill my boys and search the house himself. The fact that he dared to show up in New York meant my father knew everything, and there wouldn't be a single rock left unturned until they had me back.

Glancing over my shoulder, I caught a glimpse of Marco glaring up at the staircase. Still as beautiful as ever, though the roundness of his youthful cheeks had gone, and time had hardened his eyes.

A decade under our father, serving as the Moscatelli underboss, had changed him in all the ways this life of ours reshapes a first-born son.

In that moment, seeing what Marco had become, I had no doubt about what lay ahead. My time pretending to live freely outside of my family had come to a screeching halt.

I had faked my death, lived for so long under an assumed identity, and still, fate let them find me.

Fate was a mean bitch.

I'd always belonged to a monster, one or the other, but always a monster.

Blood rushed to my cheeks.

I gnashed my teeth.

All his fault. Stefano, the arrogant, impatient prick.

My father found me because Stefano led them to me. He had that fucking announcement published without even talking to me, telling the whole world he planned to marry me.

Me, Valerie Salera, or so he thought. A woman he would've known didn't exist if he had bothered to run a proper, mafia-style background check.

Of course I knew what he would say.

I should be thankful he gave me a hall pass—not because he trusted me but because he wanted to trust in my innocence.

Innocence that I'd faked.

Damn him. He had the resources to find out anything. He was so much smarter than that. If he'd checked into me, he never would've made that public declaration.

So yeah. It was all his stupid fucking preventable fault.

Stefano caught my arm from behind and stopped me.

He stared at me for a minute without saying a word. His mouth flattened into a hard line, and his frown deepened, but before he could say a word, I yanked away and headed for Enzo's room.

A vicious growl rumbled from deep inside his chest.

Mother of Christ—why had I thought marrying a man as dangerous, volatile, and self-centered as my father was a good idea?

Because I loved him.

Because he lit my body on fire and soothed my soul with nothing more than a sweep of his dark eyes.

I just... I fucking loved this man.

If we survived, I would kill him. And he would finally meet Valentina Moscatelli—the real one. After that he would never mistake me for an innocent little girl again.

But first, we had to survive.

Stefano stalked after me, caught my arm in his bruising grip and yanked me back against his body.

"You're going to stop running and tell me what the fuck's

going on. Who the hell is brave enough to pound on my fucking door like that, Val?"

My heart dropped into my stomach with a heavy thud.

My legs quivered and nearly gave way.

I shook my head, keeping my voice level and low. I didn't want him to know how deep my fear ran.

And I didn't want Marco to hear me either.

"I need you to go downstairs and make him leave," I whispered. "When he's gone, I'll explain everything. I swear. Just please—make him leave."

Stefano shoved me into a bathroom and closed us in.

"Give me a name, Val. What the hell did you bring into my house?"

I jabbed him in the chest.

So very stupidly, I poked the bear.

"I didn't bring anything. I didn't come here willingly. You forced me, and without doing your homework. God, Stefano, I hid your son from you. Did you ever stop to ask what else I might be hiding? How could you be so careless? Your carelessness brought this down on us."

He slammed me against the wall. My back hit the plaster, and I lost my breath. He held me there with his hands on my throat. No blue irises—just darkness. He clenched and relaxed his jaw. Clenched. Relaxed. Clenched.

"I know why you hid my son from me," he snarled.

He did, but he was only partially right.

He had no idea about the horrors I'd lived through. Even at his worst, a monster in his own right, Stefano didn't scare me like the one haunting my nightmares. Even the psycho teacher who shot and tortured me didn't top the list of my worst miseries.

I didn't have time to explain any of it.

I had to get away from him. I clung to one of my nonna's old pieces of advice, leaning into it so hard I almost fell over.

Men need to be heroes. It's our job to make them believe they are.

The idea struck me as wrong or maybe just outdated. But I had to do something. What else could I do? I pressed my palms to his chest and dipped my chin as much as I could with his hands still around my throat.

Gazing up at him from beneath my lashes, I waited just a second, hoping his eyes might soften, hoping he might listen. Maybe even hear me out.

"If you love me, Ace," I rasped, "you'll make him leave."

He shook his head, eyes narrowing, the crease between his brows deepening until it nearly folded inward. Then he dropped his hands from my throat. Still pinning me to the wall with his body, he let out a dark chuckle.

It vibrated in his throat.

"You really think you can manipulate me that easily, Valerie? I thought you were smarter than that. Now, who the fuck is at my door, and why do you think he's here for you?"

Well, damn. I should have known better.

I nodded. "His name doesn't matter. He's my past. You're my future."

Not technically a lie, but not an accurate picture either.

I hated implying there'd been something romantic between Marco and me. But if a little misunderstanding made Stefano jealous enough to get rid of him, I could fix it later. If it kept our son safe, I wouldn't correct Stefano's assumptions.

In any case, Marco wouldn't leave empty handed. So if he and Stefano fought over it before the truth came out, maybe I could grab my son and get him out the back door.

Enzo and I would have to run for our lives, this time finding underground help. Still, it beat dying.

Guilt knifed through my stomach, stealing the breath from my lungs. I didn't want to take Enzo from Stefano.

More importantly, I didn't want Enzo to lose Stefano.

My child had his father now. He had his father's strength. And Stefano was the one who had to teach him how to wield it —like a man, not a child.

Stefano gripped my arms hard as a wave of emotions crossed over his handsome face. He seemed to recognize exactly where my thoughts had strayed.

He relented with a low growl.

"Fine. I'll get rid of him. Can't guarantee he'll walk away. But first, you promise not to leave."

I shook my head, pretending I'd changed my mind. I had to get him downstairs before Marco came up.

"I won't leave without you," I lied.

Stefano scoffed. "We both know you're a liar, Valerie. You would absolutely take my son and leave if it suited your purpose. Before I deal with whatever this shit is you've drudged up, you'll promise to wait here—and our son will remain in his room. You will not run away from me like a coward again."

I stood there frozen, disarmed by him calling me a coward.

He shook me, his eyes narrowed like dangerous slits.

"You give me your goddamn word," he said.

"Don't call me a coward," I hissed. "You have no idea what awful shit I've had to run away from to stay alive. Please—just make him leave."

Stefano dropped his arms and stepped back, as if my words had slapped him.

I opened the bathroom door for him to go.

"Please," I begged.

A second male voice filled the foyer. Younger and colder but also unmistakable. Hearing it gripped my chest and squeezed my heart.

"Look, man," he said, "I don't know who you are, but I know you're not Vignali. So go get the motherfucker—now."

Santo.

The last time I saw my younger brother, he was only nine, the same as my son. Santo used to be all laughter and sunshine. Now he sounded like a stranger from one of my bad dreams. Our father had broken him.

I used to love Marco and Santo so much.

A single tear slid down my cheek.

Tony's voice cut in from the front door.

"And I don't know who the fuck you are either, asshole, so you're not getting in this house or anywhere near my boss."

Marco spoke up, cutting through the pissing match with his usual calm and confident demeanor.

"We're only here to take back what's ours. Like I said, your boss has something that belongs to my family."

"And what would that be?" Tony asked.

Stefano's hard gaze never left mine. He waited for me to answer the question, but Marco beat me to it.

"The girl. She's my sister. She's unwed, and therefore still belongs to my father. There are family obligations she's expected to fulfill. I'm sure Don Vignali understands this."

Stefano stared at me, searching my eyes for an explanation, something to ease the pain in his eyes.

Shame washed over me.

I dropped my gaze to the floor.

He'd probably pieced it together by now, and things would only get worse the more we heard from Marco and Tony.

I'd fed Stefano lie after lie. Told him I grew up as an orphan, no siblings, weaving stories about the girl I wanted to be into a fictional tale that gave me a new life.

I wanted to end the whole charade, to tell him the awful truth right there in that stupid fucking rose-scented bathroom.

"What the hell is he talking about, Valerie?" Stefano demanded.

"Please, just get rid of them," I pleaded. "Then I can explain it all. I'll tell you everything."

He grabbed my chin and tilted it up, but I couldn't bring myself to meet his eyes. I wouldn't have been able to see through the sudden blur of tears anyway.

"When I get back," he said, "you and Enzo will be here. You are mine. That boy is mine. And after I handle the situation, you will explain every-fucking-thing. Understand?"

He brushed the backs of his fingers over my wet cheeks, his gentle touch in stark contrast to his harsh tone.

I didn't want to lie anymore. I didn't want to run anymore.

But what choice did I have if I wanted him to live?

"I promise," I said.

Another lie—burning me up from the inside out.

Stefano didn't know what he would be dealing with when it came to my family. He had no idea how disgustingly savage my father could be. I wouldn't let that come down on him. I wouldn't let the cruelty and my family's sins come down on my son either. They deserved better.

Stefano pressed a hard kiss on my lips, one that almost

broke me, almost made me confess everything and beg for his forgiveness.

Instead, I swallowed the lump in my throat as he warned me one last time before he walked out, still in his plush robe, the master of his house.

The second he was out of sight, I rushed to Enzo's room.

I hated what I was about to do, taking Enzo away from his father. But I had to do it. It was our only chance.

"Gentlemen, what's the issue?" I heard Stefano ask, his tone smooth with confidence and authority.

When I opened Enzo's bedroom door, expecting to see him alone at the foot of his bed, playing the video games his father had bought him, I stopped dead in my tracks.

Two men sat there— one on either side of him.

Saul Moscatelli.

A depraved mafia monster from Chicago.

My father.

On the right side of Enzo's bed, with one hand on my son's shoulder and his other pressing a gun into my son's ribs, sat the vilest man in existence. Worse than my father even.

The demon who had tortured me throughout my childhood, who took infinite pleasure in the suffering of others, and who coveted my older brother's inheritance.

Aris Moscatelli.

My twin brother.

He wore the same wicked grin he'd had as a child.

"Hello, sister."

My breath caught in my throat.

I gripped the doorframe to keep myself upright.

A muddled mess—my mind. I couldn't think.

My gaze shifted from my father's perpetual scowl of disapproval to the stoic expression on my son's face.

"How nice of you to join us," Aris said. "I was just getting to know my nephew."

Aris placed the gun on his lap, no longer pointing it at Enzo. Now that he had my attention, he didn't need to. His unspoken threat sliced through the air as cleanly as any bullet.

He didn't need to say it. I knew. If I didn't do what he wanted, he would kill my son without hesitation or remorse.

Not one of us in the room had a shred of doubt.

Aris would do it.

I nodded.

He grinned again.

No more hiding.

I had to find another way to keep us alive.

THREE
STEFANO

Deception flashed in Val's eyes, lighting up more of her lies. Her promise to stay and to keep her damn hands off my son meant nothing. Just another attempt to manipulate me.

Mia bellissima diavoletta.

My beautiful little devil.

I moved in close to her mouth with mine.

She dug her front teeth into her bottom lip and forced me to part her pretty lips with my thumb. I pressed a hard kiss on her mouth. No tongue. No tenderness. Only a clear warning for her to stop the fucking lies or suffer the consequences.

"Make no mistake—you'll pay for the lies you tell me," I said. "Every one of them, Valerie."

Christ, ten minutes ago she'd been happy, content, ready to take on this life with me. Ready to raise our son with me.

Ready to tell me the truth.

But in the span of a minute, she'd gone from angry to terrified, her perfect ivory skin turning a stark white, the hollow of her neck fluttering with panic.

Not a moment went by when I didn't want to touch her

there, when I didn't want to hold her throat and feel her life pulsing beneath my fingers. To own it. To own her.

To own her fear...

I wanted her to fear me and only me.

Not whoever the fuck frightened her now.

I wouldn't tolerate something like that coming between us, someone else taking that from me.

Nor would I let another man hurt her.

Ah, but someone from her past waited at my front door.

God help him if he wanted to cause her pain, if he tried to ruin my future with her. I would kill him. If he'd hurt her in the past, or tried to take my family now, I would bathe in his blood.

At the staircase, I cast one more glance over my shoulder at Val and repeated my order.

"Go to our son. Stay with him until I'm done with this."

She nodded, but her eyes said something else.

Good thing I'd planned ahead. She wouldn't get far.

Earlier, I'd ordered every window, door, and gate on the estate to be locked down. Not because I worried she would run, but for my family's protection. I suspected the Commission might pull some violent bullshit to force me into taking that seat.

That security detail may have been for the Commission, but it would also keep my girl inside this house.

After realizing someone other than my own men was involved in the shit downstairs disturbing my discussion with my woman, I had first assumed the unwanted visit came from Edgardo Lordi's order to intimidate me. The dumb fuck.

Why the Commission would use threats to build my loyalty was beyond understanding. But they would do it, and it would only prove Don Lordi had become as short-sighted and foolish as my father had been.

I would deal with the Commission and their ultimatums and backstabbing after getting rid of the motherfucker making demands at my front door.

Tony, Bruce, and some of my other men stood gathered in the foyer as I approached, forming a barrier while Tony continued trading verbal jabs with our unwanted guests.

"Enough," I ordered. "Let me through."

Dread abruptly struck me in the gut as my men parted.

Fuck. I should have put Val and Enzo in the safe room and armed myself, but these men had already seen me.

Bring it on.

Whatever hell waited, I would handle it.

After that, I planned to take Val to the church and have us married in the eyes of God and the State of New York. She would go, by force if necessary.

She would come to understand one thing if nothing else.

Yes, I was indeed her fucking future.

She would learn to be grateful for it, and like it or not, she would tell me all her secrets before anything else came back to bite me in the ass.

While upstairs with Val, I had heard one man mention something about his sister. That couldn't be right.

I had a theory about what they really wanted.

Val must have stolen from them. I wouldn't put theft past my pretty little liar. It explained all the money she had hidden in her apartment.

A barista shouldn't have that much cash on hand, not even if she owned the place, not unless she'd squirreled it away for years without paying any of her bills.

Even if that were the case, I knew as an astute businessman that Con Amore couldn't be making that kind of bank without some laundering going on.

My girl. A liar, and now a thief.

It seemed cleaning up after her and keeping her tail clean could very well become a full-time job.

In the meantime, to get the immediate situation resolved, I would happily return the money she'd taken from these men and pay whatever interest they considered fair. A small price to pay for my wife to be free of Chicago's influence.

Then I planned to make Val pay her debt to me in trade.

On her knees and in my bed.

My cock twitched at the thought, and a smirk tugged at one corner of my mouth. I shook my head to clear it.

Back to business, Vignali.

One of the men had a foot and hand braced against the door to keep it open, while the older one stood there quietly.

He wasn't much older than me, mid- to late-thirties, similar height and build, wearing a black, well-tailored suit that legitimized his menacing presence.

Discomfort settled in my gut.

He had the same almond-shaped, light blue eyes as Valerie.

The asshole with his grip on my door was much younger.

His eyes matched hers too.

This one had tattoos covering his neck, disappearing into his hair. Scars marred some of his skin, and I would have wagered the ink covered more scarring. Marks that hid a story he didn't want to share.

A baby-faced thug with a past.

I could see it all in a single glance. One of the benefits that came with being the only surviving son of a crime family.

Yes, I'd seen this pairing many times before.

The businessman and the enforcer. The heir representing his family in a professional manner and the thug who broke bones when deals couldn't be brokered. One offered a dangling carrot while the other held the stick.

Christ, I was bored with their cliché-as-fuck show of force.

"How can I help you, gentlemen?" I asked.

Really, I just wanted to go back upstairs to Val and demand answers from her. Tie her to my bed and edge her until she gave in and spilled all her dark secrets. Not boring at all.

Young Thug snarled at me.

The Heir stepped in front of him and extended a hand, offering me respect.

"Don Vignali," he said, "I'm Marco Moscatelli, and this is my brother Santo Moscatelli. We're here from Chicago because you're currently in possession of something that belongs to our family, and we'd like to have that back."

I arched a brow. He could keep his fucking handshake.

"You being here on my doorstep violates the New York–Chicago treaty. I'm sure you understand I can kill you for that."

The treaty existed for a reason. Chicago lacked the civility for which the New York families were known. At least we smiled cordially before stabbing you in the back, and we did it only to protect the bottom line.

Always about the money.

Money drove New York City in every way, which meant the prominent dons could be reasoned with if profits were shared. Sure, at times some of the made men got too greedy, but even then, New York had a method to its madness.

Chicago had no such compunction. They craved violence for the sake of violence, money be damned, blood first. Anyone could find themselves in a lucrative deal in Chicago and die the next day just because one of the bosses felt like offing them.

Wars in Chicago broke out constantly. The news couldn't stop reporting all the shootings. Stupid fucks.

Not only did an underground war cost everyone millions, but it also cost lives, and a family couldn't easily replace those lives. Every made man had a dollar value tied to his experience and skill.

Wars also brought publicity.

Politicians only worked with a don they could pretend wasn't a mafioso. Hard to portray a legit businessman when your mugshot graced the front page of the newspapers.

"Who took what?" I added. "We can come up with a civil arrangement, put it behind us, and you can go back to your second-rate city."

I noted the hostility in my voice. This was my house. They were on my doorstep. They needed to keep that in mind.

Young Thug took another step forward.

Marco Moscatelli put a hand on his brother's shoulder before the kid could open his mouth. Enforcers were typically loose cannons, but Moscatelli seemed smart enough to keep his brother on a short leash.

"I assure you, I understand the terms of the treaty, Vignali. We're not here to cause New York any trouble or to disrespect you personally. A member of our family strayed, and we're only here to retrieve her. Same as you would do."

Then Moscatelli reached into his breast pocket.

Tony and Bruce raised their guns, aiming at Moscatelli's head.

The younger Moscatelli drew his pistol.

Without sparing my men a second glance, Moscatelli pulled

out a photo and handed it to me while his expression remained professionally blank.

I accepted the photo and studied the image in my hand.

Valerie. My Val.

Young, like when I'd first met her, but there was no mistaking her features. The shape of her face, her eyes, her lips.

She stood on a pedestal in what looked like a high-end dress shop, her dark hair piled on top of her head, and she wore a white wedding gown.

With her porcelain skin and her brightly stained lips, she looked like a little girl's doll.

So pretty, but with lifeless eyes.

Her rounded shoulders and her arms clasped around her abdomen revealed fear. She was a sad, frightened girl without hope. This girl was nothing like my foul-mouthed barista so full of light and fire.

Fuck. I finally saw her truth.

Val had said she didn't want to be with a killer, and I still believed that, but it wasn't the only reason she wanted out.

Now I could see it. When she left me after finding out my real name, after learning my family worked in the gray and the black, she knew our relationship was forbidden.

She knew it would bring death.

She'd been hiding from her family.

A Chicago family. My rivals. My enemies.

My girl was a runaway princess.

My goddamn head spun as I stared at the photo.

She'd had many opportunities to come clean with me, and I would have protected her.

If she had told me the truth, I would have done anything to keep her and my son safe from the Chicago syndicate.

I would have paid her father any price—or killed him.

After resolving the matter of her father, I would only have had to marry her to fully claim her. Once the church said she belonged to me, that would have been the end of it.

Yeah. So there had to be something else.

Was she already married, running from a husband?

I continued staring at her image, careful to mask my expression to hide the emotion swelling in my chest and the rage climbing from my gut to meet it.

Once these men were gone, Val had a lot of explaining to do. And punishments to endure.

Did she even understand the fucking mess she'd put me in or how easily we could have avoided the whole thing if she had just fucking told me the truth?

I handed the picture back to Moscatelli.

"The resemblance is remarkable, but you risked coming here for nothing. This isn't my Valerie."

Young Thug moved his hand to his gun.

"Her name is Valentina Moscatelli," he said.

"Yes, well, my fiancée's name is Valerie Salera. The two girls might have some similarities, but they're not the same. Now, if you don't mind, I'm busy. I have real business to tend to."

The first order of business would be getting the truth out of that beautiful, lying mouth upstairs.

Young Thug white-knuckled his weapon.

"We're not leaving without that traitorous bitch," he spat.

I made a calculated move, stepping close enough to be on him before he could pull his gun on me.

"My Valerie is not your Valentina," I snarled. "End of discussion. Now get the fuck off my property."

He sneered. He looked forward to the challenge. And if he

ever called the mother of my son a bitch again, he would get his match. I would gut the little bastard with my bare hands.

"Get the fuck out of my city, Moscatelli, now, before all hell rains down on your family."

Then I gave them the disrespect they deserved, the kind that would trigger them. I turned my back.

A blood-curdling scream echoed through the house.

My muscles tensed. I had maybe half a second to react.

The younger Moscatelli had more balls than I'd given him credit for, and his brother didn't have the control he should have had.

The little thug pulled his weapon and aimed it at my back.

Bruce reacted first, always the first, always the fastest, tackling me to the ground, prepared to take a bullet meant for me.

Acidic bitterness hit the back of my throat as I lunged back onto my feet and bolted across the floor for cover.

Tony followed on my heels.

More gunshots cracked through the house.

As we crouched behind the grand piano, I took a gun from Tony's second holster, and together we returned fire.

"Just give us our fucking sister," the young thug yelled from behind the sofa. "Then I won't have to fucking kill you."

"Let's go," I shouted. "You came into my house making demands, you fucking arrogant little prick. You think I would let that stand? Do you know who the fuck I am?"

"Some rich dick playing at being a killer? I bet you have your men do all your dirty work."

I bared my teeth in a malicious grin.

Tony shook his head, warning me to stay put. He knew I wouldn't hesitate to get my hands dirty.

When I had first taken over the family, I hated it, but these days the violence excited me. An acquired taste I'd developed, intensified by my line of work.

"Just give us the girl, Vignali," Marco Moscatelli yelled from behind one end of a bookcase, "and we'll leave."

"That option went out the fucking window when you opened fire in my home, Moscatelli."

I squeezed off three more rounds, and the resulting bout of swearing told me I'd hit the mouthy, tattooed bastard.

"This doesn't have to get any messier," Moscatelli called out. "We only want what's rightfully ours, same as you would."

"My girl is not your fucking sister," I yelled.

But she was.

She would be in so much fucking trouble later.

"Yes, she is," a deep, raspy voice said from the staircase.

I whipped my head around to find an old man with a cigar sticking out from between his fat lips. A fucking lit cigar.

The insult of any man smoking inside my home burned through my veins for sure—

But seeing Val caught up in his stubby red fingers and another man standing so closely behind her magnified my rage exponentially.

They had her.

They had my girl.

She kept her gaze on her feet, tears streaming down her cheeks, one side of her face reddened by a large hand.

Someone had dared to hit her.

Someone had hit my woman.

Images all around me turned red.

The need for violence blasted through me. It burned inside my blood, and it vibrated my bones.

I would gut them all and paint my walls with their insides.

I moved slowly in Val's direction.

Clenched my jaw.

Flexed my fists.

"Let her go," I snarled.

The younger man behind her put a gun to her head, stopping me dead in my tracks.

"She comes with us, motherfucker," he said, "or she goes with God."

FOUR

VAL

My father's calm collected voice echoed inside my head. "Hello, Princess. We've missed you."

He pressed his lips together and waited for my response, his cold, familiar greeting slapping me in the face like it had been only a week since he last saw me.

Saul Moscatelli never yelled, never lost control.

When he got angry, his voice softened. Whenever someone came crawling back to him, begging for forgiveness, he had this way of seeming like a kind and forgiving man. He made the person feel like family.

Then, the moment they turned their backs to go, believing he had accepted their apology, he would wrap piano wire around their throats and kill them.

My father's unfeeling business demeanor, his fine-tuned ability to suppress all emotions and conceal his intentions until the moment he struck, made him terrifying.

This time, though, he wasn't the biggest threat in the room.

Not to me.

Even if you disagreed with his logic, my father believed his actions had a legit purpose.

My brother Aris, however, didn't need a reason for his cruelty. It was his sport. My twin delighted in causing pain and suffering to others. Whenever I looked into his eyes, I didn't see my father's veiled calculating or anything else like it.

Only brutal, raw depravity.

And amusement.

Now that Aris had found my son, he held the most precious thing in my world on the palm of his hand, and he would end my boy's life for no other reason than because he could.

He would do it simply to devastate me.

Even just the threat of it carved out a hollow space in my soul, crushed my heart, and made me shake uncontrollably.

Witnessing my agony had always entertained my brother.

Our father had never allowed him to kill me because I had been a useful commodity for trade.

I shifted my eyes for a quick side-glance at our father.

Yes, even now it was true.

Even after I'd run away and had a son. I didn't know what had happened to his original deal with the Russians, but if it fell through, he definitely made another deal with them, and I was still the honeypot.

For Enzo, on the other hand, the bastard son of one of his rivals, he would have no real use. So if Aris chose to kill Enzo just to make me suffer, my father wouldn't stop him.

He wouldn't order it, but he wouldn't stop it either.

Saul Moscatelli wouldn't pretend to show respect for the Vignali family. My father had been acquainted with Stefano's father and still with a few of the older Vignali made men, but he had no patience for young bosses like Stefano.

Men like Stefano could command loyalty more effectively than the previous generation of dons had ever done. That pissed off my father, and for that reason alone, he would risk a multi-family, multi-city war rather than spare Stefano's son.

I had to find a way to save my son.

I straightened my spine and forced my tremors to stop.

"Why are you here, Father?" I asked.

I needed time to come up with a plan. There had to be a play here, a move I could make that might not save me from Aris but would give Enzo a chance to survive.

Stefano wouldn't let me walk out of here without a fight.

This meant I had to maneuver both men to save my son.

Aris answered my question for our father.

"We're here to collect you, dear sister. Your fiancé already married someone else, but the deal still stands... you're alive, and we're obligated to deliver you to the Russians. I'm sure they'll find some use for you. Kitchen maid. Whore. Target practice. I hear they prefer live targets for knife throwing."

"My mama isn't going with you," Enzo screamed.

He tried to get off the bed, but Aris dug his fingers deeper into my baby's shoulder, pinning him down.

Enzo winced without making a sound, quickly schooling his expression better than any nine-year-old should be able to.

Aris laughed. "Feisty one, isn't he?"

As if he were bored, my father looked down at his watch.

Feigning courage, I stood my ground by releasing a heavy breath and forcing out a threat against my brother.

"I think you mean he's strong. You should meet his father. Stefano built what's now one of the strongest families in the country. Commission members are courting him to save their own asses. Speaking of the Commission, you know you can't be here in New York. The families won't stand for it."

Aris laughed, motioning with his gun for me to continue.

"The Commission won't tolerate you threatening their golden boy. I don't know how you got into this house, but you need to leave. Stefano won't stand for you coming into his home and threatening his wife and his son."

My father stood and straightened his suit jacket, now several sizes larger. The last ten years had not been kind to him, his health seemed to be failing, and he looked so much older.

He'd always been a large man, tall with broad shoulders, but the muscle that once supported his thick frame now appeared to be fatter than anything else. His strong jaw had also softened, his skin red and blotchy, and his jet-black hair looked unnatural, like he dyed it a lot.

Maybe my father was sick, or had he just let himself go?

My brothers clearly handled all the physically taxing work now, making our father soft. Or had his regular diet of red meat, rich cream sauces, and booze caught up to him?

If he was sick, what would that mean for me? Did he see me as a loose end he wanted to tie up?

No, not a loose end. That thought was all wrong.

Saul Moscatelli had never been the kind of man who cared enough about other people, and that included his children, to worry about the burdens he would leave behind.

If anything, it might make him more reckless, less worried about long-term risk, more focused on short-term rewards.

A dangerous situation for us all.

My father's arm flew, and the back of his hand smashed against my face hard enough to send me to the floor.

"You forget your place, Valentina."

Enzo struggled against Aris's grip and cried out for me. "Mama! Mama!"

My skin throbbed with familiar pain that brought tears to my eyes. I had to get up, though. Whenever my father had hit me before, I always stayed down, but I wasn't that girl anymore.

I had become a mother with a child to protect.

A woman about to marry a king, not a mafioso claiming to be one, but the presumptive king of the cruel kings.

That made me a queen.

Now was the time for me to stand up to my father and show him I deserved the respect he'd never given me.

I got up onto my fucking feet and looked him in the eye.

He spoke before I could shape my thoughts into words.

"You've caused quite enough trouble, Princess, and you've wasted far too much of my valuable time."

I maintained eye contact, forcing my words to spill out in an even tone, even as my legs shook.

"I have no interest in your time, Father. I understand you can't stay and must get back to Chicago. I'm sure your grandson is happy to have met you."

My father let out a stupid fucking chuckle while looking at his stupid fucking watch again.

"Oh, mia piccola principessa. Here's what's going to happen. You're leaving with me and your brothers. You'll tell Vignali you don't belong to him, you're not his wife, he has no claim, and you have a prior contract to honor. Then we'll go home."

Pushing my luck, I lifted my chin, hoping he could see the strength in my eyes and not the terrified little girl he'd created.

"And if I refuse to go?" I asked.

Aris intervened, flashing one of his depraved grins.

"I'll shoot your son and his father, then drag you out by the hair. So what's it going to be, sister? Do I get playtime?"

My mind spun in a frenzied loop, working to come up with something to get my son out of the situation alive.

Enzo took advantage of the moment, leaping to his feet and jamming his fist into Aris's groin.

Oh god, no. No, no, no.

My brother grunted and doubled over in pain.

Enzo raced to me, throwing himself in front of me.

My pulse accelerated. Nausea rolled through me, bile rising and burning my throat.

I shoved my son behind my body to shield him.

With a guttural snarl coming from between Aris's teeth, he straightened and pointed his gun at me.

"You should've taught your son some fucking manners."

I gripped Enzo's arm behind my back.

"I taught my son how to fight and how to survive."

"What the fuck would a dumb cunt like you know about survival?"

Realizing that if I antagonized Aris and forced him to focus on me instead of my son, it was a step in the right direction.

"How many times have you died, Aris? Have you ever survived on your own? Oh wait, you still live with daddy, and Marco's still bailing you out all the time, because you're too stupid not to start fights you can't win."

I pushed out my bottom lip in a childish, mocking pout.

Aris stepped closer. Shit. Had he actually just growled?

"You really wanna play, you little cunt? I'll teach you some fucking manners first, then remind you where your place is— right before I do the same to your kid."

It worried me that I couldn't tell what my father was doing

in my periphery, but I didn't dare take my eyes off Aris, not when he stood so close to my son with his weapon.

I forced one of his disgusting grins onto my own face.

"But can you? I mean, you were just punched in the dick by a nine-year-old."

He thumbed back the hammer on his gun as he closed in on me. Then he settled the cold steel barrel against my temple.

My heart slammed against my ribs, but I couldn't allow Aris to see my fear. He would exploit any form of weakness.

Our father casually cleared his throat as he put his hand on top of Aris's gun and pushed it down.

"Enough, son. Don't shoot her in the face. We need her to stay pretty for the Russians."

Then the old man met my gaze.

"As for you, Princess, you're coming with us, and I don't mean to say it again. Come willingly, and the boy lives. Anything more out of your mouth, and I'll kill him myself."

Enzo ripped his arm out of my grip and rushed between Aris and me to shove him back.

Aris pointed his gun at Enzo.

My heart stopped.

"If you kill him," I blurted, "you'll have to kill me too. And then not only will you have nothing for the Russians, you'll never be able to hide your actions from the Commission. They'll kill you if Stefano doesn't kill you first."

Aris studied me, then flicked his gaze over at our father, who didn't offer a visible reaction.

My brother shrugged. "Fine. The bastard can live for now."

He started to put his gun away, but must have had a second thought, because he whipped the butt of his weapon down against the side of Enzo's head with a vicious crack.

My son crumpled to the floor.

I screamed, diving to the floor for my baby.

My father grabbed my arm and yanked me away before slamming my head against the wall, blurring my vision.

Gunshots fired downstairs.

I slumped against the wall and slid to the floor. I stared at Enzo, watching his little chest rise and fall.

How would I get him out of here alive?

My father hauled me up from the floor.

"Leave the bastard," he growled. "He's not your concern anymore. Now let's go. Be sure to tell his father on the way out not to come after you. You'll get into the car and behave yourself. If you do not, I'll send Aris back for the boy."

He had me with that, and he knew it.

I cast my gaze to the floor and let him guide me out of the room and down Stefano's grand staircase.

On the way down, the nauseating mix of overheated metal, gun smoke, and blood overwhelmed my senses.

I didn't dare risk looking at the carnage strewn across the once pristine floors. I didn't want to see Stefano lying on the cold marble in a pool of his own blood.

I'd brought death upon this house. My choices had led to this moment, with my son upstairs, unconscious, and his father likely dead. All for nothing.

If only I had told Stefano the truth from the very beginning. Maybe none of this would have ever played out. But I hadn't, so it all came full circle to slap me in the face...

Me in my father's possession again, about to be sold by one monster to another. My baby lost to me. Stefano lost.

My brother Marco's voice rang out in anger and startled me.

Stefano yelled something back at him, and a fleeting sense of relief washed over me. A sliver of hope. Stefano was still alive.

He would find Enzo upstairs and protect him.

Marco and Stefano argued. Santo interjected, insisting I was absolutely his sister, Valentina Moscatelli, not Valerie Salera.

My father pushed me down the stairs in front of him.

"Let her go," Stefano snarled.

With my eyes still downcast, I stared at the destruction of his beautiful house. Plaster, shards of glass, splinters of wood, and splattered blood all over the floor.

Stefano made a move in my direction.

Aris pushed the barrel of his gun against the back of my head, forcing my neck forward.

"She comes with us, motherfucker, or she goes with God."

"She's mine by code," Stefano said. "She's the mother of my son and my wife in a matter of hours. I've already had her, and our engagement has been announced."

"Fuck your code," Aris spat.

Nothing surprising there. My family often chose to ignore the rules established by the founding families.

"Seems my daughter failed to mention she's already been purchased. Hell, after all this, Klimov might just refuse her when he finally sees her. If he does, maybe I'll let you buy her. For now, boy, just be grateful I'm letting your bastard live."

Every time my father called my son a bastard, my blood boiled hotter, and the way I hated him grew stronger. I would dance on this man's fucking grave someday soon.

"She's mine," Stefano snarled.

My father pushed me down another step.

"No, Vignali, she's not."

My foot slipped as we got close to the bottom step, and Saul Moscatelli, my father, so easily let go of me to save himself.

Stefano caught me.

I looked up at him, hoping to see the love he'd shown me earlier. Hoping he understood why I'd done it all.

Understood what I had to do now.

But that's not what I found in those dark eyes.

The cruelty in his stare made my breath stop.

"What the fuck have you done?" he demanded.

FIVE

VAL

Stefano steadied me, then he let me go—same as my father had done—and I couldn't help but hate him for it.

At the same time, I couldn't help mourning the loss of his touch and wanting more.

His eyes grew darker, his expression so full of fury.

My lies had hurt our son.

My lies had caused death under his roof.

One of Stefano's men lay dead in the foyer.

His underboss, Tony, sat slumped on the floor, leaning against the wall, his shirt soaked with blood, his face twisted in pain as he gripped his side to slow the bleeding.

Within minutes of my family's arrival, Stefano had learned my worst truths. Truths that cost him the life of a made man and the good health of his underboss.

Aside from Enzo, the Vignali men were the closest thing to family Stefano had, and I'd hurt them.

Even Enzo wouldn't walk away unscathed.

"Please don't hate me," I whispered.

Stefano just stared at me.

He deserved an explanation, the whole truth, but I didn't have the time to give him what he needed.

He deserved more than answers. He deserved an apology.

I had judged him for his family when mine was worse. I let him believe he was the only reason I couldn't be with him—and when he came back for us, that he was the only reason I'd kept Enzo's birth a secret.

I had lied to his face over and over without hesitation. I told him that he was to blame for everything. I willingly allowed him to draw the wrong conclusions about me, about my motivations, about my past.

Stefano had shouldered the blame, the regret, the sadness, and I just let him live with it all. Alone.

Endless opportunities had existed for me to tell him the truth, to ask him for help, a thousand chances to give him my real name and tell him where I came from.

After discovering his identity, I should have revealed mine, but no, I left him like a spineless little bitch instead. And worse, because God knew I hadn't stopped there, I hid his only child from him, his son.

He was right to call me a coward.

That's exactly what I'd always been.

I blinked up at him, and he frowned, the line between his brows going deep again. Then pain flashed through his eyes, and seeing him hurt that way shattered my heart.

Stefano hadn't caused any of this.

I did it all on my own.

Just me.

I couldn't go back in time and change my bad choices, but I could start protecting him and our son now.

My life was forfeit anyway.

Accepting my fate meant giving my boys a better chance.

But my mind raced too quickly for a thoughtful plan.

However screwed up my brain might have been, I understood one thing. My behavior in front of my father determined whether Stefano and Enzo lived through the night.

SECONDS LATER OR AN ETERNITY

Saul Moscatelli hacked out a wet, phlegmy cough that turned my stomach.

Yeah. No longer would I call this depraved asshole my father. He never had and never would love me or keep me safe.

"Don't you have something to say, Princess?" he asked.

"Make it happen, sister, or I come out to play," Aris added.

Saul's words, Aris's words, the image of Enzo lying unconscious on the floor, the hurt in Stefano's eyes… it all swirled inside my skull like a hurricane, making it hard to focus on any one thing.

Why the fuck didn't Marco intervene?

I mean, of course he wouldn't act against the family, but he had always been good at softening the blows.

So much time had passed since I'd been around my brothers. I didn't know who they were anymore, or what they were capable of now. I couldn't be sure about how they would react to anything.

Saul Moscatelli, on the other hand, had not changed. His tactics seemed to be the same, so he wouldn't kill Stefano unless Stefano forced his hand. And even in that case, it might be more trouble to Saul than it was worth.

He knew starting a war with New York would be expensive, turning no profit at all for him.

He wouldn't stop the violent hands of my brothers, though. If one of the Moscatelli boys started a war, Saul would let the chips fall where they may. And if my brothers won, he would take credit. If they lost, not so much.

As we grew up, Saul often said to the boys, "Weakness gets culled from the herd."

Phrases like that helped him justify death. Even if it meant sacrificing a son, the man would wash his hands clean of blame.

My nonna had disagreed with Saul's tactics and beliefs about death, but if he caught her even thinking it, he would punish her. Still, she found ways to teach me how to be mentally stronger than the men.

She'd said men like her son underestimated women. They didn't consider us to be capable humans. We were pretty possessions to them, born to be owned and used for bargaining.

Too emotional to be their equals.

With no options left, I took my nonna's words at face value, hoping this time it didn't feel like a manipulation to Stefano.

In a moment of complete, shameless desperation, I chose to play that role for Saul Moscatelli.

I drew images of Enzo to the forefront of my mind, forcing myself to focus on him lying helplessly upstairs without me or his father, unmoving, only his small chest rising and falling.

Tears spilled down my cheeks, and pain rolled through me. I hunched over, clutching at my stomach, releasing all my fear and the pain in gushing sobs. Those emotions always roiled just beneath the surface anyway, so I did what I'd never done before.

I let all that shit come out.

Stefano lurched forward and grabbed my arms with utter confusion written all over his face. He knew it wasn't like me. I didn't get messy that way. I didn't let my emotions define me or my actions or bare my weaknesses.

I literally threw myself at him, heaving with sobs, my body shuddering, and held on to him with everything I had left.

"It'll be okay, Angel," he said. "You're mine, not his, mine. I'll fix this, I promise."

Taking in all of him, inhaling his scent, feeling his warmth, hearing his soft words, I tried to memorize everything about him. Everything from how the luxurious robe hugged his strong arms and torso to the spiciness of his cologne.

I wanted to remember this moment in his arms for however long I might live. I wanted to dig up this feeling from my soul whenever I made my mental escapes during whatever I had to endure in my unknown future.

This, with Stefano, and cuddling with Enzo on the massive leather couch at the café while reading bedtime stories together.

The memories would be the glue holding the pieces of my sanity together and the will I needed to survive another day. My family could take me from my boys, but they couldn't take away my memories of them.

I wiped my nose on Stefano's shoulder.

"Ace," I whispered. "Hear me, not the words I have to say. I have to leave to keep you and Enzo alive. Whatever happens, I will always love you both."

I straightened my back and raised my voice for Saul to hear.

"I want to go. It's a fair trade, Stefano. And I don't want you to come after me. Stay in New York and raise our son."

Stefano tightened his embrace, shaking his head.

"I'm not letting you go."

I nodded. "Yes, you have to let me. I've decided. I'm going."

Angry again—at me, at my family—Stefano shook me.

"You're not going anywhere. Do you hear me?"

Aris grabbed a fistful of my hair and yanked me back.

"Yeah, she is. This brazen whore is coming with us."

I cried out, releasing Stefano's arms to clutch my scalp and dull the pain.

Stefano raised his gun, leveling it at Aris's head.

"Get your fucking hands off her," he snarled.

Santo crept up from behind and pressed the barrel of his weapon to the back of Stefano's head.

"I don't think you're the one in charge here, Vignali."

I shut my eyes for just a second, to remember the little boy Santo used to be—so unlike the monster he'd become.

He grew up taller than Aris, and that probably drove Aris crazy. Santo's blond ringlets had darkened to a golden-brown and straightened to hang along the sides of his face. Tattoos and scars marred his skin.

He looked every bit like the killer Saul Moscatelli had raised him to be, standing there in complete confidence with a gun pressed against Stefano's head.

In that moment, Saul stepped in, his demeanor so calm and casual like the fucking sociopath he was.

"Mr. Vignali, I apologize for the intrusion. We'll leave peacefully now, so you can clean up your home."

"Peace?" Stefano snapped. "Oh, there'll be no more fucking peace on this earth. How the hell did you get into my house?"

Saul waved him off with a flick of his wrist.

"The important thing is the return of my property. I'm taking Valentina home, where she'll fulfill her obligations. I understand you weren't informed about her marriage contract. With that in mind, I've decided to be gracious and let you keep the child. You'll find him upstairs—mostly unharmed."

Stefano's jaws clenched, his eyes narrowed.

"If you've hurt my son, Moscatelli, nothing in this world will save you from me."

I squeezed my eyes shut again, this time to pray to the Virgin Mother, asking her to watch over Enzo, begging that the pistol-whipping my brother gave him wouldn't leave any permanent damage.

"Your son doesn't know how to behave around his betters," Aris said, "so I taught him a little lesson."

I couldn't see the smug grin on my twin's face, but I could feel it. I remembered that evil look well and how, in most cases, it had been followed by the same words.

No one cares what I do to you, bitch, as long as I don't mark up your face or spoil your cunt.

Stefano stepped forward.

"I assure you, my son knows exactly what separates him from a piece of shit like you."

Santo thumbed back his pistol's hammer.

Aris's grip on my hair tightened, pain shooting across my scalp as hot tears burned behind my eyelids.

Saul calmly adjusted his cufflinks, ignoring everyone.

"In any case," he said, "Valentina returns to Chicago with me today, after which she'll make good on my obligation to Klimov."

Instant recognition flashed in Stefano's eyes.

Of course Stefano knew about Klimov.

Everyone had heard about the giant, bloodthirsty Russian, how he'd come into power, and what he did to those who broke their contracts with him.

My twin's abuse and Saul Moscatelli's sociopathic behavior had driven me to desperation, yes, but neither topped the list of reasons for me to run from the horrors I faced.

Evil men had built and commanded my family. I knew this in my heart. But they didn't hold a candle to the atrocities in which Klimov delighted.

The horrors he'd had in store for me as his bride.

The man didn't just torture someone he wanted to hurt. That was a much too simplistic approach for him.

The last undercover cop discovered in his ranks had lived through the removal of his own tongue, followed by Klimov's men beating him until he was close to death.

Then, with broken ribs and legs, the cop had survived only to be nailed to a wall in his home, where he'd been forced to watch Klimov and his associates brutally rape and murder his family, one by one.

Klimov's men left him there to starve afterward, staring at the broken, mutilated bodies of his family.

Police had discovered the officer several days later. Rumor had it, when they found him, the man begged for death. He never made it to the hospital.

After that, no officer would dare take an assignment to infiltrate Klimov's organization. Other outfits had tried to rise against Klimov, but he always left a long trail of blood and gore in his wake.

"You cannot give her to that fucking monster," Stefano hissed. "He'll torture her and kill her."

Saul shrugged. "Valentina is no longer fit to be a proper

wife, thanks to you, Vignali. You've dishonored us all by taking her without marriage. You ruined her value. You took that from me. Still, Klimov is owed my daughter, and what he decides to do with her is none of my concern or yours."

"She is mine by right," Stefano snapped.

"She was yours by theft. We are rivals, and your relationship with Valentina was forbidden. You know this. My daughter's not yet wed, so she indeed belongs to me."

Saul nodded at Aris, who then dragged me to the door.

Stefano followed on his heels, but I begged him with my eyes to stop, to let me go, to stay alive for Enzo.

We both knew he couldn't win, not then, unprepared, and I needed him whole. He couldn't save me, but he could protect our son.

He held my gaze and shook his head, his stoic mask cracked by torment.

Then I looked up the staircase.

My heart stopped.

Enzo stood at the top, arms folded over his chest, a thin trail of blood trickling down the side of his face.

I swallowed back a sob.

It would be the last time I saw my son.

His last memory of me, watching strangers drag me out of his father's house.

I mouthed the words '*I love you always*' to my boy.

"No!" Stefano shouted.

Aris fired his weapon.

Stefano fired back.

Santo and Marco opened fired across the house.

I screamed over the sound of gunfire, my whole body dying from this waking nightmare, writhing to break free of it. My soul shrieked and wailed within me. Then I dared to look back at the landing.

Enzo was gone.

I had to believe he'd run away, that Aris hadn't hit him.

Stefano dove for cover in the kitchen, returning fire.

Tony, slumped against the wall, squeezed off several shots.

Aris dragged me outside, shoved me into the back of a limo, and climbed in after me—cutting off my view of Stefano's house and everything happening inside it.

I scrambled to the opposite door, yanking at the handle, but Aris hauled me back with a violent jerk.

Then he aimed his gun at my face.

"Just fucking do it!" I screamed. "Do it!"

He didn't pull the trigger. So I kept going.

"Klimov knows I'm alive. Kill me, and you'll take my place. Maybe a hired gun. Maybe he'll let his men have you. I hear they like to fuck boys, so they won't care which twin they get."

"Fucking bitch," Aris snapped. "Killing you lets you off too easy. The Russians won't count your fingers. I bet they won't even notice if you're missing an arm. Broken ribs? Legs? They won't give a shit. I may not get to kill you. But I can hurt you."

"I'm not afraid of you," I lied.

A malevolent grin turned up my twin's mouth.

"You should be. I know where your kid sleeps."

I swallowed back vomit.

"Aris, if you touch him—"

"If I go after him, you'll never know. You'll never hear a whisper about what happened to your son... or your lover."

I clenched my teeth to keep from screaming.

He was right.

My psycho demon twin was absolutely right.

"No," he added, "you'll spend what's left of your pathetic fucking life wondering if they're even alive."

More gunshots rang out again through the open front door.

I didn't know if Stefano or Enzo had been shot.

And I would never know if they survived.

SIX

STEFANO

The desperation on Val's face, the fear in her eyes, her silent pleading—those things would haunt my dreams for the rest of my life.

She had survived being shot only a few days earlier, making a conscious decision to overcome the ordeal on her terms after being chained to a wall and tortured by a psychopath.

A beautiful, fierce, determined woman.

But when her family showed up, she became someone else. Her father and her brothers terrified her. They'd broken her.

I shook my head, refusing to believe it.

Her gaze jumped from mine to the staircase.

Fuck. Our son.

He stood at the top of the landing, taunting the Moscatelli bastard clinging to his mother.

"No," I shouted at him, "run!"

The man fired at my son.

He fucking fired at my nine-year-old son...

And made himself a dead man walking.

I would kill the son of a bitch for that once the coward

stopped hiding behind Val. I needed to get a clean shot without the risk of hitting her.

He backed up through the foyer, out the front door, dragging Val along as his shield, and Saul Moscatelli casually walked out after them.

I sighted my weapon on both men, calculating the best shot at either one without putting a bullet into my girl.

Couldn't take that chance, not ever.

Marco Moscatelli and his thug opened fire, forcing me to dive into the kitchen for cover. He slammed the front door shut just as I took my shot, causing my bullet to lodge in the solid wood panel instead of Saul Moscatelli's head.

I peered around the corner at the staircase to be sure Enzo hadn't come back. Thank fucking Christ he'd had the instinct to duck and run down the hallway.

I'd watched it happen in real time, my brain transforming the scene into slow motion. My boy had just a small trail of blood dripping down the side of his face, which made it reasonably safe for me to assume he hadn't been shot.

He was safe now, for the time being, and I had to keep it that way while also fighting for his mother.

"Bella," I shouted up the stairs.

She shouted back from behind cover. Good. Smart girl. She understood the life.

"I've got him, sir. He's okay. And my aunt is here helping."

"Lock the service stairwell door and don't come down until you hear from me or Tony."

Then I motioned for my men to head out the back and come around to flank Moscatelli and his men.

Tony had been hit, but that didn't stop him. He dragged himself off the floor and followed the others outside. My second understood an attack on this house, on my family, was an attack on the entire Vignali organization.

The war I had tried to avoid now loomed on the horizon.

Seconds later, the young Moscatelli thug drew another weapon and fired with both hands like a goddamn cowboy in some stupid fucking Western. Ridiculous. And smart.

Doing so gave Marco enough cover to get the front door open again, so they could make a strategic escape.

Marco slipped through the opening, using the door as cover while firing as he and his brother made their way out.

The gunfire stopped at that point, so I sprinted to the door, but both idiots started firing behind them as they ran, making their shots wild and unpredictable.

I didn't give a fuck if one hit me.

Nothing mattered but getting to Val.

I had to get to her before it was too late.

Ducking and weaving, I charged after those retreating bastards. They piled into a rented limo, tires screaming as it tore off, but I gave chase anyway.

Later my men would hunt down the owner of that rental company and kill him for doing business with a Chicago family. A fatal mistake to make in my city.

Enraged over the loss of Val, the attempt on my son's life, the invasion into our home, I squared up and aimed for the limo tires.

The driver accelerated and moved out of range.

I fired anyway and emptied the mag, then kept pulling the trigger, gritting my teeth against the useless clicks of an empty motherfucking pistol.

I roared. "Fuck! God-fucking-damn it!"

Panting, I bent over with my hands on my thighs, trying to

catch my breath and gather my thoughts. Then I spun and marched back into the house.

Tony followed, collapsing against the wall the moment we got inside.

"Moscatelli's men?" I demanded.

My second squeezed his eyes shut.

"Both dead in the front yard, boss."

"How the fuck did they get into my house?" I shouted. "How did a fat old man get in undetected and reach my family? No way that whale scaled my walls. Someone had to see them. What about the surveillance?"

"Guards posted in the rear are dead," Tony said. "So is our man on monitor watch in the gatehouse. Necks snapped. Moscatelli used the service entrance and stairwell for access."

Dropping my gaze, I cursed at the loss of those Vignali soldiers. Good men who would be missed. I swallowed the fury burning my throat and shook my goddamn head.

Things needed doing, and only a clear mind would bring my girl back to us. Once I set a plan in motion, then I could afford to release the rage and channel it into something useful. Like a plan to kill every one of those motherfuckers.

I lifted my gaze to make eye contact with my second.

"Tony, how badly are you hurt?"

"It's fine, boss. I'll clean up in the shower and wrap myself with some bandages."

As usual, he shrugged off his injuries, ready to keep going without taking care of himself. He never seemed to get how that only led to longer, more painful recoveries.

"No, Tony, call the doctor right away. Let him patch you up right—no half-ass bandaging. I'm not going to risk you getting sick. I need you back to one hundred percent sooner than later.

And have him care for the wound on my son's head as well. Go on, get it handled."

Tony nodded. "If that's your order, Stef."

I gripped his shoulder with affection and nodded.

"There's another rat in this organization. Moscatelli had inside info—he didn't guess his way in. Look into that while you're rehabbing. Rest here and keep an eye on the boy."

Any Vignali man who could be bought by another family was a cancer. Something to be cut out fast.

I wouldn't allow it to spread.

Nor would Tony.

He needed to keep busy while he waited for the doctor, or he would take on another task and end up unconscious, bleeding out before anyone could help.

I wouldn't allow that either. I needed him.

More importantly, my son needed him now too.

"Bella," I shouted. "Find my fucking phone."

Thirty seconds later, the girl hurried down the stairs with my phone clutched in her hand.

"You and your aunt will stay here and take care of my son while his mother is gone. Don't leave him alone. Understand?"

She nodded again, then ran back upstairs to Enzo.

With her out of earshot, I made a call to one of my capos.

"Rocco, get your cleanup crew to my house. Now. I want the Vignali men handled with respect... funeral ready."

Those three men died in service to me. They would receive a proper soldier's burial, so their families could mourn.

"As for the others, you know what to do," I added. "Handle the house, whatever it takes. Don't come back to me about the money, just get it done. I want it to look like nothing happened. I won't have Val come home to this fucking mess."

Rocco cleared his throat. "Just heard. On it already, boss."

"Good. Hurry the fuck up then."

Manhattan uniforms would stop by after a shooting like this one. Corpses on the front lawn complicated matters, even if police were on my payroll.

THIRTY MINUTES LATER

Rocco and his crew arrived in a convoy of black cargo vans. He and several of his men jumped out and came directly to me.

I pointed at two who weren't yet dressed for the occasion.

"You men go inside and help Bruce. Follow his orders. I want everything you can dig up on the Moscatelli and Klimov families. Addresses. Phone numbers. Blueprints of their fucking houses. Names, addresses, earnings of their associates.

"I want to know where the two families make their money, which of their businesses are most lucrative, their strengths, their weaknesses. All legitimate and illegal cash flows. Get me every-fucking-thing."

Both men nodded. "Yes, sir."

An odd sensation, like a physical weight settling on my shoulders, gave me pause, then the urge to look up struck me.

Enzo stood at the top of the stairs again, this time staring down at me. The boy clenched and flexed his fists while glaring.

"How could you do that?" he shouted.

I recognized the judgment on his face. The same judgment my mother had passed when I refused to follow the path my family laid out for me as my brother's second. I had failed her. Now my son looked at me the same way. I had also failed him.

"How could I do what?" I shot back, my tone harsher than it should've been, considering the circumstances.

Pinching the bridge of my nose, I pulled in a long breath. My son was terrified. No need to pile more on him. I used the release from a slow exhale to soften my tone.

"How could I do what, Enzo?" I repeated.

Tears streamed down his face.

"You let them take Mama!"

He hesitated then, visibly working to rein himself in.

"From your own house," he added.

The way he forced back the anger vibrating in his blood filled me with pride. Because anger, when controlled and wielded with precision, got shit done.

The boy had inherited my volatility, and in his short time under my roof, he was already learning how to control it.

Soon, he would have to learn how to wield it.

I raked a hand through my hair and looked at the damage.

Bullet holes and blood peppered the walls. Plaster dust and tiny shards of Murano glass from my mother's vintage vase collection littered the floor.

And crimson rose petals.

The roses I'd bought for Val.

I never had the chance to give them to her.

A certain poetry lingered in the mix of blood, violence, and scattered roses—meant to symbolize my love for Valerie—all of it now laid to ruin, ready to be swept away as if it never existed.

Like my trust in her.

When I got her back, and I would get her back, there'd be a lot of necessary atonement, and it would be just as unpleasant for me as it would be for her.

I owed her as much if not more than she owed me.

"I didn't let any of this shit happen, boy."

Enzo came down and made a beeline for me.

I reached for the bruise around the gash on his temple.

"Are you hurt anywhere else, Enzo?"

My son jerked away from my touch, letting his emotions cut loose. He cocked back a fist and punched me in the gut—a solid hit, fueled by rage, fear, and sheer determination.

An image flashed through my mind. I had done the same to my father. He had laughed at me, turned his back on me.

I caught my son's next punch, pulled him into my arms, and held him while he screamed and struck me wherever he could reach. And I let him.

"She's gone again, and it's all your fault!" he screamed. "You said we would all be together. You promised to make her better and keep us safe in this house. You promised!"

I held him tighter and let him use his rage to work through the pain. He needed to process what had happened.

More than that, I deserved his anger.

I hadn't let them take her, but they took her all the same, and I couldn't stop them. To him, in this moment, there was no difference between me letting her go and me failing to stop them.

Enzo fought my hold until sobs overtook him.

I welcomed it all, keeping him safe inside my arms.

Never would I laugh at my son or turn my back on him.

After showing him to breathe slow and steady, he finally relaxed. Then he pushed himself away.

"Why did they take her?" he asked.

Thoughts of killing Moscatelli flooded my mind, forcing a wry grin onto my face. I could feel it taking control of my facial muscles, and I couldn't make it stop.

"Because they made a mistake, son."

"What mistake?"

"They thought they could come into our house, take what's ours, and walk away."

My son nodded, his eyes getting darker, his expression mirroring mine. He took my meaning. And he meant business in his own right.

Another swell of pride grew inside my chest, but Christ, how the fuck old was this kid's soul?

"What are we going to do, Mr. Vignali?"

I frowned.

I wanted to shake him. I wanted to make him call me his dad or papa or even *mio padre*.

Anything but Mr. Vignali.

I squeezed my eyes shut for a moment.

Then, right there, in the middle of all the destruction, I dropped to my knees and made my first solemn vow to my son.

Not a fucking promise, but an unbreakable vow.

"I don't care how many men I have to kill or how many cities I have to burn to the ground, Enzo Salvatore Vignali..."

And to be sure he met my eyes and knew I meant every word, I brushed his curls away from his face.

"I will do it. And I will bring her back to you."

SEVEN

VAL

My brothers flew out of Stefano's house, firing their weapons behind themselves as Stefano gave chase. They hit nothing but the concrete wall surrounding the property and maybe a tree or two. Then they dove into the limo.

I smiled.

They hadn't been able to take down Stefano Vignali.

Enzo would be safe in his father's care.

Now that Stefano knew the truth about my family, I couldn't imagine anyone ever breaching his walls again.

Aris dug his fingers into my wound.

"Wipe that smile off your face, bitch, or I'll do it for you."

But I didn't. So he shoved his fingers deeper. I had to bite my tongue to keep myself from crying out and giving him what he wanted.

He had forced me to the middle of the seat and planted himself between me and the door, gripping my arm to make sure I didn't move.

Marco shoved in next to me, breathing heavily.

"Knock it the fuck off, Aris. Let go of her arm—now."

Aris released me. "Sure."

Then he backhanded me across the mouth and grinned as he wiped my blood on his shirt.

"Told you I would," he said.

He would pay. For his cruelty.

For hitting my son.

Santo jumped onto the bench across from us and barked at the driver to go.

Tires squealed against the pavement as the car pulled away and headed for the open gate.

Gunshots cracked through the air behind us.

I twisted in my seat, peering out the rear window to see Stefano one last time. He opened fire. I doubled over my lap, unsure if I meant to dodge his bullets or ease the pain in my gut. And in my heart.

"Goodbye," I whispered before turning to the front.

When the gunfire faded, silence settled in the air.

Well, until Saul's ringing phone broke it. He always rode in the front, and he'd made it clear he did so because it gave him control. What if the driver betrayed him?

Really, though, riding in the back gave him motion sickness.

Marco yelled, making me jump.

"Christ, Santo! Why didn't you say something?"

"About what?"

Marco pointed out the growing red stain on his left side.

Santo looked down at his blood.

"Motherfucker. I just got a new piece there."

Marco rolled his eyes, then shoved me aside to get close to Santo.

"You've been shot, but clearly the more pressing concern is

the ink you etch into your flesh. Not like maybe your liver or kidney. And just forget about the risk of infection."

Saul glanced back, already barking orders into his phone, more annoyed than anything else. Then he stabbed a finger down on the button to raise the divider between the front and back seats, blocking out the noise and inconvenience of one of his children getting first aid for a gunshot wound.

"Can I help you, Marco?" I asked.

And by help, I meant push hard enough on the wound and make my little brother cry.

Marco lifted Santo's shirt, revealing the bleeding wound.

Aris's hand went back to my arm, and I clenched my teeth to stop myself from making a sound.

"You've done enough, sister. This is your fault. Our little brother was shot because you went off to play the cheap whore with no concept of family honor or duty—"

"Aris, shut the fuck up," Marco snapped.

"It's her fault he—"

"I don't give a fuck. I said shut up." Marco pointed in my direction. "Valentina, get me the first-aid kit under your seat."

I blinked. He'd caught me off guard using my real name. I shoved down the confusion in my gut, saving the emotion for later.

"Oh, come on," Santo whined. "It's not that big a deal. Not the first time I've been shot, and it probably won't be the last. It's fine. Barely a scratch."

"You shut up too," Marco ordered.

I reached under the seat, pulled out a small leather bag, and unzipped it before holding it close to Marco, so he could grab what he needed.

He started patching up our youngest brother.

Glancing at the door, I wondered if this was the distraction I needed to make a run for it.

But they knew where I lived. They knew about Enzo and Stefano. They knew I'd go back for them before anything else.

No, no more hiding. No more escaping. Accepting my fate to keep my boys alive, that was my purpose now.

Sitting in the back of the limo with my brothers seemed surreal. So much about them had changed in the ten years I'd been gone, but also, so much had stayed the same.

Marco had always been demanding, controlling. As the oldest, he'd also been the one who cared for us. The one who protected us from Saul if we needed it, and he was the only one who cared for us.

Throughout my childhood, Marco had played the role of protector, nurturer, and even parent.

That said, Marco had also perfectly mastered his role in the family, every bit the up-and-coming mafia boss he was supposed to be. He commanded respect and demanded obedience but not as brutally as the old-school bosses.

He didn't enjoy others' suffering the way Saul and Aris did.

When Marco had to kill, he didn't hesitate. He always did what needed to be done, but he wouldn't take delight in it. Nor did he look for excuses to carry out unnecessary executions.

I wouldn't go so far as to say he believed in mercy, but he did believe in fairness.

Aris, however, had become exactly what I'd thought.

The cruelty in his eyes had become stronger, intensifying his horrific combination of sadism, masochism, and misogyny.

Marco inherited Saul's leadership skills. My twin—older than me by only minutes—inherited Saul's barbaric cruelty.

Aris's once cherubic beauty, with the same dark hair and

light blue eyes as mine, had matured into something demonic. I was pretty sure the women of Chicago considered the devil a poor imitation of my brother.

Nonna used to whisper about Aris and me sharing one soul. He was the darkness, and I was the light. I believed her because it explained his needless cruelty with little or no provocation.

But now, after everything I'd learned, everything I'd seen, after everything I did to protect my freedom and my son's safety, I knew the truth.

Aris and I weren't the same.

We didn't share a soul.

I certainly had some darkness inside me along with the light, but his soul was pitch black.

Once upon a time, I thought something or someone might save him. I used to pray he would find the right woman, or a special interest, or some other purpose in his life for him to love more than himself.

I'd been certain something like that would give him light.

No longer did I believe in the naive fantasy from the Disney movies—the kind little girls clung to for hope. I knew better.

Santo had changed so completely, I hardly recognized him.

He lay stretched out on the limo's bench seat, staring at the ceiling, bored while Marco fished around for the slug in his side.

When I looked at him, I tried to see past the tattoos and the permanent scowl, wondering if that beautiful little boy still existed, the one with brilliant blond curls, electric-blue eyes, and the most infectious laugh.

But I couldn't.

"I don't do tricks," Santo said.

I blinked in confusion. "What?"

"You're staring at me like I'm about to pull a rabbit out my ass or something. I don't do tricks."

"I don't know…" Marco cut in. "You always manage to piss me off in record time. Isn't that a trick?"

Santo muttered something smartass under his breath.

I ignored their bickering and scooted closer to Marco.

"Is there something I can do to help?"

"I think you've fucking done enough," Aris growled again before grabbing my hair and yanking me back into the seat.

Pressing my lips together, I refused to make a sound.

Any sign of pain or weakness would only encourage him.

"I said shut the fuck up," Marco growled, "and let go of her arm. I need a hand, and we all know you're a shitty medic."

"It's not my job to stop the bleeding," Aris fired back. "I'm the one who makes shit bleed. If Santo's stupid enough to get shot, he deserves to bleed out."

He released my hair, letting me scoot closer to Marco, who knelt on the floor beside our youngest brother.

"Keep talking, Aris," Marco said over his shoulder, "and I'll take out your tongue."

Aris sat back and folded his arms.

"I'm not the one who got him shot."

But he didn't say anything else after that.

He and Marco fought a lot when we were young—and Aris always got his ass kicked. Clearly, nothing had changed beyond the surprising fact that Aris backed off a little faster now.

Santo scoffed and narrowed his eyes at me.

"I don't fucking buy it."

I narrowed my eyes. "What?"

"You abandoned our family and left us with a massive

fucking debt to the Russians, and now suddenly, you wanna fucking help? No way."

"I don't have anything better to do right now," I snapped.

With a shrug, I forced myself to put on a brave face.

Did Santo really think I'd meant to abandon him?

He'd been so young at the time.

Maybe I should've fought harder to take him with me. I had planned to, but the risk became too great.

"Hold this." Marco nodded at the bullet while pulling it out from Santo's wound.

I opened my hand, and the bloody, lead cylinder dropped onto my palm. Its warmth turned my stomach.

"Douse it with the hydrogen peroxide, then chuck it out the window," Marco ordered.

The peroxide would destroy the remaining DNA evidence in case someone found the slug on the street and decided to test it. Unlikely scenario, yes, but I understood exactly what my brother was instructing me to do. And why.

After finding the dark plastic bottle, I poured the liquid into my cupped hand and watched it fizz and foam around the bloody bullet. Then I tossed the mess out the window and returned to Marco's side, wiping my hand on my jeans.

Marco stitched up Santo's side with surgical sutures—his movements precise and certain like he'd had a lot of practice.

So much of Santo's skin was covered with colorful tattoos, but up close, I saw that the tattoos masked scars—puckered reminders of bullets or blades. Other scars were only skin deep.

Tears burned my eyelids as I wondered what had happened to him over the years. Some of the scars looked older, so probably from soon after I left.

Back when he was still a child.

An image of Aris and Saul 'teaching Santo a lesson' instantly came to mind. Were these scars the remnants of my baby brother's punishments? His innocence sacrificed, so the little angel could become a monster?

Or had this happened because I hadn't been there to take Aris's abuse? Had Aris turned on the only other person in the family weaker than him?

That sounded far more likely.

I pushed those thoughts out of my head. All I could do now was help Marco with the newest wound, the bullet hole that hit the center of a large, inked clock.

Santo's tattoo appeared red and raw. He hadn't been kidding about the ink being fresh. Pile on the gunshot wound, and the pain must have been intense.

He hadn't winced at all.

"Santo, are you okay?" I asked.

He opened his eyes but seemed to stare right through me. His pupils were huge. Maybe he was on something.

"I don't mind the pain, never have. It grounds me."

Santo shut his eyes, letting Marco stitch him up without complaint.

Once again, I didn't know what to say, so I just nodded and did whatever Marco told me to do.

The limo's smooth roll came to a stop.

We'd arrived at a private airstrip.

Saul got out of the car first and headed straight to the plane waiting for us while shouting into his phone in a mix of broken Italian and bad English.

He probably thought it made him seem more Italian, less like a third-generation American. It didn't.

As I got out of the car, Aris gripped the back of my neck.

"Don't even think about doing anything stupid, you traitorous cunt," he sneered.

"You have me, Aris," I shot back. "You know where my fiancé and my son live. So just where the fuck would I go?"

"You weren't even loyal to this family, and now you expect me to believe you would be loyal to that little bastard and the low-level New York asshole who knocked you up?"

Roiling heat seethed through my veins.

I sucked in a long, deep breath,

No, I wouldn't take the bait. My twin wanted a reaction—any excuse to do God only knew what to me.

I wouldn't give him the satisfaction.

Without saying a word, I let him march me to the plane and toss me into one of the leather seats.

But before Aris could get his ass into the seat next to me, Marco pushed him aside and sat there instead.

Marco raised a single brow, waiting for me to say something.

I dug my nails into my thighs, working up the nerve to ask the only thing that mattered to me, praying he wouldn't lie.

"Is my son really safe?"

"He is… if you do what you're told. Taking his life isn't worth the risk of violating the treaty again."

"What exactly does that mean?"

Marco looked over his shoulder to check on the others.

I did the same while taking in the small but luxurious jet. Losing me hadn't put my family into any dire financial straits.

Santo had kicked back on the ivory leather couch, and Aris took chair at the rear of the cabin, near the closed door that filtered Saul's continued shouting.

Satisfied, Marco sank into his chair.

"We won't go after your child unless you give us reason to.

We're not claiming him as a Moscatelli, and we have no real issue with Vignali. Don't cause problems, and it stays that way."

A flicker of relief washed over me.

"And what if I do cause a problem?"

"We'll use that leverage to put you back in line."

"I'll do what you say, Marco. Thank you for being honest."

A tear fell onto my cheek. I didn't bother wiping it away.

Then Marco leaned in and whispered close to my ear.

"You should have kept your boy away from Vignali—and stayed quiet at the café. Father never would've found you."

EIGHT
STEFANO

Hours after Moscatelli had taken my fiancée, I paced around my office like a caged animal who couldn't find its way out—seething, worrying, trying to make sense of it all. But more than anything, I was angry as fuck.

She belonged to me.

She belonged to our son.

She belonged in our home.

And in my bed.

It didn't matter to me or Enzo how many secrets she kept from us or that she came into the world a Moscatelli. I didn't even care that she'd given my son a fake name.

They were both Vignali now.

Why did her father wait so long to come for her?

I raked my hair back and looked down at Enzo.

"Back on the couch, son. Take it easy. You've been hit on the head."

Tony knocked on my office door, waited a beat, then came in and stood in his usual spot in front of my desk.

"Got some intel back on the Moscatelli family. The old man

is fourth-gen Italian. Family goes way back, like to the Capone era. His great-grandfather ran everything in Chicago, north of the river. Seems old Saul lost some footing when he took over. Still, he runs everything from Streeterville up to Old Town."

I stopped walking. Fuck. I'd focused my energy on the East Coast. Considering my original plan was to blow up shit, the Midwest syndicates never hit my radar.

"That doesn't mean anything to me, Tony. I don't know the Chicago territories or those families."

My leather chair creaked as I sat down, sparking memories of Val naked on the desktop.

I imagined her there before me, head hanging over the edge, breasts heaving, manicured nails spreading her thighs apart to offer me what was mine, her sweet-tasting wet pussy.

Tony ruined my fantasy with his big mouth.

"North Chicago. Still south of Lincoln Park, but mostly along the coast. Looks like Moscatelli runs a few legitimate real estate companies. Otherwise, he covers as a shipping company moving supplies and inventory from manufacturers across the Midwest to local businesses."

I nodded, mostly to purge the images of Val.

"What else do you have?"

"The little thug was right—your girl's name is Valentina Moscatelli. She's the family's only daughter, contracted to marry into the Russians."

"Why the fuck would an old-school mobster like Moscatelli sell his daughter to the Russians? We don't do business with the Russians."

"Hard to say, boss. But my guess is, the deal would've helped him expand without breaking treaties. Could've scaled his shipping business tenfold with a marriage like that, running his weapons and drugs through Canada to Europe and back without much trouble."

From a business standpoint, Tony's logic made sense. After nine-eleven, using ships and trains had become the most reliable way to transport arms and narcotics. TSA made international trafficking a huge pain in the ass. Border Patrol could be bribed more easily now.

New York families controlled all East Coast shipping. The families would rather slit every throat in the city before sharing lucrative Asian trade routes with outsiders like Moscatelli.

"What was in it for the Russians?" I asked.

"I believe Moscatelli was gonna help them with new transport lines moving south and west into Texas and Mexico. But the deal was broken the day of the wedding. When..."

He hesitated, then took a seat.

"When Valentina died."

I blinked at him. I had to have heard him wrong, or maybe he'd misspoken.

"What did you say?"

Tony nodded. "Yeah, big story at the time. She was on her way to the church when someone hit the car on one of the bridges. The vehicle went into the river. When they recovered a female body, everyone assumed it was her."

I understood Tony's words, but the story didn't make sense.

I looked at my son, his expression unmoved, as if he knew the story. This boy knew much more than his mother realized.

"What do you mean 'everyone assumed it was her,' Tony? There must be more to it than that."

"No positive ID on record, boss. Authorities must have been paid off."

"By whom? Are you saying she faked her death? And how the hell did she end up in New York?"

He shrugged. "It was eleven years ago. Had to be someone inside Moscatelli's organization helping her, then she skipped town. It's genius, really. Her family was too fucking dumb to look here in New York. Even if they wanted to, they would've had to risk their own lives for breaking the treaty."

It all made perfect sense and still confused the hell out of me at the same time. So the sons of bitches would break the treaty now, eleven years later, to get her back?

"I agree. Coming here was a smart move, or it would have been had she told me the truth."

Damn her. My beautiful little devil. So smart...

And stupid.

Still, Val had to be desperate enough to fake her death. Had to have known about Klimov, that she should fear for her life, which actually surprised me.

Princesses were usually kept in the dark.

Now I understood her panicked fury over our engagement announcement and why she left me in the first place.

If I had introduced her to my family, my father would have found out about hers. He would have dug into her background, and he would have sent her back to Chicago.

Val had known about the hatred between our families, that my father would return her to avoid a costly war, and she knew enough to keep herself out of Klimov's hands.

Enzo's voice pulled me out of my thoughts.

"Do you know where she is?"

I met his stare.

"Her father took her to Chicago. You said your mother had secrets. Secrets that weren't yours to share, remember?"

He nodded.

"Now is the time, Enzo. I need to know everything."

My son folded his arms.

"I told you before. Those aren't my secrets to share."

Taking a deep breath, I stood and dismissed Tony with a nod. When I reached my son, I kneeled in front of him to bring our eyes to the same level.

He needed to see the truth of the situation in my eyes.

"I know you said that, son, but to get your mother back, I need all the information I can get. Given the circumstances, she will understand. I don't think she even realizes how much you do know."

He lifted his shoulders nearly to his ears, hunching inward.

"I don't know..."

"Yes, you do. Even if she gets mad, isn't it better to have her here with us, mad but also safe with us, rather than in danger?"

I hated asking him these questions. Prying info from a child made me feel like a real shit. And this, from my own child.

It had to be done. Any information he had might be the difference between getting her back and losing her forever.

Enzo looked at the floor.

"Don't be ashamed, son, for any reason. We do what's best for your mother, no matter what it is. That's who we are."

"I guess you're right," he whispered. "I just know you're not the one she was hiding from."

I patted his knee. "That's right. She never actually ran from me. I loved her so much, I agreed to let her live without me."

His gaze met mine.

"You loved her?"

"Yes, Enzo. I did. I do."

Relief washed away the line between his brows for a fleeting moment. Then he nodded.

"All this wasn't because she wanted to keep me away from you. She had this money and all these plans for us to run away, but it wasn't because of you. Well, it was a little because of you, but not all because of you."

I nodded. "Go on."

"Someone else scared her more, and I heard her say to Nonna that you would bring them to us."

"What can you tell me about them?" I asked, careful to keep my tone even.

Whatever he knew, it scared him.

Fear was crystal clear in the glistening eyes of this brave boy who'd fought me, threatened me when he thought I meant to hurt his mother.

"The people who were in my room tonight," he said, his voice barely above a whisper. "Her father and brother—he said they're twins."

Twins? He and Val might have shared the same light blue eyes, but the man had looked empty. Val was full of light.

"Okay, so she's afraid of her father and her brother," I repeated. "Is that it?"

Enzo shook his head, staring at the floor again.

"Was she afraid of her other brothers?"

He shook his head.

"Someone else in her family, Enzo?"

He let out a heavy breath.

"I think it's the man she was supposed to marry before she had me. She had a newspaper about it hidden in her stuff."

"Klimov?" I asked.

Enzo nodded. "Yeah, maybe. I think so."

"Anything else I should know, to help your mother?"

Tony approached the doorway, papers in his hand.

While I needed the intel he'd gathered for me, I wanted to take care of my son first. I wanted him to know he was helping me get his mother back, that we would, in fact, get her back.

"I know she had a grandmother," Enzo added. "Another nonna, not the same one at Con Amore. One from before. I don't know how, but I know she helped Mama."

"How do you know all this, Enzo?"

"Con Amore Nonna told me stories. She didn't know I could tell it was true. I think she was sick."

"Okay, son, go on then."

"Like I said, the reason Mama kept me away from you was because she didn't want the monsters to find us."

"I understand," I said. "But now the monsters do have her, and we'll fight hard to get her back."

Enzo nodded again and stifled a yawn. The day had been stressful, frightening, gut-wrenching, and also tiresome, though I doubted either of us would sleep for a while.

He reached behind himself, then offered some photos.

"Here. I grabbed them from home when Mama and me got our stuff to run away. They're the only things she has left from her old life. I thought she might want them later."

I took the stack of photos from him, and the photo staring back at me on top made my chest ache.

Val looked so young, maybe sixteen, dolled up, ready for a formal event. Beside her stood a young version of the man who'd dragged her out of my house by her hair.

I brushed the curls away from Enzo's face.

"Thank you, son. Now go get some—"

"I don't want to sleep," he interrupted. "I want to go with you to get her back."

"You will," I lied. "But I don't have it all worked out yet. When I do, I'll need you to be ready. So for now, get some sleep. If anything comes up, I'll wake you."

He looked up at me with my own dark eyes.

"You said all this before. Do you promise?"

"Yes," I said.

Another lie that passed easily through my lips, sending a flash of guilt through my gut, for lying to my own son.

I couldn't bring the boy with me into a den of lions. His mother would kill me this time for sure if we made it out.

"Now go to bed, Enzo."

Yawning again, he obeyed without another word.

As soon as he left, Tony entered the room, but I lifted a hand to stop him from running his mouth. I waited a few seconds, then poked my head into the hallway to make sure Enzo had gone to his room.

He stood in the middle of the hallway.

The kid was definitely my son.

I raised a brow. *No eavesdropping tonight.*

"Move it, boy," I said before shouting for Bella.

Enzo rolled his eyes and walked away.

His attitude needed adjusting, but it could wait for a less stressful time.

Turning back to Tony, I closed the heavy wooden door behind me, and motioned for him to start.

He stared at me. "Fatherhood suits you, Stef."

I shrugged. "I have a lot to learn."

Tony smiled. "I have an address for one of Moscatelli's

houses in the Gold Coast area. And got more on Klimov, but nothing much we didn't already have."

What I knew about Klimov terrified me, but I needed to hear everything, so I nodded for him to go on.

"He's a fucking psychopath, we know that. And even the Russians are afraid of this guy. Yakuza won't go near him. He's extreme, quick to act, and shows no remorse when he gets it wrong. Jumping to conclusions is his favorite pastime, but the paranoia seems to have served him well so far.

"Good news is, boss, he's already married. So what's he going to do with an Italian bride? He can't take a second wife."

I sank down into my desk chair.

"He wouldn't marry her now anyway. She has a child, and the fucker would only take a virgin bride. It's the alternative that scares me."

I thumbed through the rest of Val's photos, looking for clues that might help me get her back, preferably without courting a war. Then I found it—my way in.

I showed Tony a photo of teenage Val posing with a group of girls in similar dresses.

"Does one of these girls with Val look familiar to you?"

He bent over my desk to peer closer.

"Which one?"

"Third from the left."

Tony sucked in a short breath.

"Holy shit. That's Benedetta Capaldo."

The woman I'd planned to marry only a week ago, before Val came back into my life. And now there she was, in a photo with Val, taken when they were teenagers.

A new wave of hot fury surged through me.

I jumped to my feet.

"She knew Val. And she said nothing."

Tony grunted. "Looks that way."

I dragged in a long breath to help control the rage burning me from the inside out.

She'd known. She'd fucking known her all along. She could have prevented this by telling me she knew Val.

Did Benedetta have something to do with Saul Moscatelli coming for my girl?

I flexed my fists.

Then I gave my next order through clenched teeth.

"You get that bitch over here right fucking now."

NINE

VAL

I sucked in a sharp breath and choked as the jet took off.

Marco had known all along.

He'd known my death was faked and where to find me.

He didn't say anything else. None of us did.

I refused to let any more tears fall, even as a lump swelled in my throat and my nose began to run.

If I sat quietly through the flight, maybe no one would pay attention to me, and I could use the time to sort through the big mess banging around inside my skull.

I spent the next two hours calming my silent frenzy and worrying about Enzo. Was he okay? Had Stefano called the doctor to examine our son's injury? Did I really have confidence in Stefano's commitment to our son? Would he keep Enzo safe?

Did my baby miss me?

Did he hate me?

"Let's go," Marco said, startling me.

Then, after leaving the plane, we climbed into another stupid fucking limo—Stefano would never use rented limos—

and I couldn't help staring out the window at the city I'd left behind so long ago.

Chicago buzzed with a different energy than New York.

Still, the two cities had a lot in common.

Neighborhoods with traditional brownstones and districts with massive high-rise buildings made of glass and steel. Beautifully preserved mansions and glorious Art Deco reminiscent of wealth and taste from an era long past.

I focused on the city as we passed through, working hard to ignore the discomfort from Aris's stare. He had something to say, I could feel the weight of it burning onto my skin, and the only reason he stayed quiet was because Marco had warned him to keep his fucking mouth shut.

It wouldn't stop Aris forever. It hadn't stopped him when we were kids. I doubted that would be different now.

No. If I knew my twin, he was biding his time. Waiting to get me alone, so he could do whatever he imagined inside his sociopathic brain.

The stop-and-go traffic slowed us down, but it was better than the constant gridlock of Manhattan. Soon enough, the rent-a-driver turned into a residential neighborhood along the Gold Coast.

As we rounded the corner onto Saul's street, a heady cocktail of emotions clawed at the inside of my chest. My throat closed again, and an intense longing swelled around my heart. For better or worse, I'd come home.

My childhood had been filled with so many horrors, so much pain. Countless obligations no child should ever carry. But a few good memories existed too.

Moments of joy, laughter, and warmth.

Those memories had all been made when my nonna was alive. So much had changed since then.

The neighborhood being one of them.

I searched for the house on the corner next to ours, the one Saul swore he would buy and tear down just because he didn't like the unruly kids who lived there. I didn't find it, because now a mid-rise tower that looked like an apartment building took up both lots.

Across the street rose a similar building instead of the duplex Saul had always complained about housing 'the wrong kind of people.'

I wondered if he preferred the mid-rise apartments, or if he hated them more than their predecessors, and why he'd allowed it in the first place.

The limo pulled up to the curb. As everyone got out, Aris gripped my neck, his fingers digging in with enough hate to leave a bruise.

He maneuvered me around the wrought-iron gated garden separating the front yard from the public sidewalk. When he knocked me into one of the sharp points of the decorative bars, I knew it was intentional.

It always was because those points never ripped my clothing or broke the skin. The perfect way to hurt me without leaving a mark.

Then he pushed me through the door, and I stumbled into a house that looked both familiar and foreign.

Cold. Empty.

I missed Nonna's voice and the smell of roasted garlic and tomatoes floating out from the kitchen to greet me. That aroma had defined the house in my memory, more than even the black-and-white marble tiles lining the foyer.

"Put her in her room until I figure out what I want to do with her," Saul barked.

"I'm gonna get some grub," Santo grumbled.

Aris marched me to my room, shoved me forward, and sent me flying. I landed on my hands and knees, my skin slapping against the rough wood floor.

Then he slammed the door and left me alone.

Pain radiated from my arm, reminding me that I'd taken a bullet only a few days before. I'd been keeping that pain masked as much as possible in front of the others. Especially from Aris.

If he saw that weakness, how much it still hurt, he would exploit it even more. He would dig his fingers into my arm again to aggravate the healing wound.

For now, at least he'd gone away.

My childhood bedroom hadn't changed a bit, either. I would have liked to think they'd kept that way as memorial, but the thick coating of dust hinted otherwise.

I pressed my ear to the door to make sure Aris had gone. Then I searched my room for anything that might help me.

Below my third-floor window lay a brick courtyard, obviously by design. This room had always been intended for a daughter. A room difficult to reach and impossible to escape, all in the name of protecting my virtue.

No electronics remained—no way to contact anyone in the outside world.

What could I have done with a phone or computer anyway?

Like a dumb fucking idiot, I hadn't memorized Stefano's number or email, and any cop who responded to a call from this neighborhood already topped the Moscatelli payroll.

I wouldn't have felt safe talking to police anyway, even if I made it out of the city and ran all the way to Joliet.

If I could find a weapon, I could protect myself when Aris came back to collect his pound of flesh.

Or maybe I'd get lucky and stumble upon a different escape.

At this point, anything was better than Klimov. I'd heard countless rumors about the man to whom my family had sold me, and if fate still meant for me to go to that monster, I might have to take matters into my own hands. Again.

The idea twisted a knot in my gut, and a cold shiver skittered down my shoulders.

My family murdered with ease, yes. They stole, cheated, schemed, betrayed, committed adultery, took the Lord's name in vain... and broke every one of the Ten Commandments time and again, but we were still Catholics.

Devoutly—hypocritically—Catholic.

Which meant I deeply believed that if I took my own life, my soul would burn in hell. I'd never meet my son in heaven.

I sat on the queen-size canopy bed, and a cloud of dust rose from the duvet.

I had to laugh.

Taking my own life was a sin, but suffering through whatever horrors Klimov had in store? Perfectly fine.

Hilarious.

Surely, faking my death had already earned me a spot in hell. If not, disobeying Saul and running away might have warranted the same eternal damnation. Or maybe it would be the premarital sex with Stefano and creating Enzo. Or all the times I'd reveled in Stefano's touch.

Even if that wasn't enough, I'd killed a man in cold blood, and I didn't feel a shred of regret.

Fuckface Luka got what he deserved.

Lying back on the bed and closing my eyes, I pictured Enzo

and prayed to my grandmothers, and once again, I had to ask for their protection over my son.

I prayed to the Virgin, asking for her guidance.

I prayed for my son to be different, for him to find a way out. And if escaping this life wasn't possible, that he found a way to be better than the men who came before him.

I had to believe I'd done my job as a mother well enough for Enzo to survive his father and strive for something greater.

I shook my head and squeezed my eyes shut.

It didn't matter what I believed.

Stefano would shape him.

The bedroom door slammed open so hard, the brass knob hit the wall and left a small dent in the plaster.

I scrambled onto my feet, chest heaving, and glared at Aris.

He strolled into my room like it wasn't an invasion.

"You've caused a lot of trouble."

I bit my tongue as he pulled a knife from his pocket, opened it, and stabbed the blade into the apple in his other hand.

Juice beaded down the ripe flesh, and my stomach growled. I couldn't remember when I'd last eaten.

Aris had made his point, but cutting up an apple gave him a legitimate reason to keep that open blade in his grip. He wanted me to know he had it, that he could turn it on me at any second.

He lived for these pointless power plays.

If I didn't do the right thing or say the right thing, his knife would be buried in my flesh as easily as it pierced that apple.

Aris wouldn't kill me. He wouldn't even scar me. He knew better. That didn't mean he couldn't hurt me.

I offered a polite smile, hoping it sufficiently hid my fear.

"How can I help you, Aris?"

His smug grin transformed instantly into a furious snarl.

"You can't do shit for me now, you stupid cunt. They had a plan. We were gonna be the most powerful family in the country, but you just had to fuck it all up. I should kill you."

Straightening my spine, I stepped forward, holding his gaze with hope it would prove he no longer intimidated me. I was a grown woman, not the little girl who'd run away.

Either Aris would recognize that, or he wouldn't. Either way, I didn't have to stand there and listen to him belittle me.

How many times would we have this same damn kill-me-or-don't-kill me conversation?

"Then just fucking do it," I said.

He came closer, slowly, one step at a time, pulling the blade from the apple to point it at me.

"What did you say to me, you little whore?"

"I said if you're going to kill me, then just do it."

My twin's sneer tightened and twisted, hatred and malice gleaming in his eyes. It made me wonder if he might really do it this time. My death by taunting Aris into ending it for me.

Suicide by twin.

"Don't worry, sister," he said. "I'll get my moment. Father's already called the Russians. Once they confirm they don't want your traitorous whore-ass anymore, I'll do whatever the fuck I want. Sending you back to your lover and his little bastard one piece at a time sounds like fun."

Ice needled through my veins. My stomach churned. I pushed down the nausea, recognizing Aris's words not as a threat, but as a promise—one he would keep if I disappointed him.

Even with all my fear, I stared him down, silently daring him to do it now, to get it over with.

Marco appeared in the doorway.

"Aris. Father needs us downstairs."

Aris glared daggers at me, knife at the ready.

"I'll be down in a second."

"Now," Marco barked.

"We're not finished with this," Aris hissed as he pointed his blade at me. Then he turned on his heel and marched out of the room after Marco.

After they vanished, another figure appeared in my doorway. Santo stared blankly at me with a thin cardboard box in his hand. He opened the lid to reveal a deep-dish pizza.

"Hungry?"

"No," I lied.

Sweet mother of Christ, it smelled divine.

My mouth watered, but I didn't know if I could trust him. Then my stomach growled loud enough for him to hear.

Santo smiled, and that made the decision for me.

A fleeting image returned to me in a flash. I saw in that smile the little boy he used to be, but it vanished just as quickly.

My now-grown brother's smile also disappeared, taking the light from his eyes with it. The moment was over, his true self reverting once again to the mask of cold boredom.

"Shove over."

He nudged me out of the way so he could sit on the bed.

Once situated, he ripped the lid off the pizza box and tore it in half to make two makeshift plates.

Marco used to do it just like that when we were young. He'd take us to the park with a pizza, so we could spoil our dinner without anyone finding out. Every Sunday after church, while Saul met with various men at the house for business, Marco led the three of us out to the park.

It seemed like the perfect escape back then, especially from all those strange men who'd always made me uncomfortable in a way I hadn't been able to explain until I was older. I never knew who those men were, but I knew enough to stay away.

My memories soured, and I shook my head to clear them away. They made me soft anyway. Weak.

I didn't know who Santo was anymore. I didn't know what to expect, and that scared me, so my best option was to keep my guard up, no matter how many memories rushed back to me now that I'd come home.

"Why are you doing this?" I asked.

He handed me one makeshift cardboard plate with a giant slice of pizza staining the center and oozing with melted cheese and copious amounts of grease. Then he reached into a bag on the floor and pulled out a plastic fork. He stared at me for a second before handing it to me.

"Because you gotta eat, and New York pizza sucks. I don't know what the plan is yet, but if we're gonna deliver you to the Russians, I'm pretty sure they don't want you starved to death."

I considered that for a second, then shrugged.

No, I couldn't let myself trust him, but he did have a point about New York's inferior pizza crusts.

"From what I've heard," I said, "I don't think the Russians will care either way."

Santo stopped chewing for a second.

"You know it hurt her, right? When you left?"

"Who?"

He looked at me like I'd somehow betrayed her by leaving.

"Nonna."

There was no point explaining what had happened, her involvement, so I just gave him a gentle smile.

"I think she would have understood."

He sighed. "Look, you know they know I'm in here. You know they want information, and if you wanna eat your pizza in peace, I need to be able to tell them something. Just give me enough to get the old man off my ass."

Had they planned this? Aris played the bad cop to scare me, then Santo came in acting like the beloved little brother? Like he was the reasonable one?

"What do you want to know?"

"What made you think you could get away with it?"

I looked at my cardboard plate and stared at the vaguely triangular-shaped slice splattered with red sauce and cheese.

"I did get away with it."

With those words, I finally gave in and took the first huge, melty, steaming bite of Chicago deep-dish pizza.

The instant explosion of flavor elicited a primal groan of enjoyment from my throat as I chewed. The hearty combination of Italian meats and cheeses, the incredible sauce heavily spiced with herbs, and the doughy crust dusted with flour—it was what heaven tasted like.

Santo gestured at the walls of my bedroom.

"And you call this getting away with it?"

"I was gone for ten years," I said. "I had a life. I called the shots. I had a job and a child, and if it wasn't for Stefano forcing his way back into my life and making a stupid engagement announcement, you never would've known I was still alive."

"Maybe. But he did, and we found you... living with a rival family in enemy territory. With his son."

He raised a brow and took another bite.

"Yes, Santo. With my son."

None of this was new information for him or Saul, so I didn't think stating the obvious really mattered.

Santo shifted on my bed. One corner of his mouth twitched into a grimace before he let out another sigh. He'd been shot just hours beforehand, and it had to still hurt like a bitch.

I would know.

"Here's the thing, sister. I can't go back out there empty-handed. At the very least, Father wants to know who helped you. You couldn't have done all that by yourself."

"You know what? I've come to realize I'm very resourceful when I need to be. It's amazing what a woman can do on her own, when she isn't existing under the constant control of a man who sees her as a shiny object meant for brokering deals. But yeah, Santo, I did have help faking my death."

"Who did it?"

I shrugged. "It was Nonna."

Then I took another greasy bite.

I hated betraying her, but she'd been dead for years. Saul couldn't hurt her anymore.

Santo's immediate wince was even more noticeable than his grimace of pain, though it too disappeared in a flash. Just like every other expression he displayed.

"What really happened to you?" I asked. "To the bright little boy who was always smiling and laughing?"

He shrugged, and resentment filled his eyes.

"Isn't it obvious? You left. Nonna died. Marco took on more responsibility. You all left me here with Father and Aris. Alone. That's what happened to me."

I took several tries before I finally swallowed my mouthful of pizza. To my surprise, though, my voice held steady.

"I'm so sorry, Santo."

Then the sad truth fully hit me.

What I did from then on didn't even matter. Not really.

Even if I hadn't faked my death, the Russians would have hauled me away, and still, I never would have seen Santo again. Nonna still would have died. No one could have protected him from the reality of our family.

He shook his head. "Don't be. I do just fine. If you should feel sorry for anyone, it's your son."

I froze. A piece of crust fell from my fork.

"Marco said you'd leave him alone. I'm here. I'm not running. I'll do as I'm told. Leave him out of this."

Santo laughed, and not the joyful, genuine laughter of his youth, but something dark, twisted, and cruel.

I set the pizza down and looked him in the eye.

"Let me make this perfectly clear, little brother. If you or anyone else goes near my son, I don't care where I am or what it takes, I will find a way to kill every one of you."

He arched his brows at me.

"We don't have to do anything to your kid. He's being raised by a savage New York boss. What kind of life do you think the boy will have?"

The greasy food in my stomach churned.

I had wondered the same thing countless times.

To deepen my fear, Santo echoed the deeper question I had agonized over since the day Enzo was born.

"I mean, come on, what kind of man do you think Stefano Vignali will make out of his son?"

I didn't have an answer, but Santo did.

"Take a good look at me, sister... I'm your son in ten years."

TEN
STEFANO

Lying on my bed, I bent my arm and flung it over my face to cover my eyes and block the sunlight streaming in through the open draperies.

Bella had opened them. Her morning routine to wake me.

Only I hadn't slept. I wasn't sure I'd slept in ten years.

"Fuck," I breathed. "Get out, Bella. Consider yourself my son's full-time nanny and stay out of my room from now on."

Val's room. Our room.

"Yes, sir," she whispered. "Thank you, sir. Should I—"

"Close the curtains and go."

After she whipped the velvet panels shut and hurried out of the room, I opened my eyes again and stared at the ceiling.

Rage burned inside me, steadily rising closer to the surface, hour by the hour. Getting caught up in Val's scent as it clung to the sheets didn't help. It should have brought me peace. It only pissed me off more.

She should have been lying next to me.

Her father had infiltrated my house and taken her. He'd taken what belonged to me, the fat old fuck, and he would pay for it. He would pay for every mark on her body, every tear she cried, and every moment my son didn't have his mother.

But Moscatelli hadn't done it on his own. Someone in my organization had betrayed me to help him.

With every inhale, as her scent overwhelmed my senses, another kind of fury pumped through my veins.

It's all her fault.

She had put me in this position. She kept the truth from me. She brought those men into my home.

Worse than that, she had made me love her.

Before Val came back into my life, I never spent my nights worrying about anyone. I spent them scheming, strategizing, planning the structure of one of New York's most formidable empires, and calculating how I would burn it all down when the time was right.

I never gave a fuck about any girl, or about a son I didn't know existed and the legacy I might leave behind for him.

I'd been content with my decision to marry someone I didn't love, knowing I could use her family to get revenge for mine. Content to have my legacy die with me.

Not anymore.

Everything had changed in one night.

I was uncertain if this path had been laid out a decade earlier, the night of my son's conception, simply remaining dormant until the right moment struck, or if my fate forged a new path the night I found my son.

It didn't matter.

All that mattered now was getting Val back from Chicago.

First, I had to lay to rest the men who had died for me.

Rocco had managed not only the cleanup, but also the memorial service and burial. He had the necessary connections in place. Pulling these things together at a moment's notice was his superpower.

He'd quickly arranged for the families to arrive and say their goodbyes inside the protection of my concrete walls.

Even as a made man and skilled earner, this talent made him more valuable to me than anything else.

I grabbed my phone from the nightstand and checked for a message from Benedetta. Nothing.

That bitch would pay for not replying.

After jumping into the shower and dressing in one of my black Brioni suits, I headed down the hall to my office, sending a message to Tony while walking.

> You drag that bitch out of her father's house with a gun to her head if you must but you get her to my office now

Tony strode in right behind me.

"I'll go get her myself, boss. Came to tell you we found text messages between Nico and a 312 area code."

Nico, one of the men I was about to bury.

"Chicago?" I asked.

"Yep, Gold Coast... Moscatelli's residential neighborhood. Promised him fifteen grand to get them inside."

Apparently, Moscatelli had no problem breaking promises.

Or necks.

"I had the boys put his body in the basement," Tony added. "Rocco's picking it up, sending him through the incinerator."

I nodded. "Good work, Tony. Get Bruce to drive you over to Capaldo's house. I don't want you doing any heavy lifting."

Once Tony had shut the door behind himself, I stared out the French door overlooking the courtyard, working to subdue my anger while waiting for that traitorous bitch Benedetta to get her little ass up here.

I couldn't believe all the lies unraveling before me.

First Val, now Benedetta.

They had chatted in my kitchen over cookies and coffee, for fuck's sake. And they'd posed for the same photo with a group of all-Italian girls at sixteen. Yeah, they fucking knew each other.

Benedetta should have told me, her loyalty should have been to me, but instead she either played ignorant or covered for Val.

Thinking about it now, could've been she was willing to break our marriage contract because she didn't want to find herself in the way of the fucking Moscatelli family.

She should have feared me more.

And she would soon learn that.

I had to wonder how much she actually knew, whose side she was on, and if she'd shared her knowledge with anyone else.

Was Benedetta responsible for Moscatelli finding Val?

Unable to rein in my dark energy, I prowled back and forth in front of the bookcase along the far wall, pausing only long enough to grab my grandfather's vintage Dupont lighter.

With the muscle memory from years of practice, I repeated flicking the gold cap open and shut, listening to the swipe of metal on metal followed by the distinctly satisfying click of the magnets engaging again to close the top.

Open and close.

Swish, click. Swish, click.

The sound soothed me as I formulated strategic scenarios in my head while waiting for Benedetta.

Finally, Tony appeared with her in hand.

He gave her a rough shove through the doorway.

"Next time, you'll respond to him immediately," he said.

Then he nodded at me once before leaving us alone.

I'd never seen Benedetta in any state other than polished and poised. But now her messy hair hung loose over her shoulders, and her wrinkled clothing contrasted with her usual meticulously selected and tailored wardrobe.

That combined with the lack of jewelry indicated she had indeed been dragged straight out of bed.

She stumbled into the room, then stomped like a child.

"What's this about, Stefano? Your man shows up at my house and demands I come here in his car. He wouldn't even allow me to get dressed."

"You should have been here last night," I warned. "I ordered you here in the text message you chose not to answer."

She stared at me, her eyes a little wild, hands on her hips.

"I didn't get the message until just this morning. Some of us actually sleep occasionally, you know."

I narrowed my eyes, lowered my voice.

"Is that what you were doing last night, sleeping peacefully while my fiancée was taken from my house—after you told them where to find her? Of course, why should her abduction at gunpoint while they used my son for target practice disrupt your beauty sleep."

I watched her face carefully to judge her reaction.

Benedetta frowned as she looked me up and down.

"I have no idea what you're talking about. Is Enzo okay?"

I threw the lighter across the room, where it shattered a vase sitting on one of the shelves.

She jumped, but only concern filled her eyes.

I stalked toward her, my voice low and deadly.

"I want to know why. You said you had no problem with breaking off our engagement, and I believed you. You should have come to me. I would have made whatever you needed right. You didn't have to tell them where to find her."

I pounded my fist on my chest.

"You talk to me, goddamn it, and I'll fix it."

Benedetta spread her arms while shaking her head.

"Tell who where to find who? I have no idea what the fuck you're even talking about."

I didn't think I'd ever heard her swear before. My gut told me she wasn't lying, but both women had lied to me, and I wasn't sure I could trust my gut anymore.

"You contacted her family, without so much as a warning sent my way. They came here armed, broke into my fucking house, killed my men, took her, and almost killed my son."

"Who?" she screamed.

"Like you don't fucking know, Benedetta."

"No, I don't know. Either tell me what you're talking about or let me go home."

I reached into my pocket for the photo and slapped it on the desk before turning away. I couldn't look at her anymore, so I stalked across the room to stare outside.

Dead silence filled the air.

"How did you get this picture?" Benedetta finally asked.

Still peering out the glass, I managed an even tone again.

"Val kept it as a memento from her old life."

Benedetta gasped. "She's Valentina Moscatelli?"

I turned to see her face. Her eyes were wide, and her lips were parted as she stared at the photo.

"You really didn't know?" I asked.

"No, I promise. I thought she looked a little familiar, but I wouldn't have placed her in a million years. Valentina and I met only a few times. Her father never let her do much, not even hang out with the other daughters.

"And we all thought she died. I mean, there were rumors that it hadn't been an accident. She was hardly the first mafia bride to suffer a tragic and fatal accident before her wedding."

Her words struck me numb. "What?"

Tears welled in her eyes.

"I swear, Stefano, I didn't realize it was her."

"I'm asking about the 'tragic and fatal accident' thing... what do you mean by that?"

Benedetta blinked up at me.

"Oh. Well, mafia brides die before their weddings all the time. Sometimes it's suicide, sometimes homicide. Maybe the groom doesn't like what he sees. If she's dead, he isn't honor bound to marry her. Mistresses have been known to take a life as well. I know you know this."

And I did, but it never really hit me until she'd said it.

"Not so much in New York," she added, "but Chicago's still rough when it comes to marrying off daughters. Not being satisfied with a business deal is another reason for getting rid of a bride. Considering the circumstances for Valentina's wedding, I assumed that had happened to her. We all did."

Her gaze softened as she studied me.

"It's not uncommon, Stefano."

"How common is it?" I demanded.

"Common enough that the possibility of Val having me killed if I didn't back down from our engagement had definitely crossed my mind. If I'd realized she was a Moscatelli, I would have given it more serious consideration."

I crossed the room again, hanging on her every word.

"What do you know about her?"

"Probably not much more than you at this point. I know she's the only daughter of Saul Moscatelli. Her engagement was kept hush-hush. There were rumors of her marrying outside of the Italian families, which pissed off a lot of people."

"What else?"

"I know her older brother, Marco, is currently in the market for a bride. Last I heard, it still hasn't been settled. If my father didn't hate Saul Moscatelli so much, there's a chance he would have given me to Marco."

"Why does he hate Moscatelli?"

She shrugged. "He doesn't trust him. He says Saul lacks vision and any form of moral compass."

She held on to the photo as she glided across the floor to perch on the edge of the sofa, as if sitting too hard might damage the upholstery.

If she'd had any idea what Val and I had done on that sofa, she might not have treated it so delicately. Christ. I needed to focus on the issue at hand instead of a memory of lying naked with Val's pretty little body pressed against mine.

I scoffed. "That's amusing—your father judging others for their lack of morals."

"I know," Benedetta said. "My father doesn't always live up to the code. He has his own way, making clear what he is and isn't willing to do, lines he will and won't cross.

"But my father says Saul Moscatelli has no such lines. It was rumored he knew his daughter would likely be dead within a year if he agreed to the Russian wedding, but he sold her to them anyway. He drank to her engagement like the wedding was going to be the event of the century."

I nodded, my chest aching for Val.

"How do you know so much about this?"

"Remember, my family is one of the few who can move freely between New York and Chicago. I chose to be in New York, yes, but you know most of my mother's family is still in Chicago, and I am still very well informed."

I snapped my gaze over to her.

Of course. Part of the reason I'd wanted to marry her.

"Informed enough to know where Val's being held?"

I held my breath, hardly daring to hope.

Benedetta stood and wandered aimlessly around my office.

"Possibly."

"Informed enough to get me inside? To help me bring the mother of my child home?"

"That depends. How did they find out about her?"

"Seems it was the wedding announcement I put out. Tony did some digging and found out a Chicago newspaper picked it up and then wrote about the lost Moscatelli daughter."

She turned to face me.

"So her return is public knowledge?"

Something about the calculating look in her eyes set me on edge. It wasn't new, but I'd only seen it in men who feigned loyalty just before they tried to manipulate me. It never ended well for them.

If Benedetta could help get Val back, there wasn't a damn thing I wouldn't do, even allow that fucking look. Once.

I raked my fingers through the top of my hair.

"I assume so. Why does it matter?"

"Because if it's public knowledge, she'll be expected to attend specific events. I can't promise her safe return, but I can get you close enough to find out where they're keeping her. Maybe even in the same room with her. Then you can take it from there."

I wanted to believe her, but I couldn't act on blind faith.

"Lay out a detailed plan... I want to know exactly what I'm walking into."

She stared at me with a blank expression.

"I'm not just going to give it to you. If the Moscatellis find out, I'm dead. And it won't be an easy death like a bullet to the head either. They'll make me suffer for my betrayal. They'll make an example of both me and my father."

I flexed my fingers, closed them into fists.

"So you don't want to help me. Hmm. Well, I could always make you do it."

Benedetta took a deep breath and straightened, pushing her shoulders back and her chest forward.

"I didn't say that. I just want you to understand exactly what I'm risking before we start bargaining."

I stepped in close to her.

"Bargaining? Why would I bargain for anything when I could simply force you to give me what I want?"

She didn't budge under the weight of my threat.

"You could, but you really don't have the time. Not if you want this to work. Bargaining may have been the wrong word to use. What I mean is, you're going to give me what I want."

She raised a brow and folded her arms.

"Otherwise, Stefano, there's really no chance in hell you'll see Valentina again."

ELEVEN

VAL

Santo's words hung in the air between us, echoing, but he was wrong. My son would never be like him.

But how well did I really know Stefano?

I knew the charming and cocky young man I'd fallen so hard for more than a decade ago, but power and his desire for vengeance had changed him.

How many people had he tortured and killed as head of his family? Would he do it again to get me back yet again?

I questioned how much Enzo had witnessed when Stefano tracked me down to get me back from my previous captor.

The man had taken my nine-year-old boy with him on a dangerous rescue mission and gave him a fucking gun.

And I'd left my son with this man.

I didn't have a choice. I had to do it.

Stop it. You do know Stefano well enough.

My gut—no, my heart told me his had stayed the same.

Savage enemy or not, when Stefano Vignali loved, he loved very deeply, and nothing else mattered to him.

He hadn't built a massive empire because he craved power. He built it because he'd loved his family so much.

Love was the reason he'd become so hell-bent on revenge.

But now he had to defeat two cities.

My heartbeat thumped inside my ears as I stared down at my pizza slice, trying to hold back the overwhelming tremor vibrating in my bones. My stomach flipped, the greasy cheeses no longer sitting well.

My mind spiraled, and I didn't hear Marco when he entered the room, not until he sat heavily on the other side of the bed, bouncing me on the mattress.

"Did you guys save me some?" he asked.

Santo slid the pizza box across the bed.

"Yeah, eat up, bro."

Observing the calm in Marco's demeanor created an intense panic inside me, and tears burned my eyelids. I wanted to scream out loud. I wanted to fall apart. But I couldn't let my emotions take control. I had to think clearly. I had to come up with a plan.

Find a way to escape. Get back to my son.

Beg Stefano to forgive me and help me. If he killed Saul, maybe it would all be over, and for good this time.

Aris would have to die as well.

I didn't know about Marco or Santo yet.

All I did know was I had to find a way to get to Stefano.

Santo pointed at the stains on Marco's white shirt.

"Where did the blood come from?"

"Christ," Marco grumbled. "I just bought this shirt."

Santo let out a genuine, boyish laugh.

"So whose blood is it?" I asked, forgetting myself.

"Doesn't matter," Marco said, waving off my question.

Then he settled the pizza box on his lap and dug into a slice.

Santo folded his arms and smirked like he knew something.

"Where's Aris… did he learn anything this time?"

Marco sighed. "He's downstairs with Father right now, getting some things handled. You should go help."

Santo shrugged. "Or I could stay up here and avoid the sociopath altogether."

"Which one?" I blurted.

Oh mother of Christ, had I really just said that out loud? I immediately pressed my lips together.

Me shit-talking Saul to my brothers was a big no-no.

We all thought it, but voicing it crossed a line.

"Go now, Santo," Marco ordered.

Santo rolled his eyes, cursed under his breath while looking at me a little differently than before, like he was seeing me now instead of looking through me.

Then he left the room, leaving me alone with my older brother for the first time since they'd taken me.

Santo's departure prompted an instant change in mood, the tension making the air feel thicker and amplifying the silence.

Marco got up and shut the door, turned the lock, and let the overwhelming quiet suffocate me. Time slowed as he made his way back to his seat on the bed.

I once trusted him, the brother who had protected me from Saul and the leering eyes of Saul's disgusting friends.

Now Marco locked us in a room together, his shirt sleeve notably splattered with blood as he glared at me.

Had Saul turned Marco into a monster?

Had the old bastard beat the honor and goodness out of my older brother like he beat the joy out of Santo?

"You should have stayed dead, girl."

I released a long exhale.

He didn't look angry. His words didn't come off like a threat, just a stated fact. Then his stone-cold expression melted, and my brother came around the bed to stand in front of me.

The brother I'd needed in my life for the past decade.

The brother I'd missed so much.

I swallowed back the thickness in my throat.

"You mentioned that on the plane. It was the plan, believe me. How long have you known about me?"

After grabbing his pizza, Marco sat on Santo's previous spot at the foot of the bed, facing me, leaning against the footboard.

"So now that you're back," he said, ignoring my question, "some things have changed."

The permanent knots in my stomach tightened.

"Changed how, Marco?"

"Father's already contacted the Russians to let them know you're here. Part of the deal fell through after your disappearance, but not all. A few covenants must still be upheld, and one of them means the Russians still have a claim on you."

My mouth fell open, though it shouldn't have surprised me.

"A claim on me? I'm a person, not a fucking dairy cow."

Marco scoffed. "Don't act naïve. It doesn't suit you anymore. We both know how this works. You belong to Father until married, then you become your husband's property—"

Before he finished speaking, I shook my head.

"It's archaic and it's wrong."

He shrugged and finished chewing.

"Immoral, cruel, totally fucked-up, but it's still how our world operates. I can't change it for you. You know as well as I do, the family must come first."

The blood splatter on his sleeve caught my attention again, the spray pattern moving up his arm from knuckles to elbow.

I hoped like hell he'd broken Aris's nose.

"So what happens now?" I asked. "I'm expected to pick up exactly where it ended eleven years ago and marry the man who bought me? Like nothing ever happened?"

"No." Marco leaned against the tall wooden footboard, then set his cardboard plate to the side.

Relieved just a little, I let my shoulders relax until I noticed the growing concern in my brother's frown.

"Then what, Marco?"

"That ship has long since sailed and thank fuck. Klimov married another teenage bride about a year ago. You're way too old for him now, not to mention impure."

Was that disgust showing in my brother's eyes?

"Great," I muttered. "So what are my options?"

"Well, Father's still negotiating the particulars with Klimov. I don't have any specifics yet, but I do know they want to see you before they make any further commitments."

"Of course. Inspect the inventory before the final sale."

I couldn't believe it. After having been raised in this world, knowing exactly what I meant to the men in my family and which "duties" they expected me to perform, it still made my fucking blood boil.

And it hurt terribly. Marco not putting a stop to it broke my heart.

Then again, I'd also had ten years of freedom. Being forced back into this role now was sure to sting.

But in their eyes, especially Saul's, I wasn't really a human being. No one would ask what I wanted. My opinion had no bearing on the conversation, and no one would ever request it. I would never be consulted before a decision was made, but I'd certainly be informed afterward.

Fucking asshole mafia men.

"And what does Saul get this time?" I asked.

Marco blinked, then stared at me for a minute.

"I don't know yet for sure..."

He let the sentence hang, not giving voice to the horrible things already filling my head.

I released a slow breath.

"When are they coming to evaluate the goods?"

"Masquerade ball at the Palmer House in three days. They'll send someone to get the first look at you before reporting back."

"What?" I stared at him in disbelief. "I can't be there. I'm supposed to be dead."

"No, Valentina, you're not. The papers here picked up Vignali's announcement, so everyone realizes you're alive. You're expected to make an appearance, to make small talk, explain your absence, and celebrate your happy return to the family, however brief it might be."

I leaped to my feet and paced, vibrating out of my own skin.

"I don't care what I'm expected to do."

The walls had closed in on me, and I just couldn't take it anymore. Too much energy coursed through me, too many senseless thoughts swirled around inside my head.

Marco watched me, his gaze following me back and forth.

"Father wanted them here to conduct whatever inspection they wanted, which would have meant getting their answer as soon as tomorrow. But I convinced them the masquerade ball would be a better opportunity to negotiate further."

I shot him a quick glance, unable to stop my frantic pacing.

"How? Or did you really just want to show me off?"

"I think you know me better than that. Father never gave a fuck about you. He didn't care what happened to you, and he still doesn't. I made the arrangement because I would prefer the assessment be made in public, where they can't hurt you."

God, I didn't know whether to laugh or to cry, so I chose to behave like any other Moscatelli asshole.

"Yay for me. Oh, I guess I should thank you for this great reprieve, but fuck you, Marco."

With that one gesture, though, he'd already done more for me than Saul ever had or would, but I needed to lash out.

"What you should thank me for is giving Vignali a window of opportunity to claim you and take you back to his home where you belong, with your son."

"What?" I tripped over my own feet as I spun around to stare at my brother. "What did you say?"

"Come here, *sorellina*. Sit and talk to me. Let me fill you in on the plan, yeah? If this is going to work, I need to know a few things about your man. I need to know if he's gonna come through if I set this thing up."

Sorellina. His baby sister.

I wanted to throw my arms around him and sob.

He was giving me a fighting chance.

I'd been so afraid for so long, and I never let myself miss any part of my old life—not even my protective big brother.

I climbed onto the bed beside him, my heels tucked under my bottom, and gave him my full attention.

Just like when we were children.

"What do you need to know about Stefano?"

"Does he have any friends in Chicago?"

I shook my head. "Not like that. The Commission makes it

impossible. The only person he knows who can move between the two cities is Benedetta Capaldo."

"Would she help him?"

I sucked air through my teeth and shook my head.

"No, probably not. He set her aside for me. They planned to get married two days after he found out about Enzo."

"So no love lost?"

"She couldn't have avoided the scandal, not completely."

Truth be told, I didn't like the idea of Stefano anywhere near Benedetta. I didn't know her well enough to know if she would help or try to take my place.

I couldn't even be sure what I might do if I were her. It wouldn't be hard for her to tempt Stefano away from me. She came with a lot of power. A lot of influence, money, and men. Everything Stefano had ever wanted.

Would he now let her into the home he intended to share with me just a few days earlier? Would he let her sleep in my place beside him?

Would she embrace Enzo as her own, or would she become his evil stepmother?

I didn't know how far she might go to get Stefano back or if she even wanted him back. I wouldn't put it past her having been the one to tell my family about the newspaper article.

"I don't think he has any allies here," I added. "His family honored the treaty practically to the letter. Is there any way to get him a message or... would it matter even if we did?"

Marco twisted his mouth the way he always did when he was working through something heavy.

"Father's rash, but he can be reasoned with when promised something he covets. If the Russians back away from their claim, and Vignali is there to approach him with a lucrative offer around the same time, something Father expected back when you were first out... maybe you can go home to your boy."

A moment of excitement flashed through me.

"Can we make the Russians back off?"

"Don't know yet, but assuming they did, Vignali's offer would have to be incredible. Too good for Father to pass up. That's the only way I see him letting you go back to New York."

"Okay, so we come up with an offer. What's the going rate for a woman these days?"

A caustic taste of the whole idea coated my tongue and sharpened my next words.

"Lower than average because I'm not a virgin, right? Or higher because I've proven I can bear sons? Do we trade in goats, or is US currency also acceptable?"

A flash of a smile warmed his blue eyes.

"For Christ's sake, sorellina. I've protected you since birth, believe it or not. I gave you a chance to live a normal life. It wasn't forever, but ten or eleven years is still a long time. No one else in this family got a chance like that.

"I've always had your best interest in mind. Why else would I give our nonna the resources she needed to get you out? Trust that I have your best interest in mind now, all right?"

I blinked at him. "You?"

No, it couldn't have been.

Nonna had told me she wouldn't stand by and watch what happened to her daughter-in-law, my beautiful dead mother, also happen to me.

Marco nodded. "Me. I made sure the old woman who took you in gave you a good home and a job. When she passed, I transferred the deed to you."

"Why?" I asked breathlessly.

"That's not important."

"Well, it's important to me."

He shrugged as he swiped the pizza crumbs off my bed.

"I mean to change things here. I want organized crime in Chicago to be more civilized. I want the bottom line to be the most important one. And I want to end the worst practices surrounding our traditions. Because they're disgusting, yes, and because it makes us more vulnerable to law enforcement.

"We've locked ourselves in the same gutter for too many generations. It must improve before we're no longer able to survive it. But change like this takes leverage. And leverage takes alliances—even with men Father considered his enemies."

I studied him a moment longer, then wrinkled my nose.

"That still doesn't tell me why—"

"I'm getting to that."

He leaned forward to brush the crumbs off his hands onto the floor, then he stared at me, holding my gaze as he continued.

"I couldn't take over before your wedding. I wanted to, but I didn't have the skills or the support to do it then. Ten years ago, there's no way I would've won that battle. But now? I'm close. I did what I could back then to save you before you were lost to us forever."

He'd done that for me? He had helped his little sister fake her death, so she wouldn't have to marry a deranged Russian? To save me?

The backs of my lids burned like crazy as tears filled my eyes.

"Marco, I—"

He lifted his hand.

"Not important. What's important is just how far Vignali will go to have you. Will he risk everything to get you back?"

TWELVE
STEFANO

Benedetta rolled her shoulders as if she were the one in the position of power. I supposed she was... for the moment.

Her next words affected Val's future, but I didn't know how much power I could afford to let her wield without losing mine.

I sat at my desk, stunned, waiting for her demands.

"Well? What is it you think I'm going to do for you?"

"I'd like to make a deal."

I glared at her but said nothing.

Benedetta's confidence waned, her trembling bottom lip giving her away. Then she cleared her throat and came across the room, meeting my gaze without looking away, something women like her were trained never to do.

Women like her were raised to believe they could never stand on equal footing with men like me. Or in any case, they knew enough to never act like it, common sense and human decency be damned.

She thrust out her chin.

"I want you to take control of my father's men."

The fuck? I tapped my desk with a finger and stared at her.

This wasn't about me simply taking her father's empire from him. It would have been mine if I'd married her, but that was the only bartering chip she owned anymore, and it was only good for finding a husband.

Was that what this was? Had Benedetta just asked me to marry her, so I could find the woman I really wanted to marry?

"You know my father's sick," she added.

She sank into the chair opposite mine and leaned forward over the desk, a move that offered a nice view of her cleavage if I wanted it. I did not.

Still, she'd been dragged into my home like a traitor, and now she attempted to barter with me like a man while trying to use her feminine appeal to soften my disposition.

Impressive. And fucking stupid.

I wouldn't touch any woman but my Val.

Even so, it wouldn't hurt to let Benedetta play all her cards and see where they fell.

"I'm aware," I said. "Last I heard, his doctors gave him just a few more months."

"You've heard only what my father has allowed."

"Your father hasn't allowed shit. I found the information myself. I've got leverage, and I know what's going on. Trust me, your father's base isn't as airtight as he'd have you believe."

Benedetta rolled her eyes. Under different circumstances, the show of disrespect would have had grave consequences.

I would give her a single pass this time—but if she wanted to bargain like a man, I would treat her like one from here on out.

"My father doesn't have months left," she said. "He's always known the severity of his illness, and he leaked the information to rush negotiations with you, so he wouldn't have to negotiate your deal from a position of weakness."

I raised my brows. If what she said were true, the old man had made a sly move. I hadn't thought he had it in him.

Good on him.

"It's true. He picked you from an impressive lineup, and he knows you're the one to…"

She paused to carefully select her next words. Smart girl.

"To eliminate a fair amount of competition. He admires your moves—your precise targeting and your surprisingly low death toll or loss of revenue."

"Let me see if I understand your plan," I said. "You want us to get married so I can take control of your father's empire before he passes. In return, you'll get me to Chicago to rescue Val. And after all that, which of us is going to explain to her why I've made her the fool in this scenario?

"Why even bother pulling her away from her family's claim if I can't override it with marriage? Those assholes would be back here quickly to take her home again, and I would be back to square one. Worse, they kill more of my men—and maybe they kill my son."

Those last words pitched my stomach up into my throat.

Benedetta drew in a deep breath.

"That's not the plan. I want you to assume control of my father's men, yes, because they will never follow me and might even kill me, but I said nothing about marriage."

"That's the only way without upsetting the other families and involving the Commission."

"No, it isn't. It's the easiest way, but not the only way. I have another idea if you're willing to hear it."

I waved for her to continue, my pulse echoing in my ears.

"I've had a contract drawn up that will temporarily hand you control of my father's empire. Everything from his men to the businesses and the operations they cover. He's no longer able to lead, but you are.

"With this agreement, Stefano, you'll act as regent, safe-guarding my family legacy until I find a suitable husband. Then, once I'm married, control passes to my husband."

Ah. Yes, smart girl.

"I think you mean once I find a suitable husband for you."

The corner of her mouth twitched.

"Absolutely not. The contract is set up that way, but off the record, I want your word that you'll stay out of it. I want you to allow me the time and the opportunity to vet my own potential matches. I decide who I marry. You have no say in the matter."

She pursed her lips and lifted her chin ever so slightly.

"Acting regents inherit the responsibility of choosing a husband," I said.

"Well, yes, on paper. But if we have a verbal agreement—like we once had regarding not having children—and I have your word that you'll hand the responsibility to me, then we can make it work. Let the men think whatever they want.

"Because the only way this happens is if I get the right to choose my husband. Let me find someone I personally deem worthy, Stefano. Then you'll be free of me."

Her eyes misted, and at some point during her speech, she'd gone from calm and collected to openly pleading.

I folded my arms and squeezed my biceps.

"And what criteria would you use?"

Benedetta stared at the desk.

"Criteria of my choosing. It's no concern of yours."

"Oh, but it is, sweetheart. Anything that gives the Commission more power than me will be a hard no. I want the right to veto your choice."

"Do you really think I'm not aware of the cards I hold and the type of men who covet my inheritance?"

Her voice had risen in pitch and volume, approaching a level of disrespect I wouldn't tolerate a second time.

I narrowed my eyes and dipped my chin.

"Careful, Benedetta."

She thrust her fucking finger in my direction.

"No, you listen to me. I agreed to marry you. I'd resigned myself to that fate, then I allowed you to break our contract when Valentina showed up. Not only did I not complain, but I understood. Because I understand that love is rare, and when it's found, it should be honored.

"Now I'm giving you a better chance to reclaim that love. All I'm asking for in return is the opportunity to find mine. Can you honestly say I don't deserve a shot at something more than all this?"

Her eyes roamed about, tears on the verge of spilling, as she opened her arms to gesture around my office.

Tears wouldn't sway me. She should have known that.

Benedetta clenched her hands into fists then, her long nails no doubt cutting into her soft flesh. She wanted this more than I'd thought, and she made several valid points.

But she still hadn't sold me.

"Do you deserve a normal life? Probably," I said. "Can you have that? Highly unlikely. People like you and me, we don't get to be normal. We aren't made for normal.

"A mafia princess with no living brothers can't just go off and fall in love with a dentist or computer programmer, for fuck's sake, and expect him to transform into a kingpin. Nor can you expect love to fall from some goddamn tree and into your lap. It doesn't work that way. It isn't that simple."

She huffed out a breath and stood.

"Look, Stefano, I'm not expecting to find the kind of love you have with Valentina. I've seen the way you look at her, the way she looks at you. I'm not asking for that.

"I just want to marry a man I respect, a man who won't beat me, who might even be worthy of all that comes with marrying me. I haven't deluded myself into thinking it'll be perfect, but I do want to choose him myself. I believe I deserve that much."

I drummed my fingers on the desk, considering.

She was right. For better or worse, Val was the love of my life. And without Benedetta's help, I couldn't see another way to get her back. If Benedetta could provide me with the info I needed to bring my girl home, maybe I did owe her the choice.

I rubbed my chin. "Okay."

Her eyes widened. "Okay?"

Of course she didn't quite believe it. She'd probably walked into this conversation expecting to be refused.

"Have your father's lawyer finalize the contract. As far as your father—or anyone else who's aware of the situation—is concerned, I'm choosing your husband. Privately, you have my word... the choice will be yours if it doesn't fuck with my position, my businesses, or my family.

"We'll let everyone believe the decision rests solely with me. And we will together weed out the men who only want you for the power that comes with your hand. At the very least, this gives you space to find love on your own terms."

She nodded. "How would we determine—"

"If they're only after power, Benedetta, they won't court you—they'll be courting me."

She returned to her seat.

"The contract's already been drawn up."

Grabbing the leather bag at her side, she pulled out a large envelope, and handed it to me.

"You should know I was planning to come and plead my case with you this afternoon anyway."

I skimmed over the pages inside the envelope. The terms seemed in order, so I added my signature on the line above my name and handed the contract to her.

"Let me know when your father signs it."

She picked up my pen and signed her name beside mine.

"No need. He died this morning," she said. "And thanks to you, I'm now his only surviving heir. No death announcement has been made at this point. I'll leave that to you now."

As she pushed the papers back at me, she radiated a challenging vibe, the look in her eyes daring me to deny what I had done to her family.

I wouldn't deny it, not to her.

Before Val came back into my life, I was set to inherit the power Capaldo's men would have given me.

Now? I had it anyway.

I locked on to Benedetta's stare with mine, scrutinizing her intention, then, satisfied, I gave her a nod.

"Good. So how are we getting Val back home?"

My new business partner smiled, as if she'd beaten me.

"I'm glad you asked. There's a masquerade ball in Chicago in three days. The Moscatelli family always attends."

"Christ, don't tell me the extent of your plan hinges on storming their house and abducting Val while they're out at a party."

Benedetta leaned back in her chair.

"You don't need to storm any castles, Stefano. I think you'll want to do it a little more quietly. A delicate touch is the only way to get her out alive."

Out of pretense alone, I nodded at her suggestion.

"Go on. What are you suggesting?"

There was still a good chance I'd say fuck it and do whatever needed to be done anyway, gentle touch or otherwise.

"I have an invitation to the ball," she said, "and you can go as my date. Since it's a masquerade, maybe no one will figure out who you are behind the mask before you can make your play. But if they do, well, you now control my holdings in Chicago and have a legitimate reason to be there."

"Where are they keeping her?" I snapped, losing what little remained of my patience.

"I don't know what they're going to do with her, but this event will be the best place for you to make your case to her father. I strongly recommend talking to her older brother first.

"Not only is Marco Moscatelli the heir, but I hear he has big plans for his family. Rumor has it, he's been maneuvering his father for years, setting up everything the way he wants it to eliminate any confusion when he takes over."

He planned to take out his old man.

That was Chicago for you.

"He sounds like a prick," I growled.

Benedetta shrugged her shoulders.

"Maybe, but he's still your best bet to get through to Saul. I don't know how much you know about the family, but they're absolutely ruthless.

"A few Chicago families have turned against them because of their association with the Russians. Marco's trying to mend those rifts, so marrying his sister into the Bratva is probably the last thing he'll want to do."

"I knew about the Russians," I said, "but I didn't know to what extent it had isolated the family."

"They still have too much influence to be fully isolated, but it did put a strain on relations. They may have trouble securing a husband for Valentina, especially considering..."

She bit her lip as she regarded me.

"Considering what?"

"Your engagement announcement made it very clear she has a child. You know as well as anyone, a mafia bride's only as good as her innocence."

"So you're suggesting we do this the diplomatic way?" I snapped. "That I break the treaty, make it known publicly that I've broken the treaty, and try to purchase my wife from them as damaged goods?"

Benedetta winced. "I wouldn't have put it quite like that, but yes. I recommend you offer more than what's fair for an untouched bride. Her options are limited, but some do exist. Remember, you now have holdings in Chicago. If you don't kill anyone, no one should object to you being there temporarily."

I leaned over my desk.

"How many of your father's men are in Chicago?"

Not good. She pressed her lips into a grim line.

"Most are here now. Ties remaining in Chicago are mostly social. The men who stayed are older, most retired. You can probably count on some backup if truly necessary."

It all seemed too good to be true. I shook my head.

"Sounds like you're telling me we go to the party with an invitation and leave with my bride."

"If everything goes smoothly, that's right."

"What are the chances that will happen?"

She took a deep breath and released it.

"Well, that depends. What will you say to Marco to get him on your side? What price will you offer Saul?"

"What does Moscatelli want?"

"Same as you all want, I guess. More power. I don't know how you'll offer him that. That's where Marco comes in. Oh, I did hear my father say something about the Russians opening new distribution channels for Saul."

Women weren't usually privy to the specifics of another's bridal price, or to any of the other shit she'd said.

"How the fuck do you know all this?" I asked.

"We know much more than we let on," she said softly.

She'd just proven it with how well prepared she was for this meeting. This one seemed smart enough to lead her family. Too bad our ways didn't allow it.

I stood and jerked my chin toward the door.

"We done here?"

She got up, slinging her bag over her shoulder.

"Sure. I'll send a copy of the contract to my lawyer and get started on our travel arrangements."

"Good. I want to leave right away. Let me know how many men I can put on the plane."

Benedetta stared at me for a minute.

"You're absolutely sure you want to do this?"

"Do you know of another option I'm not aware of?"

"You've considered all the consequences, right?"

"Listen, if shit hits the fan, I'll keep you safe. The only real consequence of concern is my son not getting his mother back."

She blinked. "No—I mean, you're breaking the treaty, and you can only argue for an exception if the Commission decides to listen. If they find out before you can plead your case, they'll likely punish you. Severely."

"The Commission will be a problem only if I fail, and if I fail, they'll be the least of my problems. I won't fail."

I couldn't look my son in the eye if I did.

Benedetta nodded and turned to leave.

"Okay. I'll text you the details when it's all settled, Stefano."

"Thank you."

Then, before she made it past the doorway, I put out my arm to stop her. Anger and violence vibrated in my blood.

"One more thing," I snarled. "If you interrupt me again, or raise your voice to me, even roll your eyes—I'll kill you. You want to negotiate like a man? Fine. That's how I'll treat you."

Her face paled, and she gave a small nod.

I dropped my arm and let her scurry out of my office.

Benedetta Capaldo just made a deal with the devil.

THIRTEEN

VAL

The evil, vile, and most self-serving people in the city filled the State Ballroom at the Palmer House hotel. Mobsters and their sanctimonious, publicly-elected counterparts.

Every man had a beautiful young woman on his arm, and every beautiful young woman drank as much alcohol as she could knock back, pretending not to listen to the men as they whispered about their schemes.

Women either made themselves appear insufferably bored or busied themselves with useless gossip while the men plotted for world domination, wheeling and dealing in lives like human beings were nothing more than Monopoly money.

So fucking disgusting.

Also a good distraction.

How far can I get?

I scanned the massive ivory-and-red ballroom, memorizing the location of each exit. The place dripped with luxurious gold details and had dimmed but sparkling crystal chandeliers.

The perfect darkly elegant setting for a masquerade ball.

It might have been more than a decade since I'd last been

inside the room, but it didn't take long for the memories to slap me in the face. The galas, balls, and charity events Saul had demanded we attend to improve the family image within the community.

Really, though, he didn't care what anyone thought. Our presence had served as an excuse for him and his thuggish cohorts to rub elbows with elite businessmen and politicians.

Chicago's politicians might have liked to believe they were above all the corruption, but it ran as deeply through their veins as it did through the city itself.

This masquerade ball marked my first public appearance since faking my death, but I knew the drill. Be seen, not heard. Look pretty. Act like a perfect doll to draw the highest bid when auction time came.

Saul's maid had delivered a stunning, crystal-and-red-silk evening gown to my room. Pretty sure it set him back about five grand. Didn't matter. He wanted attention, and my red dress would get it for him. It also made it much more difficult for me to blend in and get away.

And the dagger-like stilettos that were killing my feet? They would definitely impede a quick getaway. At least until I found a dark corner where I could ditch them. Then again, they might come in handy if I needed to defend myself.

The dainty silver mask they'd given me did little to hide my identity, and that was how Saul wanted it. Even if no one recognized me, they would recognize the choker. Three strands of pearls and a huge, dangling ruby, last worn by my mother.

The damn necklace had its own reputation, its own infamy, and it labeled me as a Moscatelli as much as anything else.

But a bad idea still played in the back of my mind.

What if I just walked out?

What if I made my way to the restroom and slipped between the crowds to hide in one of the coat closets? What if I took off the dress, the pearls, and the shoes, stole someone's coat, and found my way out of the hotel?

How far could I get?

Would Aris notice I'd gone missing before I even finished ditching my Moscatelli costume? Would he catch me as I hurried down the cold Chicago streets?

Santo appeared out of nowhere, startling me out of my thoughts. He handed me a tall champagne flute, which I absently accepted.

"You have to be here, yeah, but no one said shit about you staying sober. Drink up, sister."

I preferred cocktails over champagne but didn't mind watching the little golden bubbles rise to the top. It kind of completed the full illusion of the grandiose ballroom.

"Thanks, handsome." I winked. "Having a good time? Any of these lovely ladies catch your eye?"

He shook his head as if he had no time for silly games.

"I'm working tonight. I guess Father thinks a certain asset might be thinking about making a run for it. Again."

I plastered a fake smile onto my painted lips.

"I have no idea what you're talking about."

Santo fixed me with a deadpan stare. "Right."

I sipped on the champagne to stop myself from laughing, enjoying the way the delicate bubbles danced over my tongue. Maybe if I drank until my feet went numb, it would be a little easier to survive the night.

Maybe if I got wasted, the Russians would decide I wasn't worth the hassle, that I wasn't enough of a lady for whatever they planned to do with me.

With my luck, my plan would backfire, and they might think I was spirited and entertaining, or some other ridiculous shit. But then I would face retribution at home. The kind that required me to wear long, uncomfortable opera gloves with my dresses to cover the bruises.

Wouldn't be the first time, certainly not the last.

A woman in her sixties wearing a goth-like black gown and matching mask rushed in my direction, her jewelry clinking with her every hasty step.

"There you are, Valentina, darling. It's been so long. You must tell us what happened."

It took a minute before I could place the face behind the mask and caked-on makeup. I smiled politely.

"Mrs. Gallagher, how are you?"

An unbearable gossip like Mrs. Gallagher was only tolerated in these circles because her late husband left her a massive fortune. The running joke was that she'd talked him to death.

I used to think it was an exaggeration until I'd had the misfortune of stepping into the ladies' room while she rested inside. It had taken me thirty minutes to find an acceptable break in the conversation, so I could make my escape.

She waved off my question, her diamond rings twinkling in the light from the chandeliers overhead.

"My dear, no one cares how I am. I'm fine. I've always been fine. The real question is, where have you been for so long?

"We all thought you died in that horrible accident. Imagine my surprise when I opened the paper one day to read about the dead Moscatelli girl's miraculous return. And she's not even a zombie or Jesus Christ, or anything of the sort."

Then she lifted her chin and raised her penciled-on brows.

"So where exactly have you been, dear?"

I fixed her with a tight smile.

I had to think fast about what to say.

"Well, the car accident was unfortunately very real. And afterward, as I'm sure you can understand, I was in no fit state to be married. My face was practically purple with bruises. It took countless hours and several exclusive, expensive surgeons in France to put me back together again."

She clicked her tongue.

"Oh, how horrible. It must have been a nightmare, but my God, they did a fabulous job. You must tell me who did it."

The champagne and my lack of fucks to give helped me out.

"In Paris, it was Dr. House," I lied. "Horrible disposition—grumpiest man you've ever met, but his talent makes up for it."

She nodded like a bobblehead doll.

"Oh, yes, Dr. House in Paris. I've heard of him. I had no idea he did such fabulous work. I'll have to look him up."

"A simple Google search will do."

I grinned, enjoying my own made up story.

"I'm sure if you contacted your granddaughter, she would be more than happy to help you, Mrs. Gallagher."

"Yes, what a lovely idea."

Then she frowned, scrutinizing my face.

"But really, dear, it's taken them all these years to put you back together? That seems like a rather long time."

"Well, you know... the swelling and the infections, one after the other. After that, of course, rehabilitation for the painkiller addiction. Can't make it through the kind of work I've had without them. But finally, here I am..."

I gestured at myself. Well, mostly at my breasts.

"All dressed up for the party and ready for Sau—I mean my father to figure out what the rest of my life will look like."

She blinked at me and nervously licked her lips. The smile she'd so quickly offered me flickered out.

"Yes, right, well, I'm just going to go check on Mrs. Vander. You understand."

"Of course. Don't let me keep you."

"Fucking hilarious," Santo whispered as she walked away.

The woman shot me another quick look over her shoulder, clearly unsure what to make of our encounter.

"I don't think I've ever seen her end a conversation in under an hour. That's a new record," my brother added.

"Watch and learn, brother. You haven't seen anything yet."

I clocked another meddlesome gossip headed my way, looking desperate to get something straight from the Moscatelli horse's mouth.

"Mrs. Sanders. How are you?"

She stopped short to look me up and down.

"Very well, dear. We're all very surprised to hear about your unexpected resurrection."

"It's really less of a resurrection and more like an official return to society," I said.

She leaned forward, as if I were about to serve the most piping-hot tea the world had ever been served.

"Oh? Return to society? What do you mean? From where?"

"Well..."

I leaned in, cupping a hand around the side of my mouth, like I actually cared whether anyone bothered to read my lips.

She met me half way. "Yes?"

"The car accident was tragic, but I didn't die. Just washed up on the riverbank under a bridge."

Then I switched to a whisper that Santo could hear.

"And that was when the river trolls took me hostage."

She clamped her fingers around the pearls dangling from the single strand around her neck.

"I don't understand?"

"Oh, listen to me complain," I said, then mustered a deliberately annoying giggle. "I actually miss a few of the nice ones."

The woman gawked at me in bewilderment.

I tipped back the rest of the champagne into my mouth, savoring the tickle of the bubbles and the one small bit of freedom that couldn't be taken from me tonight. Just because my life wasn't my own anymore didn't mean I couldn't have a little fun.

Santo gripped my elbow to lead me away.

"I'm sorry, Mrs. Sanders. Please excuse us."

I turned back to wiggle my fingers at her, but he jerked me forward again, biting back laughter.

"Fucking trolls?"

I snorted so loudly, I had to cover my mouth.

"Well, I had to tell her something. Saying I faked my death and ran away to be a barista in New York wouldn't have packed the right punch, you know? The Starbucks benefits just aren't the same in Chicago."

Santo pressed his lips together.

"Girl, you got problems. And you're also a light weight."

"Nothing another flute of champagne won't solve. Or make me forget for the next several hours... I'm gonna need more than one glass."

"I think you've had enough."

Santo took the empty flute and set it on a nearby table.

"Correction, I haven't had anywhere near enough."

I grabbed a full flute from a server's passing tray.

"Know what, Santo? I've found my mission for tonight."

He gazed out over the crowd.

"Your mission is to impress the Russians. Whenever the assholes bother to show up."

"No, that's Saul's job. Let's be honest, this deal has little to do with me. I'm just the cherry on top. Well," —I snorted again — "maybe not the cherry anymore."

Santo's mouth twisted into a grimace. "Gross."

"Agreed. But back to my point, little brother, my goal for the night is to break you."

He looked down at me and squinted.

"Break me? What the hell did I ever do to you? Well, other than the obvious."

I took a gulp of champagne.

"Kidnapping me, you mean? You're always so stern and grumpy, like you tattooed a permanent scowl on your face with all the other ink. And when something funny happens, you won't even let yourself laugh. So yes, I'm going to break you tonight. I'm going to make you laugh."

"Great life goals." He rolled his eyes. "Good luck with that."

What the hell else did I have to do anyway?

I smiled as he offered me his arm and led me around the ballroom, stopping here and there to make small talk when someone approached.

God, I'd missed him so much. My childhood might have been horrible, but the moments that had made it bearable, at the very least, included being with Marco and Santo. Time with them more than made up for having none with Aris.

My heart ached. I hated having my brothers back in my life, even by force, because I would only lose them again.

It was almost as cruel as taking me from my son, a reminder that few people in my life genuinely cared about me.

It would only hurt that much more when the Russians took me away.

But I pushed the depressing thoughts away and refocused on the evening with Santo, dreading the moment those sick fucks showed up, but refusing to let it destroy the time I had left with my brother.

I'd almost started to enjoy myself, to forget about the reason we were there—until I gazed across the ballroom and saw her.

Benedetta Capaldo.

In Chicago.

Right there in front of me.

And she looked stunning in her floor-length silver gown, her caramel-blonde hair perfectly piled on top of her head to show off the gorgeous diamonds dripping from her ears.

As she lifted her hand to adjust her mask, an even larger diamond flashed brilliantly from her finger.

I squeezed my eyelids shut for a second.

No, no, no. This can't be happening.

When I opened my eyes, a tall man in a beautifully custom-tailored tuxedo and a black mask moved closer to Benedetta. He rested his hand on her lower back.

Nausea overwhelmed me. Vomit burned my throat.

Even with the mask, I would recognize this man anywhere.

Everything about him was a part of me. I could never forget the darkness in his eyes, the perfect symmetry of his broad shoulders, the fullness of his lips, or his confident swagger.

Stefano.

With her.

Literally with her.

Benedetta wore the kind of dress women chose to announce an engagement—I couldn't do a goddamn thing about it either.

What had Stefano done?

Had he allowed so much as a drop of blood to dry after my family took me? How long had he waited after the limo drove away with me inside before deciding to marry her again?

And where. The fuck. Was. My. Son?

My eyes filled with hot, angry tears.

My heart thrashed wildly.

No. Hell no. Stefano would not get to see me cry.

In fact, I didn't want him to see me at all.

I grabbed Santo's arm to maintain my balance while reaching down to slip off my stilettos beneath my dress. Then I shoved the shoes against my brother's chest.

"I need to use the ladies' room."

"You know I can't let you out of my sight," he muttered.

"Take my fucking shoes. How far can I get without them?"

"Yeah, no. Probably a lot farther without them."

I didn't wait for Santo to say anything else.

Stefano was getting too close.

He pushed through the crowd, his eyes locked on me.

I let go of the shoes and ran for the closest door.

I had to get out of there.

FOURTEEN

STEFANO

I spotted her from a distance on the Moscatelli thug's arm.

Valerie. Valentina.

Whatever her name was, it didn't matter to me. Val could use any name she wanted. I just wanted to call her mine.

She looked stunning in a sparkling red gown. Even the pearl and ruby choker at her neck, as impressive as it appeared to be, paled in comparison to her beauty.

The only way she could've been more beautiful might have been if her dress lay on the floor by my bed while she rode my cock in that red lipstick and the diamonds I'd bought her.

Benedetta nudged me with her elbow.

"Stop staring at her, Stefano."

"Never," I snapped without taking my eyes off Val.

She hadn't seen me yet.

I drank in the sight of her, moving my gaze up and down her body, taking in every detail, inch by inch. Her hair, her lips, the shape of her ass, her hips, and her breasts, her...

At first glance, there seemed to be a shadow beneath the

pearls, but when she shifted, and the light hit differently, I saw the fucking bruise on her neck.

Then another. And another. More bruises marked her perfect skin, some leading down into the long gloves she wore. Once I'd seen the first mark, I couldn't stop seeing others.

The gloves covered the bullet wound on her arm, but it couldn't hide the bruises on her neck and shoulders. Some were faded, which I supposed she'd gotten from Cozza.

I guessed she'd been told to cover them with makeup, and to obey her father but rebel at the same time, she used as little concealer as she could get away with.

My heart now raced for a different reason.

Someone in her family had dared to hurt her. They dared to touch what belonged to me. Another man or men had put their hands on my girl.

I would kill them all, slowly, until they begged me for death.

"You should calm down," Benedetta whispered. "You look like you're about to murder everyone in the room. You're going to draw the wrong attention."

"Someone hurt her," I snarled.

My feral response echoed through my head as my mind replayed it again.

"She has a few bruises, but she's fine," Benedetta said. "I promise you, she's been through much worse. Honestly, I'm surprised her twin didn't take it further."

I clenched my jaw and flexed my fingers to subdue the monster rising from the darkest part of my soul.

"Yes, I've heard about Aris Moscatelli's reputation and his violence against women."

A reputation so well earned, it was the first thing Tony had dug up on the son of a bitch.

Benedetta lowered her gaze to the ivory-and-black carpeting.

"It's all true. He was even more violent with his sister. Some in this very room say it went as far as—"

"No, it fucking did not," I said.

"How could you know that?"

I shot her a knowing look, and she understood my meaning.

"Oh, she was... I mean, you were her, um... Are you sure?"

I dragged my gaze away from Val to meet Benedetta's.

"I was the first man to touch her. I don't care what happened between then and now, but you can be sure I'll also be the last man who touches her. And I swear to Christ, no other man will leave a fucking bruise on her body again."

Only my bruises were acceptable—my fingerprints on her thighs from holding them open. My handprint on her ass the next time she even considered lying to me again.

"Don't make promises you can't keep," Benedetta whispered, a note of melancholy in her voice. "It's cruel."

"One way or another, that's one I will keep. Enough. I need to get to her and tell her about the plan."

Then I made a beeline in Val's direction, forcing my way through the crowd.

Benedetta grabbed me. "Stop... look who she's with."

I halted.

The young thug still stood close to my girl.

No doubt he was armed.

Of course he would be the Moscatelli assigned to escort her. Enforcers guarded the goods. He'd certainly been tasked with making sure she didn't leave or say the wrong thing, and equally as important, with preventing undesirable advances toward her.

"I'm not going to just stand here all night," I said.

I had to get a message to her. It had to come from me.

"Please, Stefano, wait. You have to pretend you're enjoying the party. Remember, you're here to conduct a business transaction. It's the only reason you can be here. I'll get you closer to her but let me do it the right way."

I turned to her and stared daggers through her.

"You promised me you would—"

"I promised to get you in the room with her. You're in the room. I've met my obligation, but I'm willing to keep going if you can be patient. If they find out you're here for any other reason before we have Marco on our side, well, I don't think it will end well for either of you. Or me."

I gave her a curt nod despite my nerves burning with impatience. I had no other option but to trust her. For now.

So, if milling around the ballroom is what she needed to do, to make small talk and gather gossip about Val's assumed future while looking for Marco Moscatelli, then so be it. For fucking now.

She grabbed two glasses of champagne from a passing tray and handed me one, smiling as if we were a happy couple about to announce our engagement.

Fuck. I had to play into the room's assumption if I wanted to get to Val, even if it hurt Val when she discovered us.

As we listened, I realized my girl had been having a little fun spreading some tall tales of her own. Everything from a decade's worth of plastic surgery in Paris—as if anyone but God could craft that kind of beauty—to having been held captive by trolls, to spending years in a drug recovery facility.

I couldn't help but grin.

She'd found a way to survive with her sanity intact.

She knew I would come.

Finally, we ran into an old gossip with some information.

An older woman with gray hair styled so tight on top of her head that it pulled back the skin on her face, making it look like she'd been the one surgically altered.

The woman hugged Benedetta.

"It's so lovely to see you again, dear. To answer your question, well, I can't speak to what that girl got up to, but I know the Russians aren't happy about it.

"Why it's such a problem for them is quite odd if you ask me. The man she would've married has a wife. In fact, he's had three brides over the last decade. And despite all that, seems the Russians won't drop their claim."

"Will they be here tonight?" Benedetta asked.

"I hear they've sent an emissary, so he can get a look at her. If it were my husband, the deal would be entirely void. And as for that brash little girl, she could die unmarried, and I wouldn't shed a tear." The woman sniffed. "Once her beauty fades, she won't be desirable anymore."

I set my jaw to keep from strangling the old fucking bitch.

"Will there be a deal with the Russians or not?" I asked.

She stared at me for a minute.

"A few of the families tried to convince Don Moscatelli not to work with the Russians. But a woman like that, after all that's happened? She doesn't have many prospects now, does she? Shame, really. Such a beautiful young woman unmarried because no one wanted the baggage that comes with her."

Her critical tone scraped at my patience—she was talking about my son, referring to him as baggage.

The haggard old bitch. How dare she.

I'd never hit a woman like her in anger. But this wrinkled cunt was begging for a beating. She preferred a loose tongue?

Fine. I'd loosen it from her mouth permanently. Maybe then she'd finally learn a thing or two about the art of silence.

Benedetta must have picked up on my rage. She squeezed my arm, steering my focus back to the conversation.

After several pointless excuses, the woman finally wandered off to spread her shit somewhere else.

Benedetta turned to me. "I have an idea."

I hoped it involved violence. "Go on."

"I just saw Marco leave the ballroom. I didn't see him come in, but now I can follow him. I'll talk to him and see if he'll get you an audience with his father tonight. Saul is here somewhere for sure. He's not socializing, so he's taking meetings somewhere in this hotel, right?"

"You can count on it. What else do you know about the old man that might be useful?"

She nodded. "He'll want you to make an official offer to marry his daughter with his blessing. He's simple, motivated by greed. Offer him an obscene amount or a lot of power and influence or something. I think that's the best way to get her back. After all, that's why she's here."

"What?"

"Her father dolled her up and put the family jewels on her. If the Russians back out, this becomes an auction."

"So you want me to line up like one of these second-rate motherfuckers and pretend I don't already have the right to the mother of my child?"

She shrugged. "Well, yes."

"And if he refuses my offer? I lose the element of surprise, and he'll expect my attempt to steal her back. And I will take her by force if necessary."

"I'm out of suggestions, Stefano."

We had to do something at this point, like it or not.

"Do it then. Go talk to Marco."

She squinted as she stared over my shoulder.

"Oh—he's back and actually coming this way."

Then Benedetta skirted around me, flashing a brilliant smile as easily as if it were another mask.

"Marco, hi. I was hoping to see you."

I took a side-glance and instantly recognized him.

He kissed Benedetta on the cheek.

"It's good to see you. What can I help you with? Finally coming back to Chicago? You look great, by the way."

She chuckled politely. "Not quite, and thanks. But can we talk? I'd like to know what your father wants most right now."

His gaze flickered in my direction.

"Hmm. Well, I can come up with several answers to that question, but none of it's fit for mixed company. Why would you ask about that anyway, beautiful?"

Turning to face him, I interjected and answered for her.

"I want the mother of my child back where she belongs... with me, in my fucking house."

Marco stared at me, past my mask, and the asshole grinned.

"She told me you would show up. Not sure if you're stupid or brave, but I'm glad to see my baby sister chose someone who won't give up on her. I mean, it would've been better if you were on the outside but fuck it."

"What does your father want?" I hissed.

"More power than he has or deserves. You should know if the Russians want her, and just looking at her... of course they will, my father will go with them. I've tried to change his mind, but he's a stubborn old man."

"What are they offering?" I asked. "I'll beat it."

Marco looked me up and down, chewing on the corner of his lip, showing me his false tell.

This fucker liked playing games.

"Money," he answered. "Same offer he'd get for a bride of her worth ten years ago."

"She's worth more than two and a half million, Moscatelli. Any asshole here could offer that much. Stop fucking around and tell me what'll work for your father."

Marco grinned again like an idiot.

"Once upon a time, the deal included a lucrative shipping allowance for my family. Offer him the money and promise you'll join the Commission. I know they've extended a standing offer to you. Tell my father once you take your seat, he gets some leeway for shipping on the East Coast.

"It's a big fucking ask, Vignali, I know. I know about your history with the Commission, but that's what it's gonna take. And there is one other stipulation, because if you want a chance in hell, you'll need me to push him for you."

Fine. I would play his game.

"And your price for this favor?" I asked.

"I'm my father's heir. When I take over—"

"Assuming your brother doesn't stab you in the back."

Marco offered a half-hearted shrug.

"Aris will be dealt with when the time comes. When I run this family, I want you to be the voice that opens the door to dissolving the treaty. Men like my father are on their way out. Cooler, smarter heads will soon prevail in Chicago. We're all losing money with the treaty intact, and I want to see it gone."

Smart man. Something I might have asked for myself had I been in his shoes. I extended my hand and nodded.

"She comes home with me tonight, and we have a deal."

Marco grasped my hand for a firm shake—like we'd just signed a multibillion-dollar deal. In a way, long term, we had.

"I have to make my rounds," he said. "You'll get your sit down with my father tonight. Stay close."

Marco left us to continue his business around the ballroom.

While scanning the room for Val again, I rested my hand on Benedetta's lower back.

"I need to talk to her right now. I might not get another opportunity."

There—my girl. I fixed my gaze on her.

Benedetta sighed and touched my shoulder.

"Seems there's nothing I can say to stop you. Just be careful, Stefano. I'll be around when you're ready to go."

"Thank you," I called after her as she walked away.

Exactly right. Nothing could stop me. I focused on Val's location again, but now her brother stood there by himself, holding a pair of women's shoes like a dumbass.

Then a flash of red slipped along the wall.

She was slipping out of the ballroom.

Good. That made it easier for me to see her, to tell her I would get her back. Maybe even to give her a piece of my mind for dragging me through this bullshit with all her lies. She had forced me to break the treaty and chase her to Chicago.

And where the fuck did I find her?

Not locked in a cell, pining for me. Not on the street, running from her family to get back to me and our son.

No. I found her dressed like some beautiful mythical creature, a goddess, trying to attract potential husbands at a stupid fucking masquerade ball.

As discreetly as possible, I made my way through the sea of sequined dresses and tuxedos to the other side of the ballroom.

When I stepped through the same double exit doors Val had used, the hallway beyond felt far too empty.

With every step along the red carpet runner, following her, my blood boiled hotter and hotter.

She had caused this mess.

Now I had to risk everything for her—again.

I watched her enter the ladies' room and headed that way.

Before I could grab the ornate golden handle, the door opened for me. Then a hand darted out and clamped down on my arm to yank me inside.

No light. The room was pitch black.

Someone shoved me against the wall and held a knife to my throat.

The lights came on—and there she was.

Valentina Moscatelli, furious, glaring at me while wielding a fucking butter knife.

I grinned. "Found you, mia bellissima diavoletta."

FIFTEEN

VAL

I held the blade to his throat, not because I could do anything with a stupid fucking butter knife, but because I feared what he might do to me.

Stefano wouldn't hurt me the way Aris and Saul had, and I knew that. He had every right to be angry with me, though. Furious even.

And I couldn't stop myself from trying to stay ahead of it.

I had my own reasons to be pissed off anyway.

"How dare you?" I hissed.

He bent his neck, dipping his chin, pressing the dull knife more firmly against his throat.

"How dare I what, Valentina Moscatelli?"

I winced, then corrected my expression.

"How dare you show up here with her."

Tears burned my eyelids, but I willed them away.

"I should slit your throat and let you bleed out on this floor for betraying me like that. Were you the one who called my family? Did you set this up to get me out of the way? So she could raise my son?"

Stefano pushed my hand down and took the knife.

"What the fuck are you talking about?"

His dark eyes flashed in warning behind his mask.

"Once again, you've fucking lied to me about a life-or-death situation. Now you want to blame the mess you created on me? I don't fucking think so, not this time, woman."

"You brought her here to rub it in my face," I shouted. "Why else would you break the treaty? No, wait—you probably got the Commission's permission. Why else would you leave our son in New York without a parent, huh?"

He blinked, then frowned. "You think I betrayed you? If anything, you betrayed me. You lied about your name, your family, why you left me, everything, all lies."

While he kept his voice low, his tone still seethed with fury. He grabbed my wrists and pulled me against his chest.

"I don't even know who the fuck you are right now or what I'm supposed to call you."

I yanked myself free. Then, while absently rubbing my left wrist, I remembered to subdue my expression. His grip wouldn't have hurt as much if Aris hadn't twisted the same wrist a few hours earlier.

I couldn't let Stefano see the bruises Aris had left on me, all the painful, dark patches, or the purple marks around the wound on my arm.

It would send Stefano into a full-blown fit of rage, much worse than what he expressed in his eyes already, and he would go after Aris. He might succeed in killing my sickass brother, but he might not make it out of Chicago alive, maybe not even out of the hotel. Enzo would be left all alone.

So I had to lie more.

An omission of truth... that sounded better.

"I had to lie," I said.

"Bullshit," Stefano snapped. "You had plenty of opportunities to tell me everything, but you chose the lies before me. You put me at risk and endangered our son's life—and then I find you at a fucking party dressed like a high-end hooker trying to lure some rich Russian."

He ran his finger over my breasts.

"Or maybe this is the backup plan, in case the Russians are no longer interested."

"Fuck you," I snarled.

"Ah, so that's it... You're dressed like this to catch some politician's eye. Tempt him to the dark side. Drag him into your father's debt with your perfect tits and seal the deal with that magic little cunt of yours."

He brushed his fingers over the pearls and the ruby.

"Too bad you forgot something, Valerie."

My vision blurred with another rush of hot tears.

It was bad enough he could see through the person I wanted to be, but now he stared at what Saul had made me... so no, I couldn't let him see me cry. He didn't get to talk to me like that and then witness the pain he caused.

I swallowed hard to push back the emotion.

"What's that... what did I forget this time, Stefano? And you can call me Valentina now. That is my name."

Stefano swept his gaze down the length of me, his fingers now following his eyes, tracing along my curves.

"You forgot this is mine. All of it."

"I'm not yours," I spat.

His mouth curled into a sinister grin.

"You've always been mine... Valentina. You let me fuck you even after I told you how it works with me. Mine. Only mine."

"Stefano—"

"Mine."

He slid the pearl choker higher on my throat while narrowing his eyes. So dark, so dangerous. And he knew to look for the bruises on my neck.

"The man who touched you, who marked you like this, dies by my hand. It won't be quick. I'll make it last. I'll make him suffer a much greater level of pain than he inflicted on you before I let him have his death."

I swallowed and shook my head.

"You can't promise that."

"But I can, little girl. I'll watch the life fade from his eyes as he begs for the sweet release of death. Do you know why I can make that promise? Because you are mine."

I pulled back, meaning to open the door, to send him away.

"I'm not. I wish I could be yours, but I can't be. You should leave. Please, Stefano. You need to go before they—"

He grabbed the back of my head and slammed his lips against mine, claiming me with a kiss that stole my words, my thoughts, my breath—and set my body on fire.

My mind fought, screaming for me to push him away, but I didn't have the strength. I could only bring myself to grip the lapels of his jacket and pull him closer.

Then he broke the kiss and demanded my obedience.

"You belong to me. Repeat it," he ordered.

I slipped my hands inside his jacket. It wasn't enough. I wanted more. I wanted all of him. I dragged my fingers lower, down to the front of his shirt, to the six hard ridges on his abdomen. I couldn't not touch him.

"Repeat what?" I asked.

He surged forward, closing the gap between us, devouring

my lips with his as he shoved me into one of the empty stalls, shut the door behind us, and locked it.

"Say you're mine."

The ladies' room at the Palmer House had floor-to-ceiling wood panels and doors, making each stall feel like a cozy little room—a dangerous illusion of privacy.

I gave in to his kiss.

It would be the last time I felt his touch, tasted his kiss, or knew his kind of love, so I gave in just once more. I would let him do what he wanted with me.

Like every other addict in the world, I promised myself this would be the last time. I just needed to feel him, to let him make love to me, to let him claim me the way only he could.

One last time.

Only then could I give him up forever.

As if reading my mind, Stefano slid an arm around my waist to find the zipper on the back of my dress, then he opened it with a single pull, and the dress floated to the floor.

I stood before him in nothing but the silver mask, my long, black gloves, and the pearl and ruby choker.

Stefano tore off his mask and stepped back, taking in the sight of my bare body as if he wanted to memorize every curve. The heat in his eyes faded when his gaze landed on the mottled black-and-purple flesh covering my ribs.

An icy rage replaced the heat.

He reached out and brushed his fingers over the proof of my family's abuse, his touch almost ghostly in its tenderness.

His gaze dropped to the burn on my thigh.

"Which one of them did this to you?"

"It's nothing."

What a lie. It hurt like fucking hell.

What else could I say?

Most of the bruises were from the first night after I told Aris to go fuck himself—he came back to my room a few hours after Marco left to have his fun.

The burn, though, was fresh.

Aris's work again. I'd refused to help him iron his shirt, and his explosive reaction included literally ironing my leg instead of his shirt. Thankfully, the iron hadn't reached full heat, so the burn wouldn't leave a lasting mark.

That didn't mean it wasn't painful.

Stefano seemed unable to look away from my torso, but honestly, that one looked worse than it felt. A bruised ribcage, courtesy of Saul.

He'd hit me with his fist, two quick jabs to the same spot, because I had the audacity to ask what would happen if the Russians didn't want me.

Saul's wordless message had been perfectly clear.

If the Russians refused me, if I couldn't entice a suitable replacement, the bruises covering my ribs would cover every part of my body.

The threat didn't really matter. I was certain if I went with the Russians, or any other man Saul deemed acceptable, bruises would eventually cover my body anyway.

A low growl rumbled in Stefano's throat as he studied me.

"Who touched you?" he asked again.

I pushed him toward the stall door.

"Stefano, please. I need you to leave. Go home and raise our son to be better than this." I gestured at my body. "Please. He needs his father to guide him. You're so strong. Show him how to rise above all this."

I picked up my dress, feeling exposed and vulnerable.

"Our son also needs his mother," Stefano said.

Faster than I could track his movements, he grabbed my hand, forced me to drop the dress, and kissed me again, the taste of sweet champagne and dominance on his tongue.

Every time Stefano touched me, kissed me, looked at me for too long, my heart thrummed, my head spun, and my soul and my body ached for him. I craved this man like a drug.

"I need to hear you say it," he said against my lips.

Bunching his crisp shirt fabric, I gripped it with my fists, wanting to get lost in the undeniable pull between us.

"What do you want me to say?"

I began working on the buttons of his shirt. I didn't want it unbuttoned because I planned to fuck him next to a toilet, but because I needed to feel his skin. To lay my face on his chest. To feel his warmth on my cheek. To hear his heart beating vigorously in his chest.

"Say you're mine," he breathed onto my neck.

"But I'm not."

My heart clenched around the truth behind my words.

Stefano slid his hand down and rolled my nipple between his fingers, creating a little sting. The good kind of sting.

"Say it."

"No. I can't say it. I want to, but it's... saying it hurts too much. The lie physically hurts me."

He swept his fingers down to softly trace over my ribcage and my waist. He pressed his erection against my stomach, nipping my skin and leaving sweet kisses on my neck.

"Say it," he demanded.

His hot breath against my ear made my knees tremble.

"No." The damn word didn't come out like a refusal. Weak and airy instead, kind of like I didn't even believe myself.

He kissed me again while sliding his fingers between my thighs and into my wet, pulsing core.

"Your body tells me you're mine."

"My body lies," I moaned.

"No, it doesn't. It's telling you what you already know. You belong with me. Under me. Beside me. Above me while riding my cock like a good girl. Or my face," he whispered between kisses. "It knows the truth. Don't fight it. Honesty can be so much more rewarding for you, Angel."

"I have to fight it."

My breath hitched as he swirled tight circles around my clit, sending wave after wave of pleasure through my body.

I pushed open his jacket and his shirt, peeled them from his arms, letting it all drop to the floor, then gripped his shoulders to pull his body against mine.

Feeling him—skin on skin, chest to chest—made heat bloom from deep within me and intensified the shock that always surged between us whenever we touched.

Stefano pressed his forehead to mine, then drove his fingers deeper inside me, using his thumb to circle and circle and, oh, sweet mother of Christ, faster and harder.

"Say it."

It had been only a few days, and still, he had me melting into his hands. But damn it, it had to stop.

We didn't have much time.

I needed to know his plan for Enzo, and I wanted to apologize. He deserved more, but it was all I had to give. Saying the words he wanted to hear would hurt too much.

Maybe I could even show him how much I wanted him, loved him, wished I could be his wife.

His lips traveled to my chin, then to my neck, kissing that

one spot that always made my toes curl as he circled his fingers around my clit with the most exquisite pressure.

I reached down to feel him. His hard cock pressed against the zipper of his pants. With one hand on his chest, I eased him back a little and shook my head.

"I can't say it, Ace. But let me show you how I feel."

I leaned in and kissed his shoulder, his chest, his abs. I continued downward with my lips, my tongue, lowering myself onto my knees. Then, biting on my lip, I stared into his eyes and unzipped his tux trousers.

"Let me apologize to you for what I've done."

I took the tip of his thick cock into my mouth and swirled my tongue over and around the tip, closing my eyes, savoring the sweet and salty sensation.

With a primal grunt, he grabbed the back of my head, filling his hands with my hair, and pulled me away from his cock.

"Uh-uh, no way. Open your eyes and look at me."

When I looked up, wide pupils had overtaken his beautiful blue irises.

Stefano tightened his grip on my hair to hold me in place.

"Open your mouth. Stick out your tongue."

I did what he said.

He gripped the base of his shaft and traced the tip along my lips. Then he tapped it against my tongue, reminding me which of us actually held the control.

"Now take it all," he ordered.

He thrust his cock to the back of my throat, pulling my head down, forcing me to take him deeper.

I fought the intense urge to gag and choke.

"That's it. Relax around it, Angel. Take more."

My pulse hammered in my ears as I followed his command,

though we both knew there was no way in hell the entire length of him would fit without me literally swallowing it.

I pulled in useless air through my nose.

Stefano might push me to the very edge, but he would never break me. He had never hurt me, and he never would.

"Good girl. Now I'm going to let you go, and you're going to sit back and tell me why the fuck you think sucking my cock would get you off the hook. You'll do as I say, Valentina."

He released my hair, and I rocked back, gasping, taking a moment to catch my breath before saying anything.

Tap, tap, tap.

His shoe on the tile echoed around the stall.

I couldn't say what he wanted me to say. I couldn't destroy my soul, not when I needed it the most to save myself.

Before he anticipated my reaction, I sprang forward and sucked him back into my mouth. I took in as much as I could without passing out from a lack of oxygen. Then I drew back, sucking all the way down to the head before thrusting up the length of him again.

He braced himself between the walls, eyes squeezed shut as I took him in deeper.

"Fuuuuck..."

I smiled or tried to anyway.

I'd made this strong, intelligent, usually articulate man lose himself to me, and it filled me with a rush of warmth and pride.

It didn't take long for him to regain control, though.

He grabbed handfuls of my hair and yanked me up to my feet, and while panting, he reprimanded me. Threatened me.

"Try it again, and you'll be very sorry you did, little girl. You will tell me what the fuck I want to hear. You belong to me. And you won't forget it while we're apart. Say the words.

"Say my cock is the only one you'll ever suck... that only my fingers and lips will touch you... and as soon as I get you back in my bed where you belong, you'll give me another child. You're mine, and you will tell me this, one way or another."

God, I wanted to. The words sat at the tip of my tongue. I wanted more than anything to tell him that I loved him, that I belonged to him. That he would always own my body, my heart, and my soul.

But then the pain hit me. It shot through my chest and twisted inside my stomach. I bit down on my tongue and closed my eyes, forcing my mind to imprint every second, every sensation onto my brain.

Stefano pressed his palm against my clit.

"Be my good girl now, and I'll let you come before I fuck you. I'm going to fuck you so hard, my cum will wet your panties for a week."

"Stefano, plea—"

The bathroom door opened.

Stiletto heels clicked across the marble floor.

Stefano drew little circles with his fingers.

If someone caught us, it would be over. Saul would kill him for being in Chicago and for touching me when, as far as anyone else knew, I was protected by my family.

Neither of us would survive Saul Moscatelli.

"Stop," I whispered, begging. "Stefano, please, stop."

He didn't stop.

He didn't care about the same consequences I feared.

This man wanted what he wanted, and he'd get it.

Even if he had to die for it.

He smashed a hand over my mouth to shut me up and increased the intensity of his circling fingers.

My knees weakened.

Panic stole away my breath—or had he done that?

I didn't know.

Between the lack of oxygen and knowing we might get caught at any moment made every sensation more intense.

"Say the words," he whispered into my ear.

I shook my head, tears streaming down my cheeks. Tears from being so overwhelmed, so wracked with emotion and stimulation all at once.

"Give me what I want, Val. Then I'll let you come on my hand," he promised, the evil fucker.

I tried to block the sensations, to listen past his voice to the movement on the other side of the stall door.

"Say it," he growled only loud enough for me to hear.

No, I wouldn't do it. I made myself focus on the footsteps of the woman inside the restroom, on the thundering of my heartbeat. To hold back my orgasm, I willed my muscles to tighten and not release.

I'd gotten this far. I couldn't give up now.

Sweat trickled down my back. Heat blistered my skin in waves. I fought to steady my breathing.

Stefano took the back of my head into his hand, pressing me against him as he pushed my body to its limit.

"You're shaking, Valentina," he breathed at my ear. "How much agony can you withstand? How long before your body gives in to my command?"

Fucking sadist, he was right.

Every inch of me trembled as I struggled to prevent release.

Why did he have to make this so difficult for me?

Well, because he knew it made me want him more.

Yes, I wanted him. I wanted to come. I needed to come.

I wanted to bathe in the bliss Stefano could give me.

But I couldn't let him win this time, so I used everything I had to hold on a little longer.

Then those fucking heels clicked across the floor again—and it seemed like the woman headed straight for us.

The danger of her discovering us increased my desire.

It intensified my urgent need to come.

I wasn't sure who the sick fuck was now.

"That's right," Stefano whispered with a smirk on his face. "Come for me now, Angel."

The tension, the anticipation, they were killing me.

My desperation to unravel in his arms overwhelmed me.

I couldn't take the delicious agony any longer.

SIXTEEN

STEFANO

Hinges creaked, followed by a soft rush of air as the ladies' room door shut behind the woman who had entered.

Her presence wouldn't have stopped me.

I had every intention to make Val cry out my name.

I shoved two fingers inside her as she came and kissed her hard, swallowing her scream and her moans. Then I dragged my lips along her jaw to her neck and continued teasing her clit.

"Now say it," I ordered, noting how her thighs shook. "Then I'll let you come again on my cock. I know that's what you really want, so give me what I want, and we'll call it even."

She dug her nails into my shoulders.

"Yes, sir," she gasped.

There she is... my good girl.

"Go on. Say it."

"I belong to you. Only yours."

I nodded. "Who am I?"

"Stefano Vignali."

"And what does that make you?"

Val stared at me for a minute, and I guessed she was considering my reaction to how she chose to answer.

"Your bride... and a Vignali."

I grinned. "That's my good girl, yes. See? Everything's better when you obey me."

After pulling my fingers from her hot pussy, I painted her lips with them, then sealed my mouth over hers again.

Fuck, she tasted good. I wanted to drop onto my knees and worship her sweet little cunt and get my fill.

But I didn't have the time. I didn't have the fucking will.

I spun her to the wall with her dress still pooled at her feet. I kicked the red silk out of my way, then pushed her shoulders forward, bending her over at the waist.

She flattened her hands on the wall and braced herself.

I halted in my tracks.

New bruises surrounded the wound on her arm.

Had to be her twin—motherfucker had used the injury to hurt her. When I got my hands on that prick, he wouldn't beg for mercy. He would beg me to send him to hell.

First, I needed Val to be safe.

She peered over her shoulder, her bright eyes pleading with me. For so many reasons.

I needed to be inside her. She needed me there.

Without bothering to go in easy, I rammed my cock deep inside her with one harsh thrust.

My girl wanted to be fucked hard, and my own impatience would serve as a lingering reminder for her. I wanted her to feel me for days. I wanted her to know, if the shit with her brother didn't work out, I would come back for her.

My eyeballs rolled back. "Fuck," I groaned. "Christ."

The way her tight little pussy gripped onto my cock became everything. And it confirmed all that she'd just said.

I went still to collect myself and give her a second to adjust. Then she arched her spine, her hands still on the wall, and rocked back onto me, taking what she wanted.

Sexiest thing I'd ever seen.

Her pretty ass bounced against my hips as she took everything I gave her. I couldn't resist the temptation—I slapped that ass. She deserved to be spanked. For all the lies. For not obeying me the first time when I commanded her to say she was mine.

Val moaned into it, pushing back harder, moving her hips faster, gliding up and down my cock. I gripped her hips and met her thrusts with mine while she rode my cock like she owned it, demanding and taking her pleasure.

At that moment, I finally saw her. All of her.

No masks, no pretenses.

This girl wasn't the gorgeous, foul-mouthed barista I'd fallen for as a young man. Not even the fiery mama bear who captivated me as a grown man. This was my beautiful Valentina, the real woman who'd hidden behind a mask for so long. So much more than I'd ever given her credit for.

Fire and vengeance.

An unyielding mafia princess made to conquer the world. A survivor, thriving where most would have curled up and died.

Smart, sexy, powerful. My perfect match in every way.

This woman didn't belong in a coffee shop or PTA meeting. Valentina was meant to rule with an iron fist by my side.

The first true Vignali queen.

Mine.

No one would ever convince me that God himself hadn't made Valentina Moscatelli for me. Only me.

I loved watching that ass bounce on my cock, but I needed more. I needed to see her face when I made her come on me. I needed to see those brilliant eyes and feel her lips against mine when I filled her with my cum.

I swung her around, so she faced me, and pinned her against the wall. She wrapped her legs around me as I lifted her, then I slammed my cock into her.

She parted her swollen lips, her red lipstick smeared around her mouth, and ripped off her mask. She paused and stared into my eyes, demanding more.

I traced my fingers over her lips. Val leaned into my hand, her gaze still locked on mine as she closed her mouth around my fingers and sucked them clean. Then she grabbed a fistful of my hair and pulled my mouth back to hers.

She wanted control. Maybe one day I would let her play that game, but not here. Not now. She'd fought me too damn hard to give her that indulgence so soon.

With one hand, I grabbed both her gloved wrists and pinned them above her head. With my other, I fondled her breasts, loving the way her pussy tightened, squeezing my cock when I rolled her sensitive nipples.

Not many women could survive what Val had gone through and come out the other side stronger, bolder, and fueled by a hotter fire. No other woman could take my cock like she did.

I didn't care what I had to do, who I had to kill, how many houses or cities I had to burn to the motherfucking ground.

For her, I would do it.

This woman was mine. She would spend her life with me.

I sealed my lips over hers, muffling her cries while thrusting into her at an angle that drove her crazy, hitting that one spot deep inside her with my cock.

She arched her back, taking short, gasping breaths.

"You looked perfect on your knees with your lips around my cock," I growled. "I want to see it again. Next time, I'll bind your hands behind your back with one of my neckties."

She moaned.

"When I get you home, I'll take my time claiming every part of your body. Tie you to the headboard and eat your pussy until you're wrung out with pleasure."

I slid my hand under and around to her ass to press the back of my knuckle against her asshole. Nothing deep, never entering her, only circling with light pressure, reminding her of the pleasures that awaited us there.

She arched into another orgasm, her wet little cunt pulsing around my cock and setting me off, making me come right along with her. I kept thrusting through my release, stretching it out, making sure to satisfy her completely and take the edge off as much as I could.

Afterward, I pressed her back to the wall with my chest, leaving no space between us, savoring the feel of her body becoming part of mine. But I wouldn't be fully satisfied until I buried myself in her every night.

I pressed my lips to her temple.

"I love you, Angel."

"You shouldn't," she whispered.

Her words punched me in the gut.

"I love you," I insisted. "It's not some fucking choice or an opinion or even an option, Val. It's one of the few things in my life I can't control or change. There's nothing either of us can do but accept it. Your life will be easier once you accept the truth—I love you and our son."

Her gaze fell to the pile of red silk with my shirt, jacket, and mask tossed into the mix.

A tear ran down her cheek.

"You shouldn't love me. I'm not worthy of it. You'd be happier if you just forgot about—"

I covered her mouth with my hand to stop her.

"Apparently, you've forgotten who I am. This is your only reminder and your only warning... If you ever disrespect the woman I love again, if you ever say anything derogatory about the mother of my child, there will be uncomfortable consequences. Understand?"

I removed my hand from her mouth, let her to slide down the front of my body, and grabbed her waist.

"Tell me you understand, Val."

"But I don't."

Her tears fell faster, and I wiped them away with my thumb.

"Why me, Stefano? You're here with her."

"Her?" I blinked, then remembered Benedetta. "I'm not here with her like that. She isn't you."

"She's stunning and calm. She knows what's expected of her, and she doesn't—"

"Watch it," I warned.

Val pressed her lips together, the way she did when she wanted to choose her words carefully.

"She would be a good wife."

"For someone else, she would be a fantastic wife. For me, marrying her would only make for a cold, lonely life. And she would always know she was second best. I know you don't like her, but that's a cruel fate to wish on anyone."

"She'd be easier."

"Easy is the way of lazy men and cowards. I'm neither."

"It's just—"

I cupped her cheek, keeping my touch soft.

"I'm here for you. Only you. I will only ever be satisfied with you. Now are you going to help me or not?"

"Help you?"

She stepped around me to pick up her dress before slipping into it. When she turned, I drew the tiny zipper up and smoothed the fabric in place to conceal it.

"Yes, I need information."

She spun to look at me. "About?"

Damn, she looked beautiful in that dress. Knowing my cum ran down her thighs under that silk made it even sexier.

I grabbed my shirt, then shrugged it on.

"What are the Russians offering your father? I've heard rumors, but I want to know what you know."

I didn't plan to tell her about my conversation with Marco because I didn't trust him. It seemed too easy. All smoke and mirrors. Why did he take her just to tell me how to get her back?

Maybe he cared about her and had to play a role to keep his father in the dark. Or maybe that was what he wanted me to believe. I didn't buy it. Not yet.

He could just as easily have been setting me up, which is a risk I'd take, but if Val could give me something that helped me make a better move, I'd take that too.

She shrugged. "I don't know much. Only that the original deal would've allowed Saul's empire to grow into Europe without violating the treaty."

I finished buttoning my shirt, then reached for my mask and jacket on the floor.

"Through Canada?"

Val nodded.

"Okay, that's useful."

I finished dressing, then turned back to her.

"Take a few minutes to clean up. I'll see you soon."

I placed a kiss on her cheek and unlocked the stall, stopping long enough to straighten my tie, mask, and jacket, so I didn't look like I'd just had incredible sex in the ladies' room.

"Where are you going?" she asked.

"We've been over this, kitten. You belong to me. One way or another, I'm taking you home to our son. You'll marry me—no one else. That's where I'm going. To make it happen."

After one final searing kiss, I left my girl alone in the restroom to freshen up, taking a moment to check myself in the mirror and wipe the red lipstick off my face.

Saul Moscatelli would see me and consider my offer.

I didn't care what I had to do to make that happen. If I had to murder people in the fucking ballroom, I would do it.

He would listen to me, and we would make our deal.

When I stepped into the hallway, I found Benedetta leaning against the wall with her arms crossed and a bored expression on her face.

She raised an eyebrow.

Any attitude from her about what I'd just done wouldn't be tolerated. I had no regrets.

I straightened my tie.

"Can I help you with something?" I snapped.

With a knowing look, she wiped lipstick off my chin.

"If you're quite finished fucking his daughter, Saul will see you now."

SEVENTEEN
VAL

Stefano marched out of the ladies' room, ready to conquer the world, and I collapsed onto the toilet seat lid, stealing another minute to catch my breath and collect my thoughts after watching him go.

A wave of intense sadness rushed through me.

Sex with Stefano was always earth-shattering, but nothing compared to this time. We had connected on a different plane, like our souls had come together in the same place, at the same time, to become one after existing alone for so long.

Why now, though? How cruel could God be, letting me find my everything, all I'd ever wanted, the man I needed, only to rip it away from me? Why did my last moments with Stefano have to be so incredible?

Tears flowed from my eyes, rolling down my cheeks, each one faster than the last, and I couldn't make them stop.

The aching in my chest intensified.

My nonna had taught me that crying was an expensive luxury, an indulgence women like us couldn't afford in large portions or with any frequency. Of course, she was right.

But fuck it—I couldn't prevent the overwhelming eruption of emotions from taking me down nor did I want to. The pain, the stress, sorrow, anger, fear, and even regret imploded within me, my heart breaking into tiny pieces all over again.

I allowed myself three gut-wrenching sobs before straightening my spine and moving my ass out of the stall.

I frowned at my reflection in the mirror.

Mother of Christ, how did one sort out makeup and hair like the mess Stefano and I had made of mine? I thanked God, though, for waterproof mascara and a complexion that required little foundation if any.

After doing my best to clean up all the red lipstick smears and reapply it where it belonged, I smoothed and straightened everything else.

I tilted my head, gazing at myself again. I actually looked more presentable than I'd thought possible... and yet somehow still freshly fucked, as Stefano would say.

Taking in a deep breath, I strode out of the ladies' room to go find my little brother and my shoes.

The long hallway with its soft, red carpet running down the center felt like an invitation to run to my freedom. I stopped and stared at the fire exit door at the far end.

If only this princess could have her fairy tale moment on the palace stairs as she escaped at the stroke of midnight. Sadly, the warden of the night kept my shoes nice and safe.

No Cinderella moments for me. Not even if my own Prince Charming thought he could make a deal with the devil.

When I entered the ballroom, classical music filled the air. Guests drank, danced, laughed, whispered secrets, and hatched their schemes for world domination.

These events were all the same. Nothing out of place, as if no one had noticed my absence at all.

Well, Santo had for sure, and he now waited just inside the door with my strappy heels dangling from his fingers.

"Thank you," I said.

I gazed at the floor as I took my shoes from him, hoping he couldn't read my face and figure out what had happened.

There was no telling what Aris or Saul would do if they found out.

No, I knew exactly what they'd do. It would start with them killing Stefano while I watched and then end with my death.

Or something even worse.

I slid my shoes onto my feet, wincing as I put weight on the new blisters they'd already given me, and tried to act normal.

Santo raised a brow and looked me up and down.

"So... have fun in the restroom?"

I shrugged, feigning innocence.

"Yes, actually, I did enjoy it. I ran into an old friend."

"Huh." He rolled his eyes. "Just wondering how often you entertain men in public ladies' rooms."

My cheeks burned as I grabbed an ice-cold champagne from the tray of a passing server.

"I don't know what you're talking about."

My brother gave me a knowing smile.

"I saw your man walk out. I know what you were doing in there. Who would've thought you had a sex-in-public kink? I mean, fucking gross because you're my sister, but also ballsy. You're playing with some serious fire. It's impressive. Or really stupid. We'll have to wait and see how it turns out."

"You don't know a thing, Santo."

I poked him, then pressed the glass to my cheek, hoping it would cool away some of my flush.

He looked down his nose at me.

"Yeah, no, let me tell you what I know, Valentina. I know you spent thirty minutes in that restroom, and although it's one hundred percent understandable to need a break from the gossipy bitches in this room, that's a long time. I worried at first you got sick or made a break for it without your shoes."

"And in Chicago, in the winter," I added.

Then he gave me a deadpan stare.

I fingered the pearls hanging around my neck like he'd accused me of something scandalous. Well, he kinda had.

And he wasn't wrong.

"Okay, just stop it now, Santo."

He didn't stop, though. My brother had much more to say.

"I stopped worrying after a very familiar man stomped past following you. I didn't need much else to figure it out. Especially when the asshole came out grinning like an idiot. Like a satisfied idiot, but still."

If Santo had seen him, who else had noticed? I couldn't help but wonder how many other people knew. And why did my little brother take so much pleasure in my embarrassment over getting caught?

"Please stop," I murmured. "Please. Please. Stop."

"But I haven't even gotten to the best part yet," he said.

I gulped champagne before signaling for him to continue.

"See, as soon as he stormed out of the restroom, he picked up the girl he came with. She didn't look pissed at all, just bored, maybe a little annoyed. And she went with him into the room where Father's holding his meetings tonight."

I sucked in a shaky breath and nodded.

"What are the chances he walks out breathing?"

"Not bad actually," Santo said. "He's got a fifty-fifty shot because Marco's also in there. I know he's pulling for you. And just between us, our brother's planning something. I think he's hoping your boyfriend can be useful to him in a few years."

"Wait—really?"

Interesting. Maybe I had a chance at that Disney moment.

"Yeah, really. So I'd say he does have a good chance, but..."

"But?"

Santo sighed. "Aris is in there, too, and he's off his meds. If I were you, I'd be more worried about Aris antagonizing your baby daddy enough to make him lose his shit. How good is the man with temper control?"

"We're all fucked," I said, shaking my head. "Wait—when did Aris start taking meds?"

Santo scoffed. "I fucking wish. Figure of speech."

I took another drink, needing more alcohol to dull my mounting anxiety, and stared at the doors, wishing I could see through them and past the next wall into that meeting room.

"There's some hope, right, since we're in public? Maybe that'll keep Saul somewhere in the 'no felonies' civility zone."

"I don't honestly know what's gonna happen in there, sister, but I think he'll walk out. Just not sure if he'll walk out with the good news you're hoping for. I don't know if the Russians have talked to Father yet, so who knows."

"Have they arrived?"

My nerves itched with the need to get that little meet-and-greet over with, so we could all move on.

Santo's gaze followed someone approaching behind me.

"Shit. I think they're coming this way now."

My breath hitched, and I turned just in time to see a large man with blond hair and pockmarked skin in a red tuxedo.

"No one ever said they had to be attractive, but Christ, would a little style kill them?" Santo murmured.

"Maybe," I said under my breath. "So why risk it?"

"Good evening," the man said, his voice heavily accented.

He stepped in close, extended his hand, and took Santo's with forced cordiality. I wasn't offered the same courtesy. Instead, the Russian looked me up and down like I was a piece of meat or an expensive doll before turning back to my brother.

"This is the one, yes?"

Santo put his hand on my lower back.

"It is. Ivan, allow me to introduce my sister, Valentina."

The Russian stared at my cleavage, speaking only to Santo.

"She is very lovely. Like a woman made to fuck."

I bit down on the inside of my cheek. The champagne in my stomach surged up to my throat, and I swallowed hard to keep from spraying the creep's ugly tux.

My brother clenched his jaw muscles.

"Listen. This is my sister, and she still belongs to my father at this point, so show some respect."

Ivan slapped his belly, threw back his head, and laughed.

"I mean no disrespect. But we all know the circumstances. She's no longer pure or worthy of marriage or giving my boss his heirs. We hear she gave some low-level Italian a bastard."

My blood burned like fire through my veins.

How dare he speak that way about me while I stood right there? How dare he talk about Stefano and Enzo like that?

A menacing gleam darkened Santo's eyes.

"Regardless. Look around. Some civility is in order."

The Russian laughed again and waved him off.

"Women bought to be whores do not deserve civility."

Santo's hands flexed at his sides. I shot him a warning look, though I would've really preferred to offer him my help.

The stupid Russian didn't seem to notice. He was too busy circling me, like a buyer at a car dealership or a starving man at a butcher shop. I half expected him to request a test drive—in which case I would've broken his big, ugly nose. Judging by its crookedness, it wouldn't have been the first time.

The idea of anyone but Stefano touching me made my skin crawl. Everything about it felt wrong. Mortal sin wrong.

"Yes, I think she will do nicely," Ivan added. "Many of the men like women with... how do you say? Extra in the trunk?"

Did this asshole just call me fat?

"When looking for a wife," he continued, "we prefer slender Russian women. But for a whore, more junk is a good change."

Never mind his nose. I wanted to break his fucking cock.

Ivan got out his phone and circled me again, making a video, then snapped photos of my chest and the way my dress hugged my ass before slipping his phone back into his breast pocket.

"Yes, I think the boss will be happy to add this one. I will send him the video and my recommendation. He will call your father with an offer. Good evening."

With his evaluation now completed, Ivan walked away.

I'd never felt so violated in my life.

Fuming, I turned to Santo.

"Is it just me, or did being in his presence make your trigger finger like super itchy?"

"Yeah," Santo admitted. "I love how you say it like you've actually killed a man before."

I stared at him over my glass with a raised brow.

My brother lifted his chin as if impressed.

"The fuck? Really? Who?"

"The last man who thought I was his property to abuse. I shot him with his own pistol."

I winced. I'd said it so matter-of-factly.

Maybe because it felt like it happened a long time ago, to someone else. The trauma had joined all my other nightmares, lurking in the recesses of my mind, the hiding place for the things that should have broken me but hadn't.

But these nightmares had a way of opening the deep, dark pits beneath me—even years later—and some could drag me down kicking and screaming.

Which was how I'd ended up here.

Santo nodded. "Well, good for you, sister. Not sure that'll work on the Russians, though."

I snagged yet another full champagne flute.

"I'll just need to get a bigger gun."

"Huh. That might work," he agreed.

"What are the odds Saul agrees to Stefano's terms before the Russians reach out to him?" I asked.

When my little brother's gaze met mine, I didn't need to hear whatever platitude he considered giving me.

I saw the truth in his eyes.

It didn't matter what Stefano offered.

Didn't matter how much cash he offered or how lucrative the connections he could provide might be.

Saul Moscatelli planned to make me go with the Russians.

And there wasn't a damn thing anyone could do about it.

EIGHTEEN
STEFANO

While approaching Moscatelli's private meeting room, I noticed Marco leaning against the doorframe, staring at his goddamn phone like something awful had happened.

I removed my masquerade mask and pocketed it.

"What is it? Have the Russians sent their demands?"

Marco shook his head but kept his eyes on the phone.

"No, but several other bids have come in from other families. I'm guessing it's an attempt by the Italians to keep our deal with the Russians from going through."

"What do the Russians get from this... other than my wife?"

"What? Isn't she enough?" Marco asked.

"For me, yes. If she were going to be Klimov's bride and give him heirs, maybe for him as well. But those other families wouldn't be hell-bent on stopping this transaction if that was all Klimov wanted from your father."

Marco studied me, seeming to evaluate how much he might choose to trust me.

I leaned in to intimidate him into my favor.

"I'm going in there to make an offer that does more to set

up your power than his. You know exactly where I stand. You know what's on the line for me, so tell me, what the fuck's on the line for you?"

Marco straightened and jammed his phone into his pocket.

"You're right. I know what you stand to lose, but it doesn't mean I'm going to tell you what I stand to gain. I've already said enough. And I think you know the Russians want a bigger piece of Chicago, that they're already in California and Texas and now grabbing at more presence in New York and Boston."

"Yes, they want more of Chicago to link future East Coast interests with their western activities," I said.

"Right. Access to the lakes, rail lines, and other amenities."

"Buildings that sell like Manhattan," I added, "but cost less to build, would make laundering money a hell of a lot easier."

He raised his eyebrows.

"You know a lot about Chicago for a man who's technically not allowed to be here."

I fought the urge to punch him in the fucking face.

I hated it when people underestimated me.

"I don't have to conduct business in this city to understand its benefits... or its disadvantages."

I didn't want to openly disrespect a man who didn't have to help me. My answers had put him in his place well enough. He knew to take me more seriously, that I wasn't the fool his family had made me out to be when they infiltrated my home.

Marco matched my intense stare, then the corner of his mouth twisted into a sly grin. Fucker had set me up. He wanted to know how intelligent and cunning I might be.

Fair enough. I wanted to know the same about him.

Someone knocked on the door from inside the meeting room, but before Marco opened it, he hesitated.

"I hope you can make this work, Vignali. Marry my sister immediately and put an end to all this. You and I can profit a great deal from that kind of relationship."

Then he opened the door and led me into the room.

Don Moscatelli's bloated body filled his massive chair as he played at being a king, sitting in the center of the room as if he were taking petitions from his subjects.

Val's twin brother stood close to Moscatelli's chair, one step behind on the right. The psychopath eyeballed me, never moving his gaze away from me.

Marco took a seat on the velvet sofa nearby, pulled out his phone, and continued with what he'd been doing before.

Searching for more incoming bids.

"Why is the weak second son of a dead bastard here in my presence?" Moscatelli asked.

I gnashed my teeth and set my jaw. He could spew that stupid shit all he wanted. It didn't make him more powerful.

Nor would it keep him alive.

If his heir didn't kill him first, I planned to do it myself.

When I was a young boy, people whispered about Saul Moscatelli. They had called him "The Pianist" and trembled in fear at the sound of his name. Seeing him now, realizing how stupid he turned out to be, I couldn't believe it.

"If you think I'm weak, your family hasn't been paying enough attention to New York," I said. "You should probably see to that."

Moscatelli scoffed but didn't say anything.

Aris spoke out while scrutinizing me with his icy blue stare. Cold, empty eyes—similar to my girl's only in color.

"How 'bout I rephrase the question? What's the father of

such a weak little bastard doing in my father's presence? You have no right to be in this city."

I bit back a grin but just barely. Aris couldn't get over the fact that my son got one over on him.

"Hmm. Didn't my son punch you in the balls and put you out for a good five minutes?"

Aris's expression darkened.

"Is that what the lying little bastard told you?"

"He didn't mention you at all. But after you abused a woman half your size and dragged her out of my house, I did see it on the security footage. I wonder, did hurting your sister make you feel powerful again after a child took you out?"

Marco snickered but kept his mouth shut. Good. If he interjected, it might raise red flags and make Moscatelli question whether his son and I had something planned behind his back. Of course, we did.

I stepped deeper into the room, closer to the old man's chair, a slow, casual move, my light footsteps silent on the thick carpet. As much as it killed me, I nodded once at Moscatelli to show him respect.

"I'm here, sir, because you took something that belongs to me. I understand the situation is somewhat messy because your daughter lied to us all. I don't know why she lied, but it doesn't matter at this point. I'd like to make an offer for her hand."

"What could you offer me?" Moscatelli asked.

"Ten million, wired to an offshore account tonight. I'll take immediate possession of her."

Aris laughed. "This fucking clown. She's not worth that kind of money."

I narrowed my eyes, taking a second to rein in my anger.

"Let me be very clear, boy. Valentina might not be worth

that much to you, and that's your business, but her value to me is not the same, nor is the reason why it's not any of your business. Ten million is my opening bid. Counter or shut the fuck up and let the grown-ups talk."

The asshole lurched forward and drew a pistol from beneath his jacket, but Moscatelli lifted his hand, stopping his son dead in his tracks.

Fucking overzealous dog on a leash.

Moscatelli leaned forward in his chair, at least as much as his fat gut would allow, and nodded.

"All true enough. One man's trash is another's treasure. You say ten million is your opening bid. What if I want more?"

"More money? Or shall I offer something more lucrative?"

He tilted his head. "Are you in a position to offer me something more than cash for the mother of your bastard?"

He continued insulting my son to see if he could get under my skin, provoke me into making a mistake. I refused to let him. Val's life was on the line.

I nodded. "I can offer better terms than the Russians."

Moscatelli's reddened face twisted into a smile.

"Well, then. Now you have my attention, Mr. Vignali."

"Good. Let's get to it then. The Russians once offered you two and a half million as well as a business deal for expanding your shipping activity through Canada into Europe."

He shrugged. "You did your homework, and I'm supposed to be impressed?"

"Not impressed, concerned that I can give you something better. That is, assuming you've done your homework as well. I think you know I'm in a position to join the Commission and take my father's seat as one of the highest-ranking members. This gives me a great deal of influence."

I paused to drive that last point home.

"Not only can I complete that wire transfer tonight, but as soon as I take my seat on the Commission, I'll provide you with a direct shipping route from the East Coast into Europe. You won't have any issues dealing with Canadian border patrol, and I own the customs agents in New York Harbor."

Moscatelli sat back and regarded me with cold indifference.

"Why would you do that, Mr. Vignali?"

"Because you have something I want."

Aris sneered. "You're willing to join a committee you hate, work with us, and give up that much cash for someone like my sister? Kinda makes you a little simp bitch, yeah?"

I grinned. "It makes me an intelligent man."

Moscatelli intervened with a dismissive flick of his wrist.

"Yes, yes. So, Vignali, tell me why my daughter's worth all this trouble to you. Consider it a token of trust. I don't get into bed with any man I can't trust."

A fucking lie. He couldn't trust Klimov either. But fine—I could rationalize my offer if it made him get on with it.

"You met my son, your grandson, the nine-year-old who challenged you and Aris. The boy will be a strong leader, and he deserves to be my heir. I can't make it so until he's legitimate. I do that by marrying his mother."

Aris threw back his goddamn head and laughed.

"Can you believe this guy?"

I will kill that son of a bitch when Val's safe.

"Then she'll give me more children," I continued. "I'll expand my empire in New York and move into Boston. With more sons as smart and fierce as Enzo, I can achieve that more easily. Valentina's proven she can provide what I need. To me, that's worth ten million and opening those trade routes."

Reducing my girl to a proven broodmare who could provide me with more children made my gut burn. Beyond that, I had no plans for Boston, but that lie didn't bother me.

Valentina could have been unable to bear more children, and I still would have offered just as much. And Enzo could one day choose not to follow in my footsteps, and that wouldn't make me regret this decision either.

But men like Val's father and her twin brother, who might have looked like her but lacked her intelligence and grace, would never understand.

So, to get them to agree to my terms, I had to barter on their level and speak their asinine, archaic language to be sure they understood me word for word.

Marco jumped into the conversation.

"This may be more profitable for the family than anything the Russians can accomplish when it comes down to it. And it's a lot cheaper... we won't have to pay off Canadian border patrol, and I'm assuming since Vignali's boasting about owning the customs agents, that means we wouldn't pay those bribes either."

I shot him a warning look. That was not the plan.

He smiled, the meaning in his expression crystal clear.

"If you want my sister, this is what it's going to take."

Fuck.

Don Moscatelli turned his head in Marco's direction.

"Yes, son, but how do I know he can come through like the Russians can? You doubt them, but I do not."

I did the intervening this time.

"You know I'll come through because unlike the Russians, I'm an Italian, same as you, and my word is my vow, same as yours. I have a reputation to maintain—"

"Your father squandered that reputation," Aris spat.

I smiled, maintaining my composure. I could keep my shit together a little longer, for Val's sake, but I wouldn't take any bullshit from the cocky little pissant who put bruises and burns on my woman.

It didn't matter what deal Marco and I came away with, because when this was over, I meant to kill Aris myself.

"His, not mine," I said, "Since his death, I've rebuilt my family empire from the ground up. My empire is much greater in size and worth more than my father's ever would have been."

"Mr. Vignali..."

Moscatelli's proper use of my name in such a calm collected manner ignited something akin to hope in my chest.

Then it died beneath the weight of his cruel glare.

"I appreciate your generous offer," he said, "but it doesn't change the fact that the treaty forbids exactly what you're suggesting."

"True enough, Mr. Moscatelli, for now. But the men who formed the treaty and the men it was designed to control are all dead. We've entered a new era. The world has changed. Capone is no longer an issue. Neither is Luciano."

Moscatelli dug his elbows into the chair's wide leather arms and formed a steeple with his fingers.

"Maybe, since you've rebuilt your family from nothing and have no senior members to guide you, you don't understand the importance of tradition."

Fucker's looking for any excuse.

"Not at all, sir. I absolutely value tradition, provided it doesn't impede progress or profit. The treaty was intended to prevent wars from spanning across state lines, to keep the government's attention elsewhere.

"But now, thanks to RICO, those lines are irrelevant. New York and Chicago don't have to remain enemies. It would be more profitable to work together."

"Well, be that as it may," Moscatelli said, "the treaty was established for a reason. I don't think the reason is any less valid now than when it was first proposed."

Then the stupid man raised his hand.

"I know, I know. There're many in my community who don't like the idea of me dealing with the Russians. Frankly, I don't give a fuck what the other families think. I only care about what I want, what it'll take to reach my goals, and everyone else can go fuck themselves."

He'd just talked himself into a corner. Not giving a fuck and only caring about his own goals contradicted tradition.

Seems he worked pretty hard to present himself as a savvy businessman, and a rational man, but the more he opened his mouth, the more I realized this dumbass just talked in circles.

He must have confused people quite often.

Whether by design or through ineptitude, who knew.

I spread my arms wide as if to bow. I didn't.

"I'm offering you a much better deal than the Russians, and when you're not even sure they're still at the table. I'm offering a hell of a lot more capital up front with the promise of direct trade routes soon."

Marco looked up from his phone.

"Yes, exactly... a promise. I also did my homework, Vignali. You say you're joining the Commission, but my source tells me you turned down the seat."

What the fuck was this guy doing?

I shot him a scowl, then quickly composed myself.

I needed to be calm. I couldn't allow a breach in my resolve or a fissure in my usual poker face.

"It's a standing offer, and now that I've taken over two other families, which makes me the strongest don in New York, by the way, I'm taking that seat. Within five years, I'll sit at the head of the table. Opening your trade routes by the middle of next year won't be a problem unless you make it a problem."

Marco focused his attention completely on me, narrowing his glowing blue eyes.

"Which families?"

"Capaldo and Malta," I said.

He scanned the room for Benedetta. She sat alone at a table near the far wall. She met his gaze and nodded with a smile.

"Bullshit, Vignali. You don't have any claim on those men. You would have to marry Benedetta to take over those families, and you set her aside for Valentina. After all, isn't that why we're here in the first place?"

"Benedict Capaldo is dead," I said. "He died two days ago. Hours after his death, I took control of his men and all business operations. And until Benedetta marries, I control his entire empire. It's being folded into mine as we speak."

Don Moscatelli cleared his throat.

"Then you're only a steward until his daughter marries. That kind of power is inflated and temporary, and maybe the only kind you have. A princess like Benedetta won't have any trouble finding a husband."

Son of a bitch then gave Marco a long, knowing look.

Fuck that. No way would Marco get her.

I shook my head to shut down their game.

"You should know, I'm the one who chooses her husband and when she marries." I raised a brow. "If at all."

Moscatelli slammed his fists on the chair arms.

"You're telling me you'll let that beautiful girl become an old maid and keep the power for yourself?"

As if the fat prick cared about Benedetta or any other girl.

He abused his own daughter, for fuck's sake.

"I have no problem turning over what I took at the time of Don Capaldo's death—when I'm good and ready, and not a moment before. Once I've consolidated my achievements, I'll consider a marriage to the right man, for the right price. After I've taken New York, the Commission, and Boston."

I could have done it all.

It could have been my plan from day one.

A great strategy as far as empire-building plans went.

No, I didn't intend to do it, but the pretense of it all was what Moscatelli could understand and needed to hear.

Aris glared at his phone, then handed it to his father.

Moscatelli stared at Aris's phone for at least twenty seconds.

"I admit," he said, "I am impressed. Now I see you're the type of man who's strong enough to manage my stubborn Valentina. You could keep her in line and provide for my grandchildren nicely. But you see, I just don't trust you when it comes to business. You're still your father's son. I can't ignore that."

"Then don't. You don't need to trust me. You're much smarter than that anyway. You're also smart enough to know you can't trust the Russians either. Christ, those assholes don't even trust each other."

"You're right, I don't trust them. They're Russians."

He paused and turned his wrist to check the time.

"But I gave those nasty fuckers my word first, and they've sent over another good offer. So I'm inclined to... what is it they say? To leave with the date who brought me."

Moscatelli's boisterous laugh filled the fucking room.

Aris joined him.

He would get more time to torture his sister.

All the air rushed out of my lungs.

I knew what Moscatelli would say next.

"Mr. Vignali, you won't be purchasing my daughter today."

Aris walked over to me, and we stood toe to toe.

"But hey, you might be able to buy her dead body from the Russians once they're done with her."

My heart accelerated.

A razor-sharp pain shot through me.

Then the rage came.

NINETEEN
VAL

I had been locked inside my room for two days after we got back from the masquerade ball. Saul's maids took turns sneaking in buttered bread and water for me.

While praying day and night for Stefano to make it out alive, I waited for Marco or Santo to visit me, to tell me what had happened.

No one ever came.

It had been easy enough to let myself believe Santo and I reconnected that night, that he still cared about me, and so easy to think I could trust Marco. But now, left alone with no support and nothing but my thoughts, I realized I didn't really know anything at all anymore.

I didn't know whether my brothers really had my back or if they'd simply chosen not to flaunt their cruelty in the same way Aris did.

Aris's brand of savagery was almost preferable at this point, because at least I knew where he stood. And he didn't waste his time giving me any hope.

Hope was the cruelest thing my family could give me.

A small part of me had hoped, though, at least until the fashionably late but unfashionably dressed Russian emissary showed up at the Palmer House.

I'd hoped Stefano would buy me.

But when fuckface Ivan confirmed his boss had planned to make a new offer after all, my hope instantly died.

Saul would go with the Russians. I believed it in my heart. Even if Stefano beat their offer, and he would, Saul would still choose the Russians rather than risk appearing inept to the other families while standing beside an up-and-coming young rival like Stefano Vignali.

Quit whining and figure out how to get back to Enzo.

I nodded to myself.

It's not over until it's over. So I got off the bed and paced the perimeter of the room, shuffling my bare feet across the wooden floorboards, sorting through all the information in my head to come up with a plan.

A productive plan, not one that would endanger my son.

I paced and cursed because my brain wasn't giving me what I needed. I hadn't eaten anything except those small portions of bread since before the ball.

The grandfather clock in the hallway chimed ten times.

God, I swore that old thing looked just like the Cogsworth character in *Beauty and the Beast.*

Then, as if Saul had an appointment for ten o'clock sharp, he turned the lock on my door and entered.

Followed by Aris, of course.

"Father." I said in greeting, ignoring my twin's existence.

Saul stopped in the center of the room and squinted.

"You've had a couple days to think about what you've done

and the name you've dishonored more than once. So, Princess, what do you have to say about your actions?"

A headache throbbed violently behind my eyes.

I pressed a palm against my temple, hoping the pressure would ease the pain enough for me to think for a minute.

"Which actions?" I asked.

Saul sneered. "Yes, you have a few options, don't you? Start with the ridiculous tales you spread about where you've been."

"Well, I didn't think you wanted me to tell everyone the truth, that you'd sold me to a bloodthirsty Russian monster, forcing me to fake my death to stay alive, which led me to give a rival boss in New York his first son."

The old man huffed out a low chuckle, then, within like a millisecond, he was in front of me, his hand flying, the back of it crashing into my face.

His favorite move, and still I never saw it coming.

Blood spilled out of my mouth.

I toppled to the floor.

My head spun, and my ears rang.

Mother of Christ, the pain in my head.

As my vision returned, I pulled myself up onto my knees, then onto my feet.

"That's why you're so angry? Because I made up some silly stories at a party to amuse myself?"

Aris snorted.

"That's the least of it." Saul said. "Let's talk about the how you decided to fuck some random man in the ladies' room, a man that no one can seem to place. You're a stain on this family's name. I don't understand why you do it because it's also your name."

He flexed his fingers, and his face turned a darker shade of red with every passing second.

I shook my head. "I didn't fuck just some random man in the restroom," I said. "The only man I've ever been with is the father of my son. The man I was about to marry."

Saul leaned in, looming over me like a dark storm cloud.

Did the man just growl?

"Are you telling me that son of a bitch Vignali came into my city, defiled my daughter once again, and then had the balls to ask me for your hand? That fucking arrogant New Yorker!"

He lifted his shoulders to stand even taller above me.

"And they say they're more civilized than us. Well, let me tell you, daughter, that man's blatant disrespect is as savage as anything we do here."

Laughter bubbled up into my throat. I covered my mouth, but I couldn't hold it back. It burst out against my hand.

They stared at me. Maybe they thought I was insane.

"He didn't ask for my hand," I said, "and neither did the Russians. Talk about civilized behavior all you want, but you are selling me, your only daughter, like I'm livestock."

My cheeks burned. Anger had crept up on me.

"They came here to buy me," I screamed.

Aris chuckled. "You are livestock, you stupid cunt. Women like you are made for breeding and keeping bloodlines strong. You have one job, sister, that's it. Lie on your back, conceive babies, and raise them."

"What the fuck would you know about it?" I spat. "Is there another woman in this house I haven't met? Your wife? Mother of your children? No, that's right... you still follow your daddy around like a pathetic little man-child."

"Enough," Saul said.

Aris and I shut our mouths and locked our gazes on him.

Coming from Aris, the behavior was a show of respect, but for me, it was just an old habit I couldn't shake.

"Fact is," Saul continued, "for whatever reason I can't begin to fathom, the Russians still have an interest in you. You may be a disgrace to this family, but Klimov's emissary enjoyed your beauty. Another man will come by and look this afternoon.

"The son of the *pakhan* you were supposed to wed. If he likes what he sees, then we will sign the contract. And from this moment, you'll keep your mouth shut and do as you're told."

The ringing in my ears intensified, bringing with it a stronger wave of lightheadedness.

"Or what? What will happen to me?"

"Excuse me?" His eyes widened with hatred.

"What exactly will you do if I don't keep my mouth shut?"

Despite being on the verge of passing out, either from hunger or a concussion, my voice sounded steady and calm.

"I mean, if I misbehave, won't you just sell me to the next highest bidder? So why should it even matter to me?"

"The next highest bidder is Stefano Vignali," he said. "Well, technically he's the highest, but you will never see him again. I don't care if he offers me the fucking moon. If this meeting with the Russians doesn't go as planned, I have no problem selling you to sex traffickers to get rid of you...

"And sweetheart, you don't want to know what they do with disobedient little bitches like you."

Then Saul turned on his heel and left the room.

Aris did not.

As soon as the door closed, I backed away from my brother. I understood what came next.

Saul knew I'd been with Stefano at the ball.

Worse, others had brought it to his attention.

This meant Aris would get away with more than usual.

"Leave, Aris," I ordered.

He let out a low, sinister chuckle.

"Oh, I can't leave yet, sister. Not until I've punished you. You need to learn your lesson."

"Lesson for what, exactly? Shaming our father at the ball or pointing out your lack of real manhood?"

He bared his teeth at me.

"What the fuck did you just say to me, you little slut?"

I wouldn't get out of this without more cuts and bruises or worse. It was already a done deal. The best chance I had was to piss Aris off more. When emotional men got angry, they got sloppy. For Aris, that meant a few things.

Either he lost his temper and knocked me out faster than he intended, so my pain wouldn't last long.

Or he might injure me where it did finally affect my looks.

The Russians wouldn't care about a red welt left on my face by Saul's hand, a temporary mark. But if Aris broke my nose or tortured me in a way that left permanent marks, that would be a different story.

A woman—even an unmarried one with a child like me—could only be physically damaged so much before becoming completely worthless.

Either way, I wouldn't get out of this room without more pain, but I could try to lessen it or make it count for something.

I hoped he left a deep scar on my fucking face.

"You heard me," I said. "You're not a real man, just a little lapdog. Your daddy shouts a command, and you go fetch like a good little boy. Do you think if you're obedient, he'll finally love you? Do you think that'll make him forget you're a sick, fucked-up asshole who likes to wear Mom's old shoes?"

"You shut the fuck up!"

He leapt at me and slammed an uppercut into my ribcage faster than I could take another breath.

I doubled over and wanted to drop to the floor. It hurt like a bitch and forced all the air out of my lungs.

It wasn't enough. He needed more provocation.

I coughed, increasing the pain, then forced myself upright.

"I've been wondering. Do you" —I coughed— "go full drag now, or do you still lie in your room, tugging on your tiny dick while sniffing the used stilettos you buy online?"

Yes, my twin had a foot fetish and liked women's clothing.

Truly, I couldn't have cared less. My words weren't about how it made me feel. It was about provoking him, using his perversions and the shame that turned it into his weakness.

"Fuck you!" Aris screamed.

He launched his fist into my face, and I flew onto the floor.

My teeth ached inside my spinning head, and I immediately recognized the taste of more blood in my mouth.

I spat it on the filthy area rug and pulled up onto my knees.

"No thanks. I only fuck real men."

His boot cracked into my stomach, the force sending me flat on my back again.

I rolled into a fetal ball to protect myself while heaving and unable to get up. Maybe it was a good thing I hadn't eaten for days.

My bedroom door burst open, and Marco's booming voice bounced off the walls.

"What the fuck are you doing?"

Aris pointed at me lying on the floor.

"This little bitch still needs to learn her fucking place."

I sucked in a ragged breath while hugging my ribcage.

"Aris needs to learn how to not be such a sensitive little bitch. All I did was mention his addiction to Payless ads."

Marco shook his head.

"You've been gone for a while. He upgraded to buying used underwear from female prisons years ago."

"Shut the fuck up," Aris shouted, "I swear to God, I'll—"

"You'll what?" Marco said, advancing on him.

I scooted out of the way as my brothers squared off toe to toe. Aris had an inch or two on our older brother, and Marco was a big man in his own right.

"What, Aris? You'll beat me like you beat your own twin? I'm not a woman who can't fight back, asshole. You hit me, I'll hit you back harder. You should understand this by now. I want you to think carefully about what happened the last time you came at me."

Aris's cheeks turned bright red, and he gnashed his teeth.

"But she needs to—"

Marco stepped forward, backing Aris to the door.

"What she needs isn't your concern," Marco growled.

"Fine, but—"

"You have work to do, so I suggest you go fucking do it."

Aris pivoted around Marco's body.

"No, someone needs to teach her a lesson. You won't do it."

Our older brother grabbed Aris by the throat.

"If you don't get the fuck out, yes, someone's gonna learn their lesson, painfully, violently, and it won't be her. Are you really that excited about another trip to the hospital?"

Marco shoved my twin toward the door.

"I hear Northwestern has an order to call the cops the second you arrive. Something about drug-seeking behavior."

"Fuck you," Aris snapped.

"Not on your fucking life."

Then Marco slammed the door in his face.

After a minute of silence, after Aris's pounding footsteps disappeared, Marco tilted back his head, closed his eyes, and took a deep breath. Then he turned and looked at me.

"God, I hate him. I know I should love him because he's my brother, but I don't."

"How do you think I feel? He shared a womb with me."

"Christ, girl, you're a fucking mess."

I flipped him the middle finger, and his easy smile appeared. The smile few people ever got to see.

He extended his hand to help me up.

"Let's get you cleaned up before your... auction... examination... I don't fucking know what to call this bullshit."

"Let's just call it what it is. It's deeply misogynistic."

My ribs screamed in protest, and my stomach turned and burned. My head swam, the ringing in my ears sharper, the pain throbbing harder than before.

But I was still alive and even conscious.

Yay me.

Marco guided me to the bed, disappeared into the en suite bathroom, returned with a washcloth, and began dabbing at my bloody mouth.

"Why do you go along with it all?" I blurted.

He stopped and stared at me but didn't say anything.

Why the fuck didn't my big brother do something about all the cruelty against women, the "bullshit," as he'd called it?

"So," he finally said. "Father didn't take your man's offer."

I sucked in air through my teeth and continued to focus on my brother's eyes. They always told me the real story.

"Didn't he offer enough?"

Marco nodded. "In fact, I think he offered too much, and if I'm being honest here, sorellina, that was my fault."

"How? What did you do, Marco?"

God, my head hurt. The pain made it hard to reach the thoughts and words hiding in the pulsing corners of my mind.

"I misread the situation. I told him he needed to offer something impressive, not just money. Vignali did that, but I never expected it to make Father believe it made you worth even more to the Russians than he originally thought."

"What does that mean?"

"The Russians said they were interested again after seeing you, so Father raised the price. He told them you're worth more now than when you were innocent."

"What?"

It didn't make sense.

Or maybe it did, and all the violence had scrambled my brain enough to make me question my own thoughts.

He shook his head and kept cleaning my face.

"Don't get excited. It's not as progressive as you think. It actually makes it worse for you."

"I don't see how," I mumbled.

"Well, he told the Russians any time they take a virgin bride, they gamble with the quality of produced offspring. But you've proven you can bear strong, intelligent sons.

"Then he told them, and I quote, 'Her son, at the mere age of nine, has already shown far more promise than his father.' He managed to convince them if they give you a chance to bear heirs, they'd be stronger for it. Because of you."

I didn't even know what to say to that.

"Honestly, sorellina, I can't believe they bought the bull-shit, but they did. Klimov's second son is coming to see you. If you meet his standards, he'll move forward with a generous offer on the spot, as if the last decade never happened.

"Seems they think if you can bear an Italian bastard strong enough to make his father willing to marry you for legitimacy's sake, then your children with a Russian sire should make perfect soldiers."

I winced as Marco dabbed at some blood on my temple.

"Ow." I pulled away. "This is fucked up. This is the twenty-first century. How do these stupid asses still not understand it's the man's DNA that determines a baby's gender? Russia has modern medicine and, like, the fucking internet, right?"

"The basics of biology are clearly still mystifying," he teased.

Then my brother's usual stony expression returned.

"I'm sorry, sorellina. The Russians will be here in about an hour, and I can't think of a way to get you out of this."

"We can't fake my death again?" I asked hopefully.

"A second time? Nah, we'll never get away with it."

He winked at me, and I smiled.

"What should I do, Marco? How do I get through this?"

He folded the bloody washcloth while avoiding my gaze.

"You put on a pretty dress. You do your makeup and cover as much of the bruising as you can. You smile like you mean it... and you hope Vignali has something else up his sleeve."

TWENTY

STEFANO

My blood and my bones vibrated with rage.

If Saul Moscatelli and his son wanted a mother-fucking war, I would bring it. If he thought the St. Valentine's Day Massacre had been Chicago's bloodiest, and Capone's war the greatest, he had no idea what the fuck was coming his way.

I stepped back into the ballroom and searched for Val. She stood in a corner, guarded by her thug of a brother. Her eyes were closed, and she seemed to be in distress.

My heart dropped into my gut.

I had to leave her alone.

If I dared to approach her—to hold her and comfort her—I wouldn't be able to stop myself from ultimately just taking her. Her brother would have to act, no matter what he and Marco wanted for her. And it would get very ugly in a public setting.

Val would get hurt.

As difficult as it was, I did the only thing I could to keep her safe a little longer. I walked out of the Palmer House alone and headed straight to the private airstrip where the plane waited.

Just before takeoff, I called Benedetta.

She'd asked to stay to catch up with her mother's family. She would be safe with the Maltas during those twenty-four hours, so I didn't see the harm in it.

I wouldn't have been good company anyway.

"Get me the fucking names, numbers, and addresses, Benedetta. Do it right now. Include all Capaldo lieutenants. Send everything directly to Tony."

Once she agreed, I didn't bother with saying goodbye. I tossed my phone onto the seat beside me, then gulped down the old-fashioned set before me by the flight attendant.

The woman swooped in for my glass with a nod to let me know she'd be back with another.

I raked my hair back.

Moscatelli refused to return my girl to me, and it didn't matter what the fuck I offered him. A vindictive asshole for the sheer pleasure of it. And he was scared.

It had shown in his eyes. The next generation frightened him. I wouldn't be surprised if he kept a wary eye on Marco.

Others had reported how Moscatelli excelled at maintaining control of his emotions, which might have been true, but even veiled emotions dictated actions. If he were truly indifferent, he would have taken my offer. My terms were better than anything the Russians could give him, and the son of a bitch knew it.

I picked up my phone and texted Tony.

On flight back

Get V and C men to the estate at noon

BC has C info

TONY

Consider it done boss

Calling BC now

That gave me enough time to wash off the failure, maybe take a power nap, and down a lot of coffee while coming up with a proper plan. At that moment, I knew only two things. I was going back for Valentina, and it would get very messy.

Find blueprint of M estate and set up private flight to C

As many seats as possible unless driving is faster

Tony would understand immediately and get everything moving. He knew how to maneuver without creating links back to me the FBI could gather too easily.

When I got Val back, and I would, I wanted time to marry her and enjoy my wife before a judge sentenced me to prison. My wife. Mine.

TONY

. . .

I got you boss

Everything done right away

Good man. Tony had always had my back since we were boys. And now he had to cover my son's back as well. Tony would never lead the Vignali empire, but his job—keeping me and my heir safe and moving forward—proved to be just as important.

TWO HOURS LATER

Back in New York, I dragged my exhausted ass through the front door of my house.

Enzo waited in the foyer, his foot tapping on the marble.

Rocco's team had repaired most of the damage already and cleaned the place up, but unfortunately, the large vase that sat on the mahogany entry table for as long as I could remember couldn't be replaced.

The absence of my mother's favorite vase made everything seem off, like my home would never be quite the same. In a way, I supposed that was right.

"You're back," Enzo said.

His tone, his stare, made it feel like an accusation.

"I am, but not for long. What are you doing up so early?"

Clearly, the boy had eavesdropped enough to know when I would return and that his mother wouldn't be coming through the door with me. Seemed he'd been doing it most of his life, listening and knowing more than Val thought possible.

"Where is she?" he snapped.

I didn't want to lie to him. He deserved to know I'd failed him and his mother.

"She's in Chicago, at her father's house."

His cheeks grew pink, and his eyes darkened.

"Why didn't you bring her back?"

"I tried, but her father refused my deal. I'm not giving up. I'm going back to take her tonight."

"You should just give up," Enzo snapped. "When are you gonna start actually protecting her like you're supposed to?"

"Watch yourself, boy."

"No! You promised us and you broke your promise again!"

I didn't have the energy or patience to deal with an angry child, but I wouldn't walk away from my son.

"I brought her home to you the first time, and I'll bring her back this time, too."

Clenching his little fists, Enzo held his position in front of me, his cherubic face now bright crimson.

"With more bullet holes in her? Is she even going to be alive this time?"

Fuck. I knew where things were headed.

"Look, I understand you're upset, but taking it out on me won't get her back any faster. I'm not the enemy."

"Maybe you are," he screamed. "You promised!"

Tears welled in his eyes, and he wiped furiously at them.

"And you broke that promise. To me—"

The truth in his words gutted me, and I lashed out.

"I've broken nothing, goddamn it," I shouted. "I'll get her back. I just need some time."

With his shoulders heaving, Enzo reached into his back pocket and pulled out the knife I'd given him.

"Son," I warned, "if you're going to pull a weapon, you better be ready to use it."

The boy charged me, willing to strike a man two feet taller than himself—and his father at that.

I grabbed his wrist, gripping tightly but being careful not to hurt him. He kicked at me, screaming, slapping with his free hand, trying to yank his arm away.

"Stop it. Enzo, stop. You're going to hurt yourself."

"No!" He wouldn't stop fighting.

He left me no choice but to squeeze the delicate bones in his wrist until his fingers opened and the knife clattered to the floor. Then I kicked it, sending it spinning away from us both with a swirling scrape of steel across the marble floor.

"You promised, Mr. Vignali. You promised!"

Tears poured from him in an endless stream, his whole body shaking with sobs. And still, he flailed against my grasp, though he'd already weakened himself substantially.

I wanted to toss him aside and escape to my bedroom suite.

Instead, I wrapped my arms around the boy, pinning his arms to his sides and holding his trembling body against my chest. My heart twisted violently as he still tried to fight me. A strange crackling sound rose in my throat, a mix of torment and yet another apology.

His heartbreak would be the death of me.

I understood what went on inside him, and I couldn't bear to witness his pain. So much like my own.

"Take a deep breath, Enzo," I whispered. "I made a vow to you, and I will keep it."

I shouldn't have yelled at him. Guilt tore at my insides, but I didn't know how to handle it. I didn't know how to be a father to the nine-year-old son I hadn't raised. I needed Val. Only she could teach me how to be the parent Enzo needed.

Seeing him like this, holding my son while he screamed and cried, reminded me I wasn't the only one who needed her back. Anything less than storming that motherfucker's house and taking her by force wouldn't cut it.

"Enzo," I said when his crying calmed, and his body relaxed against mine.

He sniffed. "What?"

"I'm leaving tonight to go back to Chicago. I'm taking her by force. I had to try the diplomatic way first. I tried running the back channels. I tried everything I could to get your mother back peacefully. Those avenues have run their course."

He pulled away and blinked up at me, tears still shimmering in his wide eyes.

"What does that mean?"

"It means that now I'm going in a second time, and I won't hold back. It means I will kill anyone who tries to get between me and bringing your mother home." I thumbed a few tears from his velvety cheeks. "Do you understand?"

"I want to go with you."

"Absolutely not. This won't be anything like last time."

"I'll listen to you better this time," he said.

I dipped my head to look him straight in the eye.

"I don't believe that for a second, Enzo. I won't be up against only one dangerous person like last time. It's not just one man's basement. I'm going into a mansion, maybe bigger than ours, filled with men who shoot at anyone. They wouldn't think twice about shooting you."

"I don't care. I want to get her back as much as you do."

"I know you do, son, but I can't bring you with me. I need you to trust me on this. It's different this time."

"How? How am I supposed to trust you? I don't even know you. You think buying me an Xbox and not making me go back to school is all it takes?"

So fucking smart, this kid.

"I know it's not enough. But neither of us has a choice in this situation. We just have to trust each other."

Enzo backed away from me, pulling out of my grasp, and this time, I let him go.

"I hate you," he said coldly.

I hated myself right then, too, enough for the both of us.

"If you need to hate me, that's okay. It won't change anything. You're still going to stay here until I walk back into this house with your mother."

"We'll see about that."

Enzo turned on his heel and stomped up to his room.

Christ. If I didn't get her back, this kid might actually try to kill me in my sleep. What was the appropriate punishment for attempted patricide anyway? For how long did I ground him? How many chores did I pile onto a list at once?

I needed Val for this. For everything. For him, and for me.

Tony crossed the foyer and picked up Enzo's knife, folded the blade, and handed it to me.

"Everything okay, Stef?"

I slid the knife into my pocket.

"No, not even a little, but thanks for waiting until that ran its course."

"Not a problem," he said with a dismissive flick of his wrist.

I wished it were that easy.

"The blueprints of the Moscatelli house are in your office."

"Good. I'll shower, then we'll get to work."

I headed for the stairs.

"But there's something else," he said.

Jesus fucking Christ.

I stopped and turned. "What?"

"This was just dropped off."

He handed me a red envelope that meant only one thing—the Commission had summoned me at the worst time possible.

Fuck my life.

The envelope looked legit, the wax seal still intact.

Only the Commission would send its correspondence in

something so fucking gaudy. For Christ's sake, I wished they would join this century and send a fucking text. No, but that would have been less dramatic and less of a waste of time.

I popped the seal and removed the heavy cardstock inside. At least the script wasn't in gold this time. It was blood red.

Stefano Vignali,

The Commission demands your presence today at 5:00 p.m. to answer for your crimes against the council. Failure to appear and plead your case will result in an immediate bounty placed on your head and the head of your immediate heir.

Don Edgardo Lordi, Council CEO

I shoved the note back at Tony and paced at the base of the stairs, waiting for him to read it.

"Fucking assholes."

"What should we do, boss?"

Damn good question. I had to think about this.

I couldn't leave for Chicago until after I dealt with the Commission, but maybe they'd help. They wanted me on the board. Edgardo had made that perfectly clear when he'd threatened to kill me for marrying Benedetta if I didn't join.

And now, I had control of Benedetta's men, and he would want my allegiance to the Commission.

They had it, as far as I was concerned. I could never allow Val to be taken from me again.

It wouldn't change my plans to eventually kill Edgardo in my family's name, but he didn't need to know that.

My living family took precedence over the dead.

Every single time.

In this case, maybe I could get the Commission on my side. Get them to sanction my trip to Chicago. It would be a hell of a power grab and more reckless than I was usually willing to be. If it went sideways, I would never have their support again.

But if I could get additional men, if I could get into Moscatelli's house and outnumber his men, that would get Val out safely. I could marry her in a church the second we hit the ground in New York. She would then be untouchable.

It would cost me my soul, but I could live with that.

"Nothing changes Tony," I said. "Get all Vignali and Capaldo lieutenants here for the noon meeting. I want food brought in for everyone. Make sure my son eats something. If he wants to, he can join us."

"But the Commission—"

"The Commission requested my attendance at five. As far as I'm concerned, what they need has no bearing on our ability to plan this mission. We'll have every detail locked down before I leave to speak with them. We'll reconvene afterward and deal with whatever bullshit they send our way after we get Val back."

"And if I can't get all the lieutenants here?"

I pinched the bridge of my nose, trying to ward off the pain settling between my temples.

"Why wouldn't you be able to?"

"Some from the Malta side are saying they should go to their cousin instead of locking themselves in with the Capaldo side."

"Fuck that. Tell them if they decide not to throw in, I'll consider it a forfeiture of their position. They get branded as rats, and I hunt them down as rats."

Had I not been in such a precarious situation, I might've handled it differently. But the situation called for action, and I couldn't let anybody sit this one out.

"Yeah, boss. I'll get it done."

Tony headed for the ops room, and I made my way to my bedroom. I paused in the doorway.

Val's perfume still lingered in the air. Her robe lay in a heap on the bed, her personal things still scattered beside the bathroom sink. Her entire essence filled the room.

My body ached, and my eyes burned, yet I wouldn't sleep. Not until she lay beside me where she belonged.

I couldn't go on a mission exhausted. Nor could I deal with the Commission when exhaustion weighed down my limbs.

Sighing, I entered the bathroom for a shower. Maybe the water would refresh my brain, so I could get to work.

It didn't.

I'd barely wrapped the towel around my waist before I collapsed on Val's side of the bed. Holding her pillow to my chest, I buried my nose in the silk case and breathed in, smelling her—wishing she was back in my arms.

4:15 P.M.

Knocking on my bedroom door startled me awake. I glanced at my bedside clock. Goddamn it. I hadn't meant to fall asleep.

How had I slept so long?

I scrambled to get dressed for my meeting with the Commission and opened the door. Tony waited for me, offering a giant sandwich on a plate.

"Why didn't you wake me hours ago?"

He sucked in a heavy breath, and I already knew I wouldn't like what he said next.

"I couldn't get the other lieutenants here, boss. Most of them aren't willing to work with a man they haven't met. They made it clear they're not withdrawing their positions or their allegiance, but you're not their boss until the contracts have been properly executed."

"Benedetta was supposed to send them to the lawyer."

"She did. Yesterday. The lawyer wasn't in the office yesterday. I called his personal line, and he said it would take at least a week for the transfer of businesses to go through. I think we're on our own for this one, boss."

I leveled him with a glare.

"You shouldn't have let me sleep that long. We need a plan to go in with a smaller team."

"That's why I let you sleep. I laid everything out. You just need to go over the details and approve. We can deal with the Commission's shit, then leave first thing in the morning. Daylight invasion. A quick in-and-out for the girl. They'll never see it coming. But if you aren't rested, it might not go as well."

Good call.

Still, I didn't like him making the decisions on his own.

I bit into the sandwich, my stomach grumbling in appreciation as I chewed and swallowed.

"All right, Tony. Commission meeting first. And when this is all over, if I'm still alive, you and I will chat about you going rogue."

He nodded. "Yes, boss."

"Listen. If I don't make it out of the meeting, see that Benedetta marries someone worthy enough to lead my empire until my son is ready. Benedetta should raise Enzo as my heir. You be there for him, Tony. Understand?"

My second seemed to stop breathing as he contemplated my wishes and their massive weight.

"And make sure Marco fucking Moscatelli stays away from them both," I added. "Kill him if necessary."

TWENTY-ONE

VAL

Wearing another expensive dress—this one bright pink, less formal, and not so revealing—I waited for someone to knock at my door.

I hated the fucking dress, with its high neckline, fitted bodice, and full skirt. It made me feel like a fifties barbie doll. Like some empty, plastic thing chosen for its beauty, bent, and moved to the will of someone else.

I needed to push beyond all my thoughts because thinking literally hurt. That kind of pain was worse than any headache or bruise or even the aching set deep in my bones.

My last bit of hope had died, leaving me with unbearable nothingness.

Thinking up a plan would only be a waste of time. Even Marco had said he didn't know how to save me anymore.

Thoughts of Enzo and Stefano hurt the most. Thoughts of Marco and his look of defeat when he left my room earlier that day made it impossible not to cry.

Oh, he'd tried to give me a sliver of hope, saying Stefano might come up with something else. Stefano would come back

—I had no doubt. If I knew nothing else, he would never give up anything he wanted so easily.

I didn't want him to come back, though. I wanted him to stay in New York and focus on raising our son.

Finally, the knock came from the other side of the door. I stood, the door opened, and Saul stepped inside, followed by another large blond man and my three brothers.

The man had cold eyes and nicotine-stained teeth. The sour stench of stale vodka and sweat followed him into the room.

Mother of Christ, I had to steel my gag reflex.

So the Russians had sent another emissary, not a decision-maker, nor the second son they'd promised. This man was more likely to spend his pakhan's money on cheap booze and women, assuming anyone actually made him pay for anything.

All mob bosses—Mafia, Bratva, and the Irish—liked to pretend they weren't criminals. They might get their hands dirty, but they dressed like white-collar elite with their tailored suits, Italian leather shoes, expensive haircuts, and luxurious colognes. Even the underbosses imitated that level of prestige.

This particular man hadn't seen a shower, let alone a tailor.

Did Saul realize this was meant as an insult? Marco might pick up on it. More importantly, did it mean the higher price Saul had negotiated would fall through?

Did I even fucking care anymore?

Without even a glance in my direction, Saul gestured at me.

"This is my daughter, Valentina. As I told your boss, we had some trouble with her before, and she has a son—he's with his father now. She's more than capable of producing more strong sons. Many good years still left in her."

I stared straight ahead, mimicking the cold, dead stare on Marco's and Santo's faces.

"It looks like you have had trouble with her very recently."

The Russian grabbed my chin, moving my head from side to side, no doubt scrutinizing the freshest marks Aris and Saul had left on my face.

"She just needed a gentle reminder of who's in charge," Aris said, smug satisfaction dripping from his words.

"In Russia, we do not hit our women. Still, knowing the purpose we have in mind for this one, maybe it's okay."

His loud, boisterous laugh followed and sent shocks of pain shooting through my damn head.

Saul and Aris joined him.

Marco and Santo stood quietly at the back of the room, blending in like wallflowers. I wished I could do the same.

The man released my chin and clasped his hands together.

"You spoke with my boss about a possible marriage to a second son. I know this. The reason you gave is understood, but it will not be possible with her reputation. Before the mask ball at the hotel, maybe yes. But people say things about her now that would follow a woman anywhere, even to Russia."

Saul huffed. "What are people saying? I can assure you it's all baseless gossip."

"They say she is strong willed. That she will fuck any man. I see these fresh bruises, and I know the first is true. The second might become an asset for what we now have in mind for her."

"What is your boss proposing?" Saul asked.

"When you first told us she was alive, we would make her a reward for soldiers who prove their worth, given her a luxury penthouse in Moscow, or perhaps Petersburg. The men who visited her would be men who pleased our leaders. Maybe an extra perk for certain others.

"She would have been provided for. Given some allowance

to spend for good behavior. It would be a very nice life. Not a long one, of course. Our men sometimes get a little rough. But it would be a good life."

"And what's the current offer?"

A note of hostility underscored Saul's voice.

He didn't care what they did with me or how they might use me. He certainly didn't care if I had a good life—or died by the hand of a man who would rather fuck a corpse.

The Russian nodded as if expecting Saul's frustration.

"We understand why you believe she is worth more. She is very beautiful. She can bear sons, yes. Seeing this, I think she can still please the second son, but not as a wife. As a mistress. She will give him sons. Bratva will raise them. They will not be heirs. They will be soldiers. Parts in the machine."

He settled his blood-shot gaze on me again.

"But first, I must know if she is up for the task."

I tightened every muscle in my body to keep from wilting under his frigid stare.

"Whatever you need," Aris said.

"The pakhan's son is particular. There must be no defects. No diseases. No curves created by padding or undergarments. No illusion of this shape."

His gaze wandered down my body, making me want to crawl out of my skin.

No one said a word to me.

No one acknowledged the fact that I was in the room.

Until Aris came up behind me, grabbed onto my dress, and tore down the zipper.

The entire thing fell to the floor, exposing the white lace someone had chosen for me to wear beneath it.

My skin flushed under the weight of their stares.

Not from Marco or Santo, though.

They kept their eyes focused on the floor.

"All of it," the Russian said. "She must strip for a full inspection."

I closed my eyes and drifted away, out of my body, somewhere else. Anywhere but there.

The idea squeezed my heart, but I forced myself to let the thoughts come anyway. Thoughts of how Stefano and Enzo would help each other through the grief after my death.

How Stefano would take care of Enzo. He might move on and have more kids with another woman, but she would be kind to Enzo. She would treat him like her own, and he would love her for it.

Not the same way he loved me, but it would be something.

Aris pinched one of the bruises on my side while he said something I didn't even bother to hear.

I squeezed my eyes shut tighter as the air shifted with the Russian's movements and let go of my thoughts again.

Enzo wouldn't call her Mama but would still give her gifts on Mother's Day. That would be enough for her.

Stefano and our son would go out, just the two of them, every year on my birthday and talk about me.

Stefano would tell him about the girl I'd been when he met me, and Enzo might share his favorite memories from when it had been just him and me.

Maybe when my son had siblings, he would read stories to them like I'd read to him. When he got older and had a wife of his own, he would tell her about me.

Aris pinched me again, harder this time, forcing me back to the present.

My fucking eyes flew open.

Saul studied me in a clinical manner, like trying to put a dollar value on a horse. The Russian looked on with thinly veiled lust, and Aris admired the kaleidoscope of colors he'd painted on my body with his fists.

Marco and Santo hadn't moved, their eyes dead as they stared at nothing, maybe refusing to see anything at all because they couldn't make it stop.

Dissociation was powerful, and I intended to master it.

The dumb-fuck Russian laughed and slapped my ass.

"She can take a beating. That will serve her well."

I bit the inside of my cheek, ignoring the sting. Just one more drop in the bucket of pain and humiliation.

"A woman must be tough to make strong boys," Saul said, like being beaten somehow earned me a badge of honor.

The Russian nodded, his eyes never straying from me.

"Yes, well, here is what I am permitted to offer... We will transfer two million. Half when we take her and half at the end of the first year. That is, if she survives. Then we open trade routes through Canada for you.

"We do not recommend American drivers in the winter. The roads get very difficult. Twenty-five percent of every ship-ment belongs to us, either in transported goods or the equal value in cash. Bribing of border patrol and any other authorities comes from your pocket."

Aris shrugged. "That seems fair."

I caught movement from the corner of my eye. Marco had straightened his posture. His fists were balled at his sides, and when I turned my head to see his face, he had his jaw clenched.

He'd lost his battle with pretending to be apathetic.

Still, my older brother did nothing to help me.

Saul extended his big fat fucking hand to the Russian.

"Tell your boss ten percent, and we have a deal."

Really? Even I knew a terrible deal when I heard one.

"I must ask his permission first," the Russian said, gripping Saul's hand, "but it should not be a problem. We will send you a deal or counteroffer soon."

Aris laughed. "You could just take her back to your hotel now and give her a test drive."

The Russian pawed at my breast before tweaking my nipple.

"Ah, it is a tempting offer, yes. But as with all new whores, gifted to a son or not, the boss always goes first."

I wanted to vomit, but there wasn't enough food in my stomach for that, which was probably why they'd starved me.

The men continued talking as I stood before them.

Naked and exposed in every way.

I tried to drift back into my fantasy, but I couldn't see Enzo there anymore. I could only see snow and blood stretched far into the distance of my future.

If this deal went through, if an opportunity didn't present itself soon—my life would end with a cold death.

Aris settled his hand on my arm and pressed his thumb against my bullet wound.

I fought to stay upright beneath the pain.

It was all I could do not to cry out.

I might not have known what waited for me over the next few days, but I did know one thing for sure.

Aris would die before I left this fucking house.

TWENTY-TWO
STEFANO

Unlike the last time I appeared before Edgardo Lordi and his Commission cronies, this meeting pulsed with tension the moment I walked through the door.

Lordi's men searched Tony and me more thoroughly and stripped us of all weapons. They made Tony wait in the empty restaurant while pushing me through the door into the back room.

The heads of all Commission families filled the room. No plates of pasta or glasses of wine sat in front of them, and not a soul spoke out of turn.

"Do you know why I've brought you here?" Lordi asked.

I would never fall for that trick.

He'd made it crystal clear. If I acquired control of Capaldo's men, I must join the Commission—or become their enemy. Or maybe he'd summoned me to discuss my trip to Chicago.

Regardless, I didn't volunteer information to anyone.

I straightened my jacket sleeves.

"I could hazard a few guesses, but we're all busy men with

better things to do. Let's skip the guessing game and get on with business."

Don Lordi narrowed his close-set dark eyes.

"Are you not aware of the laws dictating our world?"

What a stupid fucking question.

"Are we talking gravity or taxes?" I asked.

I didn't have time for this man's shit and hoped the glib answer conveyed my annoyance.

Lordi apparently didn't find my response as amusing as I had. He rose from his chair, a failed attempt to make himself the most intimidating man in the room, and slammed his fists on the table in front of him.

"You know damn well I'm talking about the laws of the Commission governing the Italian families in New York."

I shrugged. "Last time I checked, I wasn't a member of the council, which technically exempts me from abiding by its laws. Now if there's nothing else, I'll let you get back to whatever it is you do here. I'm happy to show myself out."

I turned around to exit the room.

"You will not leave," he shouted.

Enforcers appeared on either side of me, their hands clamping onto my shoulders and gripping my elbows.

A young man sitting at Lordi's left side got out of his chair.

"Is this all really necessary?"

The fuck? I hadn't seen this guy before, even though I kept close tabs on the Commission and the families in the area.

"Christ, Mr. Vignali's not going anywhere," he continued. "There's no reason to treat him like a prisoner."

Lordi shot the guy a shut-the-fuck-up look.

"Mr. Medico, I realize you're new to the committee, but you see, this is how it's done."

Ah, yes—Medico... Angelo... Victor Medico's only son.

He had disappeared several years earlier, the rumors ranging from him serving time in an out-of-state prison to the kid having been kidnapped by a rival gang.

Victor Medico never seemed concerned about his son's disappearance. He never confirmed or denied the rumors.

At the time, I hadn't paid any attention. I'd been too busy building my empire to worry about anything that didn't affect me.

I glanced around the room.

Victor had skipped the meeting, and Angelo had his seat. Whether the man had retired or died meant nothing to me, but I had to wonder if this new, younger face belonged to friend or foe.

Angelo shook his head, unbothered by Lordi's glare.

"I understand certain protocols need to be followed. I also understand Mr. Vignali deserves some respect. Hell, he's taken over the Capaldo and Malta families."

"The Capaldo girl hasn't married anyone yet," Lordi said. "And I have Mr. Vignali's word that he won't marry her."

Don Lordi's gaze jumped over to me.

"Isn't that right?"

I nodded. "It is. I've kept my word. I haven't married the girl, and I don't plan to. But that doesn't change the fact that her father's men are now under my command."

Or they would be soon. Commission members didn't need to know the transactional details.

Lordi shook his head. "No, that's not possible. Benedict Capaldo would never—"

"Benedict Capaldo is dead," I said.

Gasps filled the room. Of course, our audience assumed I'd killed Capaldo and taken his empire by force.

I jerked my arms free, held up a hand, and shook my head at the room.

"Benedetta and I signed the contract a few hours after he passed from his cancer. I control her interests until she marries with my approval and blessing. I just haven't had a chance to make an announcement. Benedetta's planning a service. You'll all be informed of the date and location."

Lordi's face turned red. He huffed out a breath.

"That doesn't change the reason why we're here today."

I gnashed my teeth.

I had to control my temper to get out alive.

Although if I failed to keep Val alive, I would come back and provoke them into killing me. Suicide by provocation.

"Then for Christ's sake," I said, "tell us why we're here. You might not have anything more important to do with your time, but the rest of us certainly do."

Fucker jabbed a finger into the air and shrieked.

"You broke the New York–Chicago treaty!"

A screaming match would be fruitless and time-consuming, so I remained as calm and collected as possible.

"I'm not a member of this council... sir. Neither my men nor the men who now report to me operate within its purview. I'm not required to abide by your treaty."

"Oh, but you are, son. Your family is a founding family, meaning you're bound by every law of this council in your grandfather's stead."

Lordi opened the leather portfolio in front of him and produced a scrolled document that looked smaller than but otherwise similar to the Declaration of Independence, complete with signatures at the bottom.

"Do you know what this document says, Mr. Vignali?"

"US declares independence from the British Empire?"

A few people chuckled, but Lordi's frigid, roaming gaze stopped them short.

"I've had enough of your smartass mouth, son. You will respect this council or suffer the consequences."

"I will respect this council when you respect my time, not to mention the valuable time of every other man in this room. Get to your point. And don't call me son again."

The moment the words barreled out of my mouth, I realized my mistake. I'd made a strategically stupid move, but my patience had diminished with every passing minute. I'd already wasted too much time. The longer I stood before this man, the longer Val remained in danger.

Lordi squinted. "You broke the treaty. The signatures shown here include that of your grandfather, and every signer's family is required to obey these rules."

"As long as the family remains under the council's influence," I added. "The influence ended in this case when you murdered my father and his heir. I was never in the line of succession. You destroyed what my family had. I've built a new empire."

He shook his stupid fucking head.

"A change in the order of succession doesn't excuse you from the influence. You're the living Vignali representative. You haven't taken your council seat as a member yet, but you're still expected to abide by our laws.

"And the fact that I haven't found it necessary to drag you

in here before now does not, under any circumstances, mean you won't be held responsible for your actions."

Interesting. Lordi said he'd never dragged me into this room before when he had. What game was he playing?

It didn't matter now. The clock was ticking, and I needed to leave. Every minute wasted in New York meant another one for my girl to suffer through more abuse.

"If you would like," Lordi continued, "we can argue this matter all night, but the end result will remain the same—"

"What's the fucking punishment?" I blurted.

He sank back into his chair as if disappointed.

"A pound of flesh. It's your first offense, so a finger will do."

A finger? Fuck it. I had nine more. Val had only one life.

Let them think they'd taken something from me. Lordi mistook sacrifice for weakness. He didn't understand the difference between a man who reacts and a man who plans.

"If it means I don't have to listen to you prattle on about the importance of tradition for six more fucking hours, then take the goddamn finger and let me leave."

The room erupted into murmurs.

What did they expect? I would never get on my knees before these men, the same men I would kill sooner or later. Nor would I ever promise to behave like a disobedient child.

The shock on Don Lordi's face as his mouth opened and closed several times made me believe he hadn't expected me to agree quite so readily.

Angelo Medico blinked like he couldn't believe it either.

"You'll willingly lose a finger here today in penance for breaking the New York–Chicago treaty?" Lordi asked. "Is that what you're telling me? You do realize that includes letting you bleed for thirty minutes before we cauterize the wound?"

"I'm aware," I lied.

I'd rather cauterize it myself while sitting in the back of my car on the way to the airport. And thirty minutes of bleeding was still faster than trying to argue my way out of his charges.

Lordi raised his bushy eyebrows.

"You'll get nothing for the pain, before or after. Only a shot of whiskey is permitted."

Shaking my head, I shrugged out of my jacket and removed the cuff link from my right shirtsleeve.

"Keep your damn whiskey, Lordi, and get on with it."

"Well, I guess if there are no objections from the council."

He gazed down along the table and around the room.

How very fucking diplomatic of him.

The other Commission members looked flabbergasted.

When I was young, my mother had taught me this trick. Whenever someone geared up for a fight, the easiest way to win would be for me to agree with them, she'd told me. They would never see it coming, and it would throw them off every time.

In this case, it meant I lost a finger.

Better a finger than my wife.

While keeping my eyes on Lordi, I rolled up my sleeve.

"Well, are we going to do this today or what?"

Some of the other men chuckled.

Lordi accepted a large hunting knife from one of his men.

"Fine. Let's get it done."

At first, I thought he planned to do it himself, but I should've known better. He handed the knife to an enforcer.

As the man came for me, another one grabbed my wrist.

I twisted my arm out of his grip and bared my teeth.

"Do not touch me."

The thug's face paled, and he stepped back. He'd intended to hold my hand down, but fuck that.

I stalked over to Lordi and smacked my right hand down flat on the table in front of him... If he was man enough to pass the sentence, he better have been man enough to carry it out.

"You really want to cut your right hand?" he asked.

"When I get my girl back, she'll want my left ring finger to be intact. Now man up and do it."

Lordi stared at me like I'd lost my mind. Maybe I had. I didn't know anymore. I just needed to get it over with.

Reluctantly, he took the knife from his man.

I folded my other fingers beneath my palm, so he would still only cut my ring finger if he missed.

He raised the knife. The glinting blade sliced down through the air and settled with a wet *thunk*. One blow wasn't enough.

I set my back teeth together, clenched my jaw, and held my tongue as I waited for the motherfucker to finish his hack job. Sweat rolled down the sides of my face. My heart ricocheted back and forth against my ribcage. The need to roar clawed at the inside of my throat, but I held it back.

Telling Lordi to do it had been a mistake. His brute could have done it in one clean shot, but it took this asshole three attempts with a dangerously sharp blade to lacerate the joint.

I'd expected him to take the whole finger, but he only took the tip. A joke lurked in there somewhere, but too many dark spots edged into my vision for me to find it.

Angelo stood and buttoned his jacket.

"Is there anything else you need to discuss before the rest of us leave and we let this man bleed in peace?"

"You're all dismissed but stay close. Enjoy some wine and whiskey on the house."

Lordi examined my severed digit as I took a seat and stuck my finger into an empty glass, so I didn't bleed all over myself.

With my left hand, I reached across my body for my phone and set a thirty-minute timer.

It hurt far more than I had imagined. I wanted to roar just to burn off the adrenaline and at least some of the pain, but I suffered in silence. I refused to show these assholes any weakness they might later use against me.

After ten minutes passed, the rest of the men had filed out, leaving only Lordi in the room with me. I'd hoped he would join the others in the restaurant and send one of his men back to cauterize the wound. Instead, he remained in his seat and poured us some whiskey.

He shoved a glass across the table at me.

"I know I've said this once before, but I truly might have underestimated you."

I ignored the whiskey and fought the urge to throw up.

"Seems to be a growing trend," I said. "It doesn't tend to end well for those people."

He nodded and sipped his liquor.

"So you now control your family's business as well as the Capaldo and Malta empires."

"So it would seem."

"You know this means I need you to take your seat on the council. Otherwise, you'll become a target, and the same goes for your son. I understand why you don't want to join us, but it's shortsighted. I believe the Commission can give you something you want even more than you want to kill me."

"What I want makes a very short list," I gritted out.

Fucker laughed.

I fixed him with a bored expression and focused on ignoring

the searing pain radiating from my finger while a cold sweat left my shirt clinging to my back.

"Aren't you even a little curious to know how I found out you broke the treaty?"

Actually, yes, but he chose that moment to bump the table with his knee. The edge of the table knocked my finger against the inside of the glass filling with my blood.

I could no longer guarantee my ability to respond without screaming, so I kept my jaw locked and my mouth shut. It worked out, since Lordi liked to hear himself talk.

"I got an interesting call this morning from Aris Moscatelli. He said you showed up uninvited at a ball to make an offer on his sister. Of course, it didn't take me long to get information and hear the rumors about her. I'm assuming the person she had a tryst with in the ladies' room was you."

I said nothing.

"It got me thinking. The treaty was a sign of weakness. New York saying they couldn't handle Chicago. Maybe it was true for the old guard, but I think it's time for Chicago to come back into the fold and get put beneath New York. I want to break the treaty, unravel it, and take over that second-rate city."

He canted his head to get a read on my expression.

"What do you think about that, Mr. Vignali?"

"I think you should have brought that to my goddamn attention before you took my finger."

"That was your own doing, Stefano, not mine. I had intended to let you make a case. I didn't think you'd let it go without a fight. Your argument was going to be the basis I used to dissolve the treaty, but you had to be difficult."

"What is it you're proposing?"

"I'm proposing you join the Commission immediately. I'll

have you sworn in right now. The rest of them are waiting in the restaurant. And then we start putting together a plan to invade Chicago, take out the heads of each family there, and restore the natural order."

"So you want a war?"

He tossed back another swallow of whiskey and shrugged.

"Not just any war. I want the bloodiest war this country has ever seen. I want to expand into Chicago, then north into Boston, and then all the way to California. There's no reason the rest of this country shouldn't be under New York control."

"Why do you need my help?"

"Aside from the fact you're now one of the most powerful men in the city, you, son, are the inciting incident for my war."

The more he called me son, the more I yearned to end him.

"This new age we find ourselves in is all about image. It's all about telling a story. If we just go attack Chicago, then we're the bad guys. Families start leaving the council. Maybe Atlantic City and Atlanta decide an attack on one of them is an attack on all of them. Suddenly, everyone's trying to restore balance."

"What the fuck does this have to do with me?" I snapped.

"You're going to be the story we tell. The young man thrust into power he wasn't ready for, but who regained his family's honor, then fell in love with a girl from a rival family. It's like the Capulets and the Montagues. You know, Shakespeare shit."

Right. Shakespeare shit.

The English Lit major in me huffed a frustrated sigh.

And the man just kept talking.

"Then Chicago is the bad guy because they're getting in the way of true love. And for those who aren't romantic, you have a claim to this woman. She's the mother of your child, and the

Moscatellis have not only stolen her from you, but they also made a deal with the Russians."

I hated to admit it, but his plan did make me look more like the hero rather than a villain if I went into Chicago, with all of New York behind me, and burned it to the ground to prevent my wife's tragic death.

However, it would also give Lordi a lot more power.

More than mine.

I never wanted to be part of the Commission. It had been my life's goal to tear it apart.

I'd already lost a finger for the woman I loved. Was I willing to lose my integrity too? Break the promises I'd made to my family? To my mother?

Yes, I decided immediately.

Yes, I fucking was.

TWENTY-THREE
VAL

Let the cold death come for me.
Warmth could never exist without him.

TWENTY-FOUR

STEFANO

In less than ten minutes, I'd gone from having to face the whole of Chicago alone—not just the Moscatelli family, but also all those who owed them fealty—to having an entire army at my back.

Promised by the one man I swore to kill.

Edgardo Lordi had offered me what I needed to get Val back home safely, and it would only cost me my soul.

I'd always believed Lucifer was a fat Italian who smelled like salami and horseradish. I'd also thought Satan's pride would cause him to hide his gluttony, but I got that part wrong.

Despite my lightheadedness, I needed to run through the options. I hadn't gotten as far as I had by making rash decisions.

If I said no to Lordi and went into Chicago on my own, I would have only a handful of men. I didn't have the time to organize some great assault. It would be just me and a handful of my men breaking into Moscatelli's home. In broad daylight while anyone could see us.

A mafia boss's estate never stood empty, and I had a feeling Moscatelli preferred to work out of his home.

Fogginess sent my thoughts in random directions as the room spun around me, making it hard to focus.

I shook my head, which only made it worse, and stared at the glass filling with my blood. My dripping finger showed no sign of slowing down.

Fuck, I should have eaten more than a sandwich.

What was I supposed to be thinking about?

Valerie. Valentina. Getting her back.

At night, with many more men, we would use the cover of darkness, and most of the Moscatelli soldiers would be sleeping, just a handful on duty. More men would make it easier to get in. Additional soldiers would overwhelm Moscatelli's men, and that meant I had a much greater chance of getting Val out alive.

Hell, I might even get her out without any more bruises or gunshot wounds.

My girl already had so many injuries, and if this fat fuck in front of me knew she and I had shared a moment of passion in the ladies' room, then so did her father.

Her twin worried me. He took pleasure in hurting her.

She would need the doctor when I got her home.

She needed to sleep somewhere safe to heal.

Her safety meant everything to me.

I refused to let Enzo down again, to walk into the house once more without his mother. I couldn't do that to him again. I wouldn't do it.

So, like a fucking fool, I asked the question of the hour.

"Where do I sign?"

Lordi gave me a shit-eating grin and slapped my shoulder.

"Good man. Let's get that finger cauterized, so we can get to dotting all the I's and crossing all the T's."

I nodded, my head pounding, my vision darkening at the

corners. I needed the wound cauterized immediately, then I needed water and food. Tony could get me both as soon as we got the fuck out of Lordi's place.

Don Lordi called two men into the back room.

One carried a metal plate with a long wooden handle, and the other held a blowtorch. It took a few seconds for them to heat the metal to a fiery red before they handed me a leather strap to bite down on.

It hadn't occurred to me until that moment that maybe the reason they waited thirty minutes was so the newly fingerless would pass out from blood loss.

A kindness disguised as a cruel punishment.

I had no time for that.

I waved away the strap. "I don't need it."

"Sir, I'm going to have to insist," one man said.

Goddamn it. I grabbed the handle from the other guy's gloved hand and pressed the metal plate to the end of my finger.

Fuuuuuuuuck.

My vision blacked out, but I forced myself to stay upright, to keep breathing. Sweat drenched my back and brow, but it didn't matter. I had to take the pain. Had to bear the nauseating sizzle of my skin and ignore the putrid smell of burning flesh that filled the room.

I held the steel plate to my finger for a few seconds before pulling it away and handing it back to the man who had heated it.

"Do you need something?" Lordi asked. "I'm sure one of the doctors here has morphine or something."

"Just water," I rasped, my mouth completely dry.

I drained the glass of cold water placed in front of me. My

vision slowly returned though with occasional white flashes. The wound burned and throbbed like a motherfucker.

"Another."

By the time I finished draining the second glass of water, my headache began to ease some, and I could think a little more clearly. The pain still muddled my thoughts, but I could piece together coherent enough sentences that no one would know.

As the other members returned to the room, they stared, watching my every move.

"Can we get this moving, please?" I asked.

"Sure. All you need to do is sign the papers."

Lordi strolled back to the leather folder with the treaty and came back with a small stack of documents.

"This is your contract with the Commission. This one makes you part of the council. This one details the laws, punishments, responsibilities, and the dues owed to the Commission."

"Dues?"

"Only upon your initiation. As you've pointed out, you rebuilt your family's business. It's not the same as it once was, so you'll have to pay the dues again."

"And what's that?" I asked, keeping my voice steady.

"A princess. We ask each family to give up a woman and to marry another councilman's woman. It honors the tradition of signing a business deal with a marriage contract. It's also a good way to blend the families and make sure each member of the council is invested in the other families.

"I guess you could say it makes us all one big happy family. Your grandfather received your grandmother as part of that deal and gave his first daughter in return."

What a disgusting and terrifying idea that I had no interest in thinking about, then or later.

"Are you saying you want the firstborn female in my line?"

"Usually, yes, but not in this case. No, I want Benedetta Capaldo. Since she is yours to give now."

"Excuse me?"

My head still swam, but I'd heard the sick fuck correctly.

"Does your wife know you have a thing for blondes?"

Lordi laughed. "Yes, as a matter of fact, she does. If I keep her in the latest Dior dresses, she pretends not to care. The girl won't be for me. But she comes with too much power for me to let her marry outside of the Commission. Marry her yourself if you want to, but if not, she's to marry another member."

"Are there any members who are currently unmarried?"

"One, but from what I understand, he's not quite ready, so it won't happen immediately. But understand me, son. I will be choosing Benedetta Capaldo's husband, not you."

Fuck my life.

This deal would cost more and more of my soul.

Not only was I betraying every promise I'd made to my mother before she killed herself and betraying myself by going against the goals that I'd had since she died, but now I was betraying Benedetta as well. She'd made me swear.

Of course, a handshake deal with her wasn't legally binding, but breaking our agreement still made me feel like an asshole.

I had to do it, had to hurt her—for my son and his mother.

Joining the Commission went against everything I was, and every cell in my body screamed for me to stop.

But signing on was the best way to get Val back. If I didn't get to her soon, the Russians would take her, and even if she survived, I would never see her again.

Enzo would never see her again.

My head pulsed with dizzying pain. I wondered if they'd

drugged the water. My three-quarters of a finger sent throbbing waves of agony up my arm, all the way to my shoulder.

I needed more time to make the right decision.

Time was the only thing I didn't have.

The longer I waited, the less likely I would get my girl back.

She deserved to be resting in our home, with our son, in our bed, tucked away safely every fucking goddamn night.

Could I do this—join the Commission to get her back?

Betraying my long-dead family undermined who I was. Even going against my word to a worthy woman made me sick.

Benedetta had shown more grace than any woman I knew, stepping away from our marriage to keep my son safe, knowing it would destroy her reputation.

She'd stood her ground when I threatened her, then offered to help. She came to me like a man with a business proposal. She showed intelligence and kindness, and I trusted her.

I didn't want to be with her, but Benedetta had earned my respect. No small feat for anyone.

She'd given me a chance with Valentina, and all she wanted in return was a chance at her own happiness.

Not control of her father's men or even a seat at the table.

Happiness.

Was I really going to be the selfish asshole who took it away from her for the sake of my own gain? What kind of man did that make me? And what did it say about my word as a Vignali?

I squeezed my eyes shut for a split second.

Yeah, it made me the kind of man who loved his family. It said I was a man with priorities that outweighed business deals, that my wife and my son trumped everything.

Of course, giving Benedetta to the Commission would make me the villain in her story, and she would hate me for it.

Still, as smart as she was, she had to know that coming to me as she had was a gamble, that making a deal with the devil could always turn into a losing bet.

I grabbed the pen from Lordi and fumbled it before realizing I needed to use my left hand to sign on the dotted line.

Three times I scribbled something that came close enough to my usual signature. Then I shoved the shit back at Lordi.

The weight on my shoulders instantly grew heavier.

I would pay the price for this for the rest of my life.

Angelo Medico came forward, as did two others from the council. The men joined Edgardo Lordi in signing as witnesses.

The four horsemen of my personal apocalypse.

It was done.

I had sold my soul to get my girl back.

Imagining her soft lips as she smiled up at me, the smell of her perfume, my hands on her pretty ass as I plunged my cock deep inside her... all of it... all of her...

Yes, she was infinitely more valuable than my soul.

Anxious to get rolling, I made eye contact with Lordi.

"When do we take Chicago?"

TWENTY-FIVE
STEFANO

Edgardo Lordi patted my shoulder, not coincidentally bumping my right hand as he reached down to pick up the signed documents and tuck them into his leather portfolio.

Pain shot all the way up to my neck.

"We'll start making plans to invade Chicago right away," he said. "It'll take a few weeks to get everything in order."

My heart raced, panic growing until it overtook the pain.

"What? I can't wait that long."

"Well, son, it takes time to strategize and set up a good plan. Rome wasn't built in a day. I'm sure you understand, after all the scheming you've done over the years to build your impressive and might I add now more secure empire."

"Your timeline doesn't work. Valentina will be in Moscow by then—or dead."

"If that's the case, your heroic tale becomes a tragedy, and the effect will be even stronger. Of course, if you can't wait, you can go in on your own. You won't have the Commission behind you if you fail, and Chicago will have the right to kill you. If you succeed, well, that's another story entirely, isn't it?"

This motherfucker.

Suddenly, even through the haze of pain and panic, his plan became crystal clear. Lordi never intended to send men to Chicago. Oh, he wanted Chicago, but he wasn't man enough to take it himself. He wanted me to run a little errand first, to see how well I fared before making a move.

If my mission failed, he would have plausible deniability. More than that, by giving him my finger, I'd made it easy for him to claim he hadn't sanctioned my barbaric act while pointing out he'd punished me for going in the first time.

Then, as a member of the Commission, all my business interests, my assets, my allegiances, everything I had, became property of the Commission, including Benedetta and the empire that came with her.

There wouldn't be a damn thing anyone could do to save my legacy and my son's inheritance.

Ah, but if I succeeded, the son of a bitch would probably march right into Chicago the next day.

Every scenario provided Edgardo Lordi with a win. The whole scheme would cost him nothing. Depending on the choice I made and how well it went, it could cost me everything.

He grinned. "Let me know what you decide to do."

"You know what I'll do," I growled.

He nodded, taking his shit-eating grin with him into the restaurant, and the remaining council members filed out of the room behind him. All but one.

Angelo Medico stared at me.

I needed to leave, but I didn't know if I could walk without stumbling. This guy needed to get out, so I could give it a shot.

"Something on your mind, Medico?"

Instead of heading for the fucking door, he took a seat.

"What are you going to do?"

"What's it to you?" I asked.

"It's nothing, really. None of it affects me personally. Not yet anyway."

"Not yet?"

Angelo leaned back in his chair and crossed his arms. His youthful, curious expression indicated he might be deciding whether he should trust me.

He shouldn't.

If I could get the fuck out the door without falling on my face, I would walk away from this guy. But I needed a few minutes for the come down from the adrenaline and for the pain to ease enough for me to function.

"How much do you know about my father?" he asked.

"Not much."

He nodded, looking around the room as if to make sure no one was lurking in the shadowed corners to listen in.

"You know this room is bugged," I said.

He waved that fact away.

"When are you going to Chicago?"

"First thing tomorrow morning," I said.

"Flying commercial?"

"Might have to if my second can't get a charter large enough for my men on such short notice."

I'd never bothered with my own since I rarely left the city.

"Use my plane. Nothing special, but it'll fit ten men. It's housed at a private airstrip about forty-five minutes outside of the city. I can arrange a flight in minutes. Just need to know what time you want to take off."

I studied him. "What do you want from me?"

"What do you mean?"

"I mean, what the fuck do you want from me? Nothing comes without a price. So what's yours?"

Angelo shrugged. "How about dinner."

I couldn't have heard that right.

"Excuse me?"

"Yeah, when you get back, invite me to dinner at your home, so we can talk business privately."

"Why my home?"

"Because, like you said, the walls in these restaurants have ears. And right now I'm unsure about who I can trust even in my own home. Give me one hour of your time, that's all I ask. We discuss a little business, and if we come to a mutually beneficial arrangement, great. If not, we part as friends."

"So you're saying you'll lend me your plane just for sitting through your timeshare pitch?"

Angelo laughed. "That about sums it up."

He pulled out his phone and held his QR code against my screen, putting his contact information into my phone.

"Text me with the time you'd like the pilot to be ready for takeoff, and I'll set it up. Hell, I'll even throw in some SUVs at the airstrip in Chicago."

"Fuck that. It's not safe to use rented vehicles in a city where you're not permitted to visit," I said.

"I use a private security service," he said, implying it might be the simplest thing in the world to do.

Maybe so, but I didn't trust him.

Still, I needed to get to Val before it was too late, and he only wanted a brief sit down at my home in return. If he pulled anything at that time, I would just kill him.

I checked the time. Already 7:30 p.m.

"It takes forty-five minutes to get to the airstrip?"

Angelo nodded.

"Have the plane ready for me by 9:00 p.m."

I got on my feet for the first time since Lordi's hack job.

Light-headed, a bit unsteady, but the haze cleared quickly.

I extended my left hand and grasped Angelo's for a firm shake, shoved my arms into my jacket sleeves, and walked into the restaurant like nothing had ever happened.

Tony sat in a red faux-leather booth with an untouched glass of wine in front of him. When he saw me, his face twisted, and he jumped up from the bench seat.

His expression went from concerned to murderous in less than ten seconds.

I must have looked as bad as my fucking hand felt.

"What the fuck happened in there, Stef?"

I walked past him. "Not here, Tony. In the car."

We made a quick stop to get our weapons before exiting through the side door. Tony started the Maybach's engine while staring at me in the rearview mirror.

"You gonna tell me what happened? Because I gotta say, boss, my trigger finger's very fucking itchy right now."

I leaned back against the cool leather seat, realizing my jacket had soaked through with sweat.

"We're officially part of the Commission."

He turned and stared in horror at my butchered hand.

"Since when is a finger the price of admission?"

"Asshole could only handle the tip," I said.

We grinned at each other like childish idiots.

"As much practice as that fat fuck's had, you'd think he could take more than that."

I nodded. "Food and water, Tony... find me a burger. Do you know where the Jamaica Bay airfield is located?"

He accelerated and peeled away from the curb.

"Yeah, Brooklyn, just off the lower belt."

"That's where we're headed. Call and get eight of our best men to meet us there, fully armed, with as much tactical gear as they can carry. A weapon for me as well."

"We're flying into Chicago tonight?"

"Not we, Tony. I'm taking the men with me, and I need you to stay behind in New York."

"What? Boss, I should be with you."

Of course I knew Tony would be unhappy about staying behind. But I needed him to protect the estate in case Lordi thought about doing something stupid while I was gone.

Not only that, but if something happened to me, I couldn't trust anyone else with my son. I didn't want the Commission raising my boy.

"You're my second-in-command. I need you here to protect my interests while I'm gone."

"But boss—"

"That's an order, Tony. I need you to take care of Enzo. You're the only person I can trust with my son."

His jaw flexed as he bit back his urge to argue with me.

"I don't like it, not covering your back, goddamn it, but yes, I got it. I know how much you love the boy."

Christ, it had become so obvious.

I swallowed back a swell of emotion.

"I need you to work on something else while I'm gone."

"Whatever you need," Tony said, his eyes on the street.

"Dig up everything on Angelo Medico. When I get back, he and I will have a sit-down at the house. I want to know who I'm bringing into my home."

"What do you want to know?"

"Absolutely everything. Look into his father as well. I don't know if Victor retired or if he's dead. Maybe the kid killed him. Talk to the maids and anyone Angelo fucks."

"Got it. Consider it done."

No sooner had the words had come out of his mouth, he crossed the Brooklyn Bridge. Heading south, he made his way around Prospect Park, hit the first burger joint in our path, then continued south to the airfield.

I needed the red meat, and the carbs and fat from the fries would help keep me stable, so I scarfed down my food while Tony made calls to round up the men.

It would be a long fucking night.

Finally, we pulled onto the small airstrip, where the plane already waited, and Tony checked his watch for the time.

"The men will be here in less than twenty," Tony said.

We got out to stretch our legs and fill our lungs with the brisk evening air while waiting for the men to pull up beside us.

Eight men climbed out of two SUVs.

And one boy.

I pinched the bridge of my nose.

"What the fuck is my child doing here?"

"He wouldn't let us leave without him, sir," Bruce said.

"He's nine years old," I shouted.

Yes, I knew exactly what he'd put them through, and why they gave in. Been there. Done that.

Enzo marched in my direction, the cold breeze lifting his curls, making them appear like a halo.

"You're taking me."

"No, I'm not," I gritted out. "Get in the car with Tony. He's staying with you."

The kid stomped his fucking foot.

"I'm going to get my mama."

Even for my son, my patience had dried up, much like the blood on my hand.

"No, you're not, and I will not stand here and argue with you about it. Get your ass in the car."

Enzo folded his arms over his chest and stared me down like a little man ready for a fight.

Perhaps a more experienced father would have handled his outburst with more restraint and grace. And perhaps even I might have dealt with it differently had I not already gone through so much.

I picked up my son, threw him over my shoulder, trapping his legs against my chest, then I tossed him onto the back seat of my car, engaged the child locks, and slammed the door before he could get out again.

Enzo screamed at me and pounded on the windows.

Turning away from the betrayal on his face, I ignored him. He could hate me all he wanted if it kept him alive.

I walked past the men to one of the SUVs and began arming myself for war. I'd already had a Glock on me as well as a few knives, so I grabbed a semi-automatic rifle, night-vision scopes, and a bulletproof vest to wear under my jacket.

"When do we head out?" Bruce asked.

"Now." Then louder, so everyone could hear me, I said, "I want to warn you all right now. This is going to be the first of what's probably going to become several bloody battles. This mission is simple. We get into Chicago undetected, invade the Moscatelli mansion, and we get my wife back.

"I don't give a fuck how many people we have to kill. I don't care if we must kill cops or innocent bystanders. We'll do what's necessary to get Valentina on this plane, in one piece, and in less than an hour. Do I make myself clear?"

"Yes, boss," the men responded.

"After this, we'll have a war to face. Edgardo Lordi is playing a game using us as pawn pieces. I don't appreciate being manipulated or maimed. We don't let that shit stand."

I held up my hand so the men could see my finger.

Christ, I still hadn't bothered to treat or wrap it. I made a mental note to take care of that while on the plane.

"Are we going against the Commission?" someone asked.

"We're part of the Commission for now, but I intend to disassemble it from the inside out. Any objections?"

Silence.

"Good. Let's get our asses on the plane, avenge the brothers they took from us, and retrieve our queen."

The men lifted their guns in a triumphant yell, then headed for the waiting plane.

I stayed behind and had Tony put down Enzo's window enough that he could see my eyes and hear me.

The boy glared at me as he swiped at the tears on his face.

"You can't make me stay here. I'm not a child."

"Yes, you are a child, Enzo, mine, and I can. That should be enough, but I'm going to go against my better judgment and treat you like a man right now."

I ducked down to his eye level.

"Think you can handle it?" I added.

Enzo nodded and sat back, listening.

"You're not going with me on this mission, not because you're too young, or it's too dangerous, though you are too young, and it is far too dangerous. You're not trained yet, son.

You don't have the skills that would make you an asset on this kind of mission, not yet.

"Untrained men are a liability. It could make the mission go sideways. People, including your mother, could get hurt."

He blinked at me, his lower lip trembling.

"So when I have the right skills, will you let me come with you on missions?"

"No," I said honestly. "You're my heir. Which means you and I can't risk our lives at the same time. You're all that's left of this family, Enzo. You're my son. You're a Vignali.

"So if I die tonight, I need you to take control of everything. Tony will teach you. He'll show you how to grow into the shoes you were born to wear. Do you understand me?"

"She's my mama," he insisted. "I should go with you."

"I need you here in case I don't come home. If I don't come back, you're to reach out to your uncle, Marco Moscatelli. If Marco is dead, then Santo. Never Aris." I flicked my gaze to Tony in the front seat, who also had his window open to listen. "Understand?"

They both nodded.

"Which one is Marco, and which one is Santo?" Enzo asked.

"Marco is the oldest. Santo is the one covered in tattoos."

He'd seen them when they invaded our home and took his mother. He probably remembered all too well.

"Aris is the one that took her?" he asked.

"That's correct. Her twin. He's a very bad man, Enzo."

"So if you don't come back, I contact Marco... but why?"

"Because he'll know where to find your mother, and you'll use his help to get her back. If I fail, I need you here for her sake, to try again. Okay?"

Enzo's brows furrowed as he considered my offer, and I imagined I often wore the same expression.

After several seconds, he nodded.

Thank Christ. Telling him this was the only thing I could think of that might keep him from trying to sneak aboard the fucking plane.

My son was brilliant, bold, and a stubborn pain in the ass, just like his beautiful mother.

He slid his fingers out and wiggled them at me.

"Just bring her back, okay?"

I took his fingers and gently squeezed, a knot of emotion tying up my throat.

"I'll do everything I can to bring her back," I promised—one I would kill to keep.

"Can you do me one more favor, Mr. Vignali?" he asked.

"What's that?"

"Kill Aris."

I smiled. "Consider it done. I need a favor in return, son."

"Okay," he whispered.

"I don't want to hear you call me Mr. Vignali again. I'm your father. Think about what you want to call me... dad or papà or whatever you like. When your mother and I get home, you can tell us what you've decided."

I didn't wait for my son to agree.

He knew I meant it.

My son understood when an option wasn't given.

And he was slowly learning to accept my commands.

I stepped back and tapped on the top of the car twice to let Tony know he should drive away.

Then, as I settled in on a plush leather seat, and the flight attendant closed the plane's main door, my phone pinged with a text message.

MARCO

Russians are taking ownership of her in the morning

I put the phone back in my pocket and prepared for takeoff. Fuck if they were.

TWENTY-SIX

VAL

Saul Moscatelli barged into my bedroom without as much as a single knock on the door in warning.

"Good news, little princess."

I'd spent the last two hours under scalding water trying to wash away not only the Russian's sickening touch, but also to erase the image of Saul examining my naked body as he put a price on it. My skin was pink and raw from all the scrubbing, but on the inside, their filth remained.

I pulled my robe tighter and hugged my abdomen.

"What news is that?"

"The Russians made their offer, and they're coming for you first thing in the morning. You'll be heading right to Moscow."

God, his expression showed such enthusiasm, like it actually was good news, and he'd struck the deal of the century.

Pain slashed through my chest. I swallowed a thick lump of emotion and bid the tears not to fall as the old fucking monster paced the room and mumbled to himself.

"Of course, I'm not getting as much as I should. The pakhan's second son refused you. Something about his

Russian wife providing worthy sons in due time, so he'll use you as a reward for his men. And you'd better last the year, so I get more out of the time and money I've spent raising you."

I wanted to roll my eyes, but I knew better. It would result in me on the floor again. But the obnoxious idea that he'd spent any time raising me made it difficult to hold back.

My nonna and older brother raised me.

The only reason Saul even allowed me to attend school was because Marco convinced Saul that education made for better wives.

Continuing his self-directed conversation, Saul wandered out. No doubt to celebrate with the expensive bourbon on his desk while deciding how to spend his new windfall.

I sat on the bed and took in a long, deep breath.

This was it. Fate had caught up to me.

I had always believed in fate.

Once upon a time, I believed fate brought Stefano to me, because he needed a mafia princess, and I needed a strong man who wouldn't beat me.

But I'd been wrong.

My fate had always been to serve a monster.

As I thought about it, I realized my once upon a time theory hadn't really been too far off the mark. Stefano could technically be considered a monster just as well.

But fuck fate. I couldn't control what she had in store—only my reaction to whatever situation enslaved me.

With my legs tucked under me, I stared outside at what used to be a fabulous view of the Chicago skyline. A brick wall now blocked much of it. It was such a shame.

The view didn't matter anyway.

Coming up with something to help me survive, maybe even to help me see my son again someday, that mattered.

The way I saw it, I had three options: run and risk being caught and killed for it, fight and risk being killed for it, or lie down and accept my fate.

If fate meant for me to die, though, and I chose to accept her option, I would definitely find a better way to go.

I would take away their satisfaction.

I closed my eyes to think through the different scenarios and outcomes to make sure I took the path with the best advantage for my son and the least amount of impact on him.

If I ran away again, my chances of making it out of the city were slim to none. But for argument's sake, if I did get out of Chicago, where the hell would I go?

I had no money, no clothes, not even a pair of shoes.

Maybe sneaking downstairs into Aris's room—to steal his shoes and a coat, as terrifying as that would be—might work.

For money, I could steal Marco's cash and credit cards.

The idea of stealing from him didn't sit well in my stomach. I would leave an apology note asking him to contact Stefano for reimbursement. Stefano had confiscated all my money anyway.

Then just maybe I would find myself in the wind, but still with no idea where to go or for how long.

Saul and my brothers would look for me. Worse, they might encourage the Russians to hunt me as well.

One thing I knew for sure? Aris would go after Enzo.

Stefano would do everything in his power to protect our son, but I worried Aris had more pull than anyone realized.

He could have developed skills and contacts no one knew about. Sadistic assholes could learn new tricks like anyone else.

Aris was dangerous. He held grudges.

Stefano would remain vigilant, now that he understood my family, but our son would always need to look over his shoulder.

I had limitations on how I could protect Enzo myself. Coming home with Saul, step one. Preventing Aris from going back for my son, undefined step fucking two.

Damn it, I needed to think. Step two.

Assuming I did get away, taking Enzo on the run might not work like I once thought. First, Stefano would never allow it. I would have bet anything his estate was now like a military base.

Stefano might have even transferred Enzo to a safe house.

He definitely had one.

Besides, I had no resources or contacts, no more fake IDs, or birth certificates. Stefano had confiscated those too.

Most importantly, what would happen to Enzo if the Russians or the Moscatellis found us?

No, running away couldn't be an option any longer. I would be a fucking fool to think so at this point, so I crossed it off my mental list.

The best thing to do was often also the hardest.

Making the full circle...

Accepting my fate.

It gave Enzo and Stefano the best chance.

I'd grown so accustomed to my independence, to freedom. Living my life while relying on myself, my wits, and my decisions to fill mine and my son's needs. Freedom meant knowing our future rested in my hands.

Managing Con Amore had taught me a great deal about self-reliance as an autonomous woman, one who made her own life choices. How did I let go of that?

Going with the Russians, I couldn't be a woman with a voice that others would hear. Just a possession meant for use and abuse. No choices left about who I wanted to be with or even what I wanted to do on a day-to-day basis.

The cold, hard truth came down to one thing. A different man would own me each day for the rest of my life, my body his personal reward for good behavior.

Saul had mumbled that they might put me up in a nice penthouse in Moscow or St. Petersburg. Maybe it would be warm, and maybe I would have food, but it would still be a gilded cage at best.

Just because a prison had a beautiful view of an onion-domed church that looked like it belonged in a stupid snow globe didn't change the fact that it was still a prison.

No more than it changed the fact that they meant for me to be their sex slave, a pretty doll who screamed when abused.

Thinking about my future in Russia made my spine vibrate with bone-deep shivers and it hollowed out my heart.

The Russian had told Saul his payment would come in two installments. Half upon delivery, then the rest in a year, but only if I lived that long.

How fucking stupid was Saul anyway?

They didn't intend to make the second payment. They intended to kill me before the year ended.

All the men involved in my transaction believed they'd won. They assumed I had no cards left to play.

They were wrong.

I'd made my decision. I planned to die on my terms. To die for my son. Die because I couldn't bear to be with any man other than my one true love, Stefano.

And I would take Aris's evil ass with me.

I choose to fight, motherfuckers.

To avoid going with the Russians, I would have to kill every man in the house. My entire family. They outnumbered me. If I dared to take them on, I would die. Fact.

Taking out Aris first was my only strategic move.

Seemed fair considering the twin thing. We came into the world together, him three minutes before me, so according to my logic, we should go out the same way. Him about three minutes before they took me out.

This was the one part of my plan that gave me any peace.

Taking Aris's life to save my son's seemed like the best way to make my final exit.

I glanced at the little antique clock on my dresser.

10:10 p.m. I needed to wait a while.

Midnight was the easiest time to get around the house.

Not only did Saul sleep before that, but also the guards changed shifts at midnight. The men would be inside the cabin in the back, swapping out weapons and reassigning duties.

I never understood why Saul gambled with his life by separating his men from the main house, but it had always been that way, and I appreciated it now more than ever.

Oh, wait—arrogance. That was why he did it.

While waiting for the clock in the hallway to strike twelve, I ran through the plan in my head on repeat, hoping something better occurred to me, cursing at the fucking clock, cursing at Stefano, Saul, even myself.

When I was a child waiting for midnight to sneak down to the kitchen, I always doubted myself, and often, I ended up going back to bed on an empty stomach.

Saul had dictated calorie restrictions for my mother and me.

On the rare occasion when I found the courage to make the trek, anxiety had nearly suffocated me before I made it back.

This time, though, complete resolve expanded inside my

lungs and gave me the breath I needed. My nerves didn't buzz, and my stomach didn't cramp from the fear.

True resolve made people dangerous—especially women. It scared men, as it should have. Oppressors should have always feared the strength of the oppressed when they had nothing more to lose.

Ten minutes before the hour.

I wished I could do something more. I couldn't contact my son or Stefano. I couldn't leave them a note. They'd never see it.

I could pray for them.

Sinking to the floor on my knees, I closed my eyes, and begged the spirits of my grandmothers to watch over my son. To keep him safe the way they once kept me safe.

I prayed to the Virgin Mother, asking her to make Enzo strong, to make sure his father gave him the tools he needed to face whatever life threw at him.

And I asked her to forgive Stefano for his sins.

Stefano had racked up quite a list for sure, and he was too proud to go to confession.

His pride only added to the list.

So I confessed on his behalf and asked the Virgin Mother to be patient with him. He never had a chance at a normal life, because his family took it from him, and he should not suffer for surviving the sins of his father.

I begged her to guide him, to show him how to be the good father Enzo needed.

"Amen," I whispered.

In answer, the grandfather clock struck midnight.

I crossed myself and rose from my knees, ready to take my fate into my own hands.

I hadn't bothered to pray for myself.

TWENTY-SEVEN
VAL

The moment my tiptoes touched the wood beyond my bedroom door, I felt like a starving sixteen-year-old girl again, risking punishment for some bread and a slice of cheese.

Same as during my childhood, I counted all my steps. Four steps from my room to the next door. Twelve more steps to the back staircase.

I didn't dare peek at any of the doors as I passed by them, some silly superstition about looking at them would make them open, and then someone would catch me.

With my heart pounding into my throat, I made my way down the stairs. Through muscle memory, I knew which of the wooden steps creaked and which didn't. I balanced on one foot as I skipped the next step and aimed for the one beyond it.

On the sixth step, I glanced up at Saul's room. No light shone from beneath his closed door.

More steps. I leaned over the circular banister and looked up again. The light from Aris's room sliced under his closed door. He could be awake just as long as he didn't come out and catch me.

I continued my slow creeping down the stairs, clutching the railing like a lifeline, listening for anyone to come around the corner at any moment.

Last stair tread—then fifteen steps to the kitchen.

After tiptoeing in, I pressed myself against the wall, ducking under the windows in case one of the guards happened to look toward the house. I couldn't risk having them come in to investigate any strange moving shadows.

Though if they did and they caught me, what would I say?

I promise I wasn't going to run away. I was just planning to murder my twin and commit suicide by shooting at you.

Somehow, I didn't think that would go over well.

Four steps to the storage closet. I opened the door and sidled in, leaving the door cracked for the moonlight and streetlights filtering through the windows to come in. A bulb hung from the ceiling, but I didn't dare risk it.

Apparently not everything had stayed the same. Someone had replaced the wood shelves with glass cabinets, secured with, of all the dumbest things, a padlock.

What the fuck was the point of having a cabinet full of guns when it took too long to get one out?

Ammo, however, laid outside of the locked cabinets, but what good were bullets when you didn't have a gun? Throwing them really wouldn't have the same impact.

My plan went to shit over something I couldn't have known.

I shut my eyes for a second to focus. I needed another plan with the same results—Aris dead by my hand, and my quick death from their retaliation. If Saul wanted to ship my corpse to the Russians, that was between him, the Russians, and God.

I nodded. I could still do it. Just had to improvise.

But I didn't know where in the house to find another gun.

Rummaging through random drawers and cabinets in any of the rooms seemed like a bad idea.

Maybe if I went back upstairs to Marco's room. I couldn't remember if his light had been on. I doubted he was asleep, though. Marco had always been more of a night owl.

I might find a gun in his room, but also get caught. If he caught me, then what? Explain my suicide mission and hope he felt bad enough to help me out?

Marco and Aris had no love lost between them, but it didn't mean Marco would help me kill our brother. He wouldn't like the message it sent to the other families.

I wouldn't even consider involving Santo. He might have been a grown man covered in ink and scars, but in my head, he was still that sweet boy from my childhood.

No, I had to do this on my own.

There had to be something else I could use as a weapon.

I retraced my steps to the kitchen. Kitchens had knives. Aris's death wouldn't be as clean—or from a distance. I would have to get up close and personal.

Shooting a person was one thing. You only had to pull a trigger, not much more difficult than pressing a button. But stabbing offered no separation between you and your victim.

Aris also had a better chance of living with a stab wound than one made by gunshot. Unless I slit his throat.

I would have to find the strength to creep into his room, pray I didn't wake him, and slice through his neck.

Mother of Christ. I gripped my abdomen.

So fucking nauseating.

For my son's safety, for Enzo, I would do it, though.

Deep satisfaction warmed my blood—Aris would know

who killed him. But if I shot him in the head, he probably wouldn't see it coming.

This way, with a knife, he would know the little girl he'd abused, the woman he tortured, won in the end. And I would even get to see the light fade from his evil eyes as his soul drifted down to hell.

Bile burned my throat. I covered my mouth.

Could I really do it?

For Enzo, yes, you can. You will.

I tiptoed back into the kitchen.

Nonna had kept her knife block on the counter, the one her mother passed down to her, brought here from the old country. About every six months, she'd sent them out to get sharpened, and she always honed the blades whenever she used them.

She had yelled at me once for touching them when I was young, then Aris chased me with one when we were a little older. I still had the faint white line over my collar bone from where he'd cut me before Marco found us and saved me.

I didn't see the wood block on any of the countertops.

Saul wasn't sentimental like his mother had been. He must have gotten rid of Nonna's beautiful knives.

As quietly as possible, I slid open all the kitchen drawers, looking for an impromptu weapon that might work just as well.

I found newer knives in the fourth drawer. A cheap set of dull blades replacing the beautiful steel and olive wood handles with perfect balance that my family had passed from generation to generation.

Saul's housemaid or whoever hadn't even bothered with the different types needed for different tasks. They just bought a bunch of generic chef's knives. I couldn't chop up a salad with the fuckers, let alone slit a man's throat.

I considered looking for something else and lost myself in thought while sorting through the options.

Male voices snapped my mind back to attention.

Aris, laughing.

I would know that psychotic laughter anywhere.

Glancing outside, I saw him cross the lawn, coming from the security cabin, and head toward the house. He couldn't just use the door into the four seasons room like everyone else, oh hell no, the asshole had to use the back fucking door into the kitchen.

My pulse thrummed inside my ears.

With a knife in my hand, I scurried to hide, diving at the table and under the tablecloth right as the door flew open.

"Nah, we're shipping the dirty cunt out tomorrow, and Marco is all pissed," Aris said. "He thinks it's bad business."

A deeper voice responded.

"I thought the Russians were paying good money?"

"Yeah, but the New Yorker offered more. A shit load more actually and better terms."

"New York? At least he's Italian then," the other guy said.

Someone opened and shut the refrigerator door. Bottles clinked together, followed by the hiss of caps being removed.

"Sadly, dude, being Italian doesn't mean he's not a little bitch. Sometimes even the best stock goes weak."

I rolled my eyes at how easily my twin parroted one of Saul's bullshit phrases.

"I thought she was with Stefano Vignali?" the guy asked.

"What the fuck you know about him?"

"Whoa... some but not a lot. He wasn't supposed to be his family's heir, but his dad and older brother were murdered at the same time. I guess the Commission let him live because no one thought he could become any kind of threat."

Aris cackled. "See? Weak stock."

"Nah, man, listen. He rebuilt that empire, and from what I've heard, it's a lot stronger now. He deals in influence, and if the rumors are true, incredible counterfeit money."

"Just how 'incredible' is it?" Aris demanded.

"Rumors say he has printing plates so good that not even the Feds can tell his shit from the real stuff. But that's not even the impressive part."

"Then what is? His shitty taste in women?"

Clearly amusing himself, my twin chuckled.

"Nah, come on. Another family tried to intimidate him and move on his territory. Guess what? They had apartment buildings with massive weed farms in the basements."

Aris scoffed. "He burned them down? So what."

"He didn't burn down anything. He strong-armed some politician into pushing shit forward to get weed legalized in New York. He took their fucking revenue away."

The guy seemed impressed.

I might have been impressed myself, just a little.

"How did they retaliate against him?" Aris asked.

"A bloody battle in broad daylight at an old warehouse. If what I heard is really fucking true, as soon as the rival leader was dead, Vignali halted the shooting and absorbed the man's assets into his own."

"Again, so the fuck what? So he owns useless weed farms."

"Dude, he's the biggest supplier to the legal dispensaries."

"How the hell do you even know this?" my twin bit out.

"I got a cousin who works for the Maltas. He helped vet Vignali when Capaldo wanted to marry his daughter to him."

"Well, don't believe everything you hear, you dumb fuck. Vignali's nothing but a simp bitch, chasing after a whore. He's even raising her son like his own."

Heat bubbled up in my chest, and I tightened my grip on the fake wood knife handle. I wanted to rush out, release a battle cry while jamming the blade into his neck, then pull it out, so no one could save him after they killed me.

"A very small part of me actually feels bad for the asshole," Aris said. "But when I sneak back to New York and gut that fucking brat of hers, dude will be back on track."

Panic clamped down on my heart. Tears spilled down my cheeks. I smashed my hand over my mouth to keep from screaming or vomiting or both.

"Why kill the kid?" the guy asked.

I noted how his voice was moving farther away.

They must have been heading to one of the living rooms. I just needed to stay quiet for a few more minutes.

"Because I can," Aris said, "and my father won't stop me."

I got out of my hiding place without them seeing me, but no way could I get upstairs without crossing in front of them. So I searched again for a better weapon.

Something much sharper that could do enough damage to kill without much force.

I fished through the drawer and swapped my knife for one with a sharper point, though it also had a dull blade. No slicing then. I would have to use the pointy end to stab him.

If he were asleep, I could jab upward between his ribs and into his heart. Oh, but Aris didn't have a heart, or at least not one large enough for me to reach with this blade.

"The fuck you think you're doing, bitch?" Aris growled.

I startled, almost jumping out of my skin.

Oh god, no, I must've made noise while rummaging, or he came in for another beer. Either way, I didn't hear him come in.

As I whirled around to face him, I hid the knife behind my back, wedging it between my robe and my nightgown. At least I didn't have to worry about the dull blade cutting the fabric.

I wouldn't win a knife fight with him. Even if I could beat him, he had a gun tucked into his pants.

My heart slammed against my bones as if breaking out.

"I'm hungry," I said. "And I wanted one last decent meal before I'm forced to live on borscht and fish eggs."

Aris took a menacing step closer, his cold eyes warning me.

"Has anyone ever told you what a terrible liar you are?"

I backed away from his advance.

"I'm not lying, Aris. I don't like Russian food."

It felt like we were twelve again, and he was coming to take out his anger on smaller, weaker me.

"No one gives a fuck what you like. You were safe in your room, you stupid cunt. Marco saw to that earlier. You shouldn't have come down here."

I tried to reason with him, not sure why. It had never worked before. What alternative was there?

"Fine. Then I'll just go back upstairs like Marco said."

He took more steps forward.

"Too late for that, sister."

I kept my body facing him, the knife beneath my robe, behind my back. My muscles twitched to draw the knife on him, but I would fail to protect myself. He would see it coming. I clenched my fingers even tighter.

"You can't touch me," I said. "I belong to the Russians now. They don't want any more bruises on me."

"The Russians bought you as a whore, and we all know

whores come in 'as is' condition." He shrugged. "I don't think they'll notice as long as you're still breathing."

He pounced on me then, grabbed me by the throat, and threw me to the floor. I landed on my back. Pain shot along my spine, and the wind burst from my lungs as he laughed.

Thank God I landed on the flat side of the knife's blade.

So close to him now, with him standing directly above me, I noticed the bit of white powder under his nose, and how his pupils eclipsed his light blue irises.

Aris couldn't control his temper while sober. There would be no stopping him while he was high.

I had to outlast him, bide my time, take the beating. Then, when he passed out, I could strike. Anything else, and he would kill me and go after Enzo.

He sneered while putting his foot on my neck.

"This is where you belong. Under my boot."

I said nothing. Didn't move. I only waited for the rest of his abuse and for him to then fall asleep afterward.

"Say something, cunt."

Spittle flew from his mouth.

"That's what I thought, you pathetic whore."

Loud, hollow booms went off outside the window.

Aris jerked his head in that direction.

Gunshots.

I thought for a second he might leave me and go.

He didn't. He took his foot off my neck, backed up, and swung his leg, kicking me over and over and over.

I choked and cried out and begged him to stop.

He drew his gun and pointed it at my face.

"What the fuck did you do, sister?"

TWENTY-EIGHT

STEFANO

I thought about the text message from Marco Moscatelli. He hadn't been warning me out of some goddamn courtesy.

His message meant more than what he'd actually said. His words urged me to dig deep and pull an ace out of my sleeve. They pleaded with me to come to Chicago and fight for Val before the Russians showed up for her in the morning.

The man cared about his sister.

And he was afraid of Klimov.

Klimov had a reputation for double-crossing his allies and business partners. He took their money, their women, their territories, broke contracts, all before savagely killing them.

Marco knew this.

He also understood my reputation just as well. My word was my word. I prioritized the bottom line. I gave fair treatment to the men who honored their word.

Had I ever killed my business partners? Of course. I had a strict, zero tolerance policy for those playing games behind my back or touching what belonged to me.

Fuck around and find out.

"Is this the correct property entrance, boss?" Bruce asked.

I refocused on the blueprints detailing the Moscatelli estate, located in the middle of the Gold Coast neighborhood.

"It is. Keep in mind, while the mansion is large, the lot it sits on is quite small. Neighbors live close on either side."

"Tony said he checked, and Moscatelli has police in that district on his payroll."

I nodded. "That's to be expected, and it's an advantage for us. Calls made by the neighbors will likely go unanswered, giving us more time to get out."

I pointed to a small building at the back of the property.

"I want this area handled first. You run point, Bruce. This is where the guards sit when they aren't making their rounds. Tony's sure they change shifts at midnight, so we're going in at exactly 12:20. By that time, men from the earlier shift should be on their way home, and the current shift will still be setting up."

"Are we to kill or maim and disarm?" another man asked.

"Usually, for an ordinary mission, we'd incapacitate and disarm. I don't enjoy killing men for doing their jobs."

But fuck—there was nothing ordinary about this one. I pulled in a deep breath through my nose and made a deliberate choice.

"In this case, the Moscatellis broke into my home, killed Vignali men, and the motherfuckers took my wife. They shot at me... and my child. Now we need to send a message. This time, I'm commanding you to kill everyone on sight, until Saul and Aris Moscatelli are dead."

Each man looked me in the eye and nodded.

"Thank you," I said. "We're in and out within ten minutes. The goal is to kill Saul and Aris Moscatelli, yes, but don't forget the most important thing... I don't want Val harmed. I swear to

Christ, if I bring her back with another bullet wound, Enzo will never let me hear the end of it.

"So once the old man is dead, his second son is dead, and the girl is safe—we get the fuck out and back to this plane."

Bruce cleared his throat, bounced his leg up and down.

"What about Marco and the youngest Moscatelli?"

I understood his frustration. Both men had taken part in the home invasion and kidnapping. I gripped Bruce's shoulder.

"Unless it's kill or be killed, leave them alone. I believe they'll either stay neutral or come to our side at some point. I can't predict which, so use caution in any event."

Taking a minute to pause, I stared at the men filling Medico's plane and thanked Christ for them. All good men. I hoped like hell no more Vignali families would have to grieve the loss of their husbands, sons, and fathers.

"And finally," I said, "I want everyone back on board immediately, and wheels up before the Chicago PD figures shit out. Do not delay. Do not fall behind."

As promised, SUVs waited for us when we arrived at the airstrip, keys in the ignition with a note to leave them where we found them when finished.

I had the men disable the GPS in the cars and enter Moscatelli's address into the navigation apps on their phones.

We drove through the city toward Moscatelli's residential neighborhood. The snow piled along the sides of the boulevards reflected the moonlight, making it easier to see. The frigid lakeside air had probably driven the neighbors to their warm beds hours earlier.

We parked one block away from our target location, arriving just after midnight. Perfect timing.

Things were going according to plan.

Once I gave the signal, we vacated the SUVs and made our way down the street, lurking to the back of the property, and observing any activity inside the small cabin-like structure behind the main house.

I made a mental note. My child lived in my house now, and with any luck, sooner than later, so would more children. I considered how separating my work from our home might be a wise move. The house would be more secure with fewer people coming and going, making my family safer.

Not for a minute did I believe that same reason explained why Moscatelli kept his men out of the house, but for all intents and purposes, it was an advantage for me.

I would never leave my family in a mansion unguarded.

After the night they'd taken Val, Tony increased security even further on my estate, buttoning it all down, locking it up, and having it patrolled like a fucking military fortress.

It was go time.

As planned, four men entered the cabin with Bruce taking point. The rooms inside were too small to clear with any more men. We would end up in each other's way, and the last thing I wanted was for my soldiers to shoot one of their own.

The remaining five of us crouched near the hedges, using the shadows to our advantage. Within seconds after the others entered the cabin, shots fired. My crew held our position.

My men exited the cabin and gave an all-clear signal.

We surrounded the house.

Bruce's crew split off to breach the front door. With all eyes on the front of the house, the rest of us would enter through the back. They wouldn't expect it, and that gave us a distinct advantage.

Divide and conquer.

There were only nine of us, and we needed to make it seem like there were a lot more men invading the property.

My crew took the back and got into position under the windows near two entry doors. I counted down the seconds, waiting for Bruce to lock it in before I moved inside.

Shots rang out from the front of the house. I held up my hand, stopping the men from reflexively rushing in too soon.

Twenty seconds later, shouting started, and I gave the signal to move, then my strongest soldier kicked in the back door.

Two young men were in a four seasons room, scrambling to arm themselves before heading toward all the commotion.

Their actions seemed disorganized and shaky. Not soldiers. Untrained boys in their twenties. Based on the pile of coke on the tabletop, the rolled-up hundreds, and their expensive clothing, I guessed they were sons of mafia leaders or politicians.

"They're that way. Move your asses," one of them snapped and pointed, believing we were Moscatelli men.

We killed them with clean shots to the heads before moving in tandem with my men into the house. Their fathers should have taught them better. My son would never get caught in a situation like this one, and I would make damn sure of it.

We marched through the first level, clearing rooms.

When we entered a grand dining room with a circular marble staircase, several of Moscatelli's men filed down in our direction. All were armed to the teeth, wearing protective vests.

In an instant, we went from clearing unobstructed rooms to being surrounded with bullets flying.

My men and I scattered, finding cover wherever we could while returning fire. I heard a few barked swears, which meant one or two men took hits but not fatally.

We gave back just as well.

Someone had clearly tipped off Moscatelli. He seemed to anticipate our arrival, happy to sacrifice the guards in the cabin to get us inside to face his hidden squad of soldiers.

Did that son of a bitch Edgardo Lordi call Saul Moscatelli? It wouldn't have surprised me. Or maybe Angelo Medico did it. They were the only men outside of my organization aware of my plans.

Fuck. It could have been Marco. He'd let me know the Russians were coming to take my girl in the morning. Maybe he counted on me coming for her. Maybe he never cared about her or wanted to do business and had laid a trap instead.

It didn't matter. Not at this point.

Once again, I'd been underestimated.

They seemed to think they owned the element of surprise, but Tony and I had trained my lieutenants and soldiers to expect such surprises. We came to fight. We didn't expect to walk out the door with the girl and a polite wave goodbye.

I didn't see the Moscatelli family themselves, the pussies.

According to Tony's intel, Val should've been upstairs, beyond the firing squad, behind the last door on the right.

The tight, circular build of the staircase made it difficult to fire up at the men coming down. They had the higher ground. But it also made it harder for them to take aim at us, and we had more cover down below than they did on the stairs.

A scream pierced the air. Her scream.

It didn't come from the second floor. It came from behind me. My blood iced over. She wasn't upstairs.

One of my men waved me on from the far side of a buffet.

"Go, boss, and I'll cover your back."

I nodded, and as more bullets flew, I made my way through an ornate marble hallway and the kitchen to a sitting room.

What I found there sent another frigid shock through me.

My girl. My wife. My Val.

Blood stained her lips. Her eyes were bruised and swollen.

Aris had her hair wrapped around his fist and a fucking gun pressed against her head.

She seemed scared. She also seemed quite pissed.

Her light blue eyes burned with fury and fear. She had one hand balled into a fist, and the other pushed inside her robe, supporting the left side of her ribcage.

A beautifully feral woman. Wild, unpredictable—hurt.

"Is this what you're looking for, asshole?" Aris asked.

"Let her go," I said. "Hand her over, and my men and I will stop fucking up the decor."

He shook his head and grinned.

"Do you really think we're going to let you take her?"

I sighted my gun between his eyes.

"Do you really think I'm going to let you hurt her again?"

Aris sneered. "I don't think you have a fucking choice. She doesn't belong to you. She never belonged to you."

"She does now. Drop the girl, and I might let you live."

"Don't you dare," Val snarled. "This fucking monster must be put down. He threatened our son. He plans to sneak in and slit Enzo's throat. You cannot let this piece of shit live."

Aris jerked on her hair, but she didn't so much as whimper, not even as tears streaked down her cheeks.

"My, those are strong words for such a stupid little cunt."

His hideous words made me hiss through my teeth.

I gripped my gun tighter.

"Let her go now, or this bullet goes between your eyes."

"You won't fire at me," Aris said. "You shoot me, and you shoot her. Do you really trust your aim that much?"

Then he swung around to cover himself with her body, ducking his head to take away my clean shot.

Fucking coward.

"I'll shoot through her if it means killing you," I bluffed. "Wouldn't be the first bullet she's taken. But unlike you, your sister's strong, and she'll be okay."

Aris laughed. "I don't know, man... she's lost a lot of blood in the last few days. Not sure how much more she can take. And then there's the other problem."

"What's that?"

"How much of her is left when the Russians come to collect her. You couldn't even fight off my family. We broke into your house, took what you thought was yours, and there wasn't a fucking thing you could do to stop us. How you gonna take on Klimov?"

I inched to the left, to get a clear aim at my target without him noticing my movement.

"And still, here I am, so don't you worry, Moscatelli. I'll do whatever it takes to protect my family."

Fucker shifted to keep Val between us.

I ground my molars together so hard my jaw spasmed.

"Lower your fucking weapon and let the girl go."

He let out an unhinged laugh, like an insane cartoon villain.

"You're not going to kill me, you little bitch."

Valentina stared at me, and as she spoke, her voice cracked.

"You can't reason with him, Stefano. He's high, and even if he wasn't snorting shit, he doesn't understand reason."

Aris sneered. "That's right, you tell him, sister. Tell him how mean your big brother is and how there's no way I'll lose this little altercation."

"My big brother is Marco. You're just an asshole," she spat.

"Bitch." He pressed the gun harder against her temple.

Hard enough to make her wince. She would have a mark there. A bruise covering her soft temple.

I had sworn my girl wouldn't bear any more fucking marks made by other men. I pulled back the hammer on my gun.

"Last warning. Lower your weapon and back away from my wife, or I'll fucking kill you anyway."

I locked my gaze on Val's to send her a message. I wanted her to drop herself down fast to expose the motherfucker, so I could take my shot.

But she didn't nod in agreement.

Her gaze shifted behind me instead.

"No, you won't," a deeper male voice said.

Then he pressed a gun into my spine.

"You're a long way from home, boy," he said. "You must be fucking stupid to come for my daughter again. Someone needs to teach you New Yorkers the meaning of the word no."

Saul Moscatelli.

My gut twisted. Sweat ran down the sides of my face.

Getting Val away from her depraved brother, killing the motherfucker, and my ever-increasing rage had made me lose track of my secondary focus.

I didn't dare lower my weapon.

"Just give me the girl, and no one has to die," I said.

"I won't be giving you my daughter ever, Vignali."

Saul let out a dark chuckle and dug the barrel of his gun deeper into my spine.

"You came into my house, attacked my men, and tried to kidnap my daughter. I'm well within my rights to kill you— now I don't even have to hide your body."

TWENTY-NINE
STEFANO

Saul Moscatelli's hot breath hit the back of my neck.

"I got the most interesting phone call earlier tonight. A little birdie I know in New York called to tell me a nine-fingered, arrogant little pissant fuck, who didn't know how to fall in line, planned to break into my house and steal my daughter."

Edgardo Lordi, I wagered. A growl vibrated in my throat.

Moscatelli continued amusing himself with his monologue.

"At first, I thought he was full of shit. I thought he was stirring up trouble again, because that's all he's good for anyway, his childish pranks and schemes. But something in my gut said this time he meant it. So I thought about it. Did I know any man stupid enough, disrespectful enough, to attack my home?"

No idea how he didn't see the irony in what he'd just said.

"And you know what, son? I didn't think anyone would really be so bold. I thought, as a man of my age, my stature, my respect in the community, no one would dare. Ah, but then I remembered the mouthy son of a bitch from New York who tried to buy my daughter but came up short."

"Let her go," I gritted out through my teeth.

"No, I don't think I will. I'm not stupid like you, boy. I won't piss off the Russians a second time."

"How did you think it would end?" I snapped. "Why do you think the Italians don't do business with them? Everyone knows Klimov can't be trusted. You've signed your own death warrant. He won't leave this house with her tomorrow before he kills you and your sons."

"Why the fuck are you here?" Saul snapped.

Was he really so fucking stupid? I slowed my breathing.

"Give me the girl, and you won't lose a son tonight."

Saul chuckled. "You really are an arrogant son of a bitch, aren't you, Vignali?"

Aris laughed his stupid fucking insane laugh, the sound of it grating my raw nerves.

"I have a gun to your bitch's head," he said, "and my father has a gun on your back, and you still think you're getting out of here alive."

Outside of the room we stood in, gunfire still popped, but fewer shots now. I could only hope my men were coming out on top against the Moscatelli soldiers.

I quickly searched my mind for a way to get Val and me out of the situation. The only option was to stall.

If my men managed to get a handle on the situation in the other room, they would come to me. I had to wait and stay alive long enough for that to happen.

"So what exactly did the Russians offer you that was better than my deal?" I asked. "I offered you ten million for her and exclusive access the New York harbor. No one else in Chicago will ever get that."

Val raised her eyebrow.

I couldn't stop myself from winking at her.

"You did," Moscatelli said. "You made quite a compelling offer. If the Russians hadn't already claimed her..." He shook his head. "No, I still wouldn't have given her to you. I don't do business with men who take what belongs to me."

I scoffed. "Oh, come on, we both know the real reason you refused my offer. You thought Klimov would let you live. And aside from that, I didn't take anything from you. I'd never even met you until you showed up in my home."

"You've taken a lot from me. My daughter and her virtue. I wonder, boy, just what your role was early on. Did you convince her to fake her death, to disgrace her family, to run away with you? Now that people know she's alive and no longer pure, her reputation is ruined.

"You know as well as anyone that a woman in this life is only as good as her virtue. So, yes, you took that from me, and you also shamed my family by making her carry your bastard."

I could've pointed out that I had no idea she was a mafia princess until he showed up in my fucking house, or that I'd shunned this life during the time she faked her death. I could have explained that women weren't cattle meant to be sold to the highest bidder. That I had no idea she'd carried my son.

But he would have only shot me faster.

"And," he continued, "you stole Benedetta Capaldo."

"Bene—what? You were trying to marry her?"

No way he was serious.

"Of course I wanted her. I had a sit-down with her father on her sixteenth birthday."

Christ, this fucker was disgusting.

She'd grown up with his daughter.

He went on. "Do you know how much power that girl

comes with? And that was before someone killed all her male relatives. Yes, she would have been a fine wife for me."

Val glared at him through her swollen eyelids.

Maybe the old bastard didn't yet know I would be the one to decide who Benedetta married now.

I shrugged. "I hear she's still unmarried."

"It's too late now. See, I wanted a young wife like her not only for the power but to start the next generation of my family, but Benedict wouldn't hear of it. Said I was too old for her."

Moscatelli snorted like the idea amused him.

I bit down hard on my tongue and kept my mouth shut.

"I settled on another plan for Marco to marry her instead. It wouldn't be as nice as having the girl warming my bed, but her power would still come to me. The real purpose, after all.

"So I bided my time and scared off suitors who approached Don Capaldo. Killed a few. When Marco was ready, I met with Capaldo and made the offer to join our houses. Ha, but he'd already made a deal that would keep his daughter in New York."

"How the fuck was I supposed to know this, Moscatelli?"

"You should have done your homework, boy."

I flexed my fingers around my gun. I hated him calling me "boy" as much as I hated Lordi calling me "son."

"Oh, I did," I said. "That's why I murdered her uncles."

"Did you bother asking about any other claims?" he asked.

"Capaldo came to me for a deal, not the other way around. If you have issues with the way he does business, take it up with him. It has nothing to do with me or my fiancée."

Saul dug his gun deeper into my back, through my jacket, almost wedging it between two vertebrae, and I quickly schooled my expression, willing myself not to react. Saul couldn't see my face, but Aris could, and he got off on others' pain.

Val's face, on the other hand, expressed my pain for me and warned me not to give her twin anything at all.

"All of this…" I said. "Making bad business deals, losing out on millions, getting in bed with the Russians, because you got your feelings hurt when Capaldo didn't agree to either of your proposals? You've got to be fucking kidding me."

Jesus Christ, could my men take any longer to show up?

I grew tired of having this man's gun buried in my back, and based on the looks coming from Aris, I wasn't the only one losing patience.

The guy shifted from side to side on his feet and rolled his eyes at every word out of our mouths. Fuck. He better not put a hole in his twin sister just for something to do.

"This has nothing to do with my feelings," Saul said. "It's about you showing your elders the respect they deserve."

Shaking my head, I lost control of a suppressed grunt.

Goddamn it.

"I never disrespected you. I didn't know you. No one in New York gives a fuck what happens in Chicago. Not many of our families even know who the Chicago families are anymore. I didn't know because I didn't fucking care.

"Valerie—Valentina became mine the moment she had my son. She might not have understood that at the time, but it doesn't matter. She belongs to me, and her father's name makes no difference in the matter."

I caught her stare. No disagreement in her eyes. Only fire.

I toed a thin line with my words, but I had to keep spouting shit at Moscatelli to keep his finger off the trigger and buy us more time until my soldiers arrived.

"Big words from a man with no family to back him up. Are you aware of the situation you're in right now, boy?"

I nodded, my subdued rage fucking fuming.

"The situation? You mean watching a sadistic motherfucker with mommy issues hold a gun to my woman's head? Or are you referring to the fat, arrogant prick pushing one into my back, because somebody hurt his feelings?

"You've overestimated your importance, Moscatelli, and because shit didn't go the way you wanted it to, you're throwing a tantrum like a child. It's no wonder your son is a psychopath who belongs in a mental institution."

Val's expression hardened. Her chest pumped faster.

"No, he doesn't," she said. "He belongs in the ground."

Aris snorted and rolled his eyes once again.

"Shut up. No one cares what a stupid cunt thinks."

I glared at Aris, done. So fucking done.

"Saul, are you really ignorant enough to let this deranged animal roam the streets? Tell me, how many millions have you paid out in hush money to keep him out of prison?"

If Moscatelli planned to shoot me, he would have done it already. It seemed he wanted to hear himself talk more than he wanted me dead.

Men like him, who inflated their importance, preferred the sound of their voice to anything else. If I gave him something to talk about, he would do it for hours.

Thing was, I'd had enough.

I wanted this night over. I wanted Val in my arms where she belonged, then on board my borrowed plane. She and I needed to have a long talk, but not until I made sure she was all right.

She didn't look all right.

He'd beaten her severely again.

After she healed, no more fucking surprises. If I had to lock her up, I would do it. Hell, I would put a fucking GPS chip in her neck to keep her from vanishing again.

Never again would she get away from me. Not ever.

The time had come to lay all our cards on the table. My cards and hers, and we would figure it out.

"What do you think, Father?" Aris asked. "Which one should we kill first? On one hand, if we kill her first, Stefano will die knowing he failed. He'll get to watch the light fade from her eyes and know it was his fault. But if we kill him first, then she'll know her son will be alone."

Aris leaned in to whisper in her ear but spoke loud enough for us all to hear him.

"At least until I take that trip to visit my nephew. I could kill him, or I could make him one of us."

The blood drained from Val's face, the same way it had when she'd heard Marco's voice in our home.

"You wouldn't," she said, her voice shaking.

Aris tilted his head. "You know I would."

If he wasn't still hiding behind Val, I would've taken my shot right then, even if Moscatelli killed me afterward.

Enzo would be safe if Aris was dead.

"My offer is still on the table, Saul," I said. "Ten million, wired to the Cayman Islands as soon as our plane lands in New York. Then you can export whatever the fuck you want through the New York harbor."

"No," he said.

I shook my head at his belligerence.

"It's a damn good offer. Far more lucrative than anything the Russians will give you. So why the fuck are you taking the lesser deal? Do you not want to leave your heir with anything? Are you content letting the Moscatelli empire die with you?"

"It is a good offer," he admitted, "but do you know what the Russians will do to me if I turn my back on them now?"

"No, tell me," I said.

I was running out of ways to buy more time.

Gunshots coming from the front were fewer, but I still didn't know which side would come out on top. I listened for movements and voices.

It had been a while, and there was a possibility of police involvement soon. We'd been there a lot longer than I intended, and I didn't know the details of Moscatelli's arrangement with the Chicago PD.

Saul huffed out a breath stinking of bourbon.

"They would wage a bloody, savage war against me."

"So you're afraid of the Russians?" I asked.

"It's not that," he lied.

I could hear the fear in his voice.

"It's about respect, something your generation just doesn't seem to understand."

"It has nothing to do with respect," I said. "I can smell your fear. If you're so fucking afraid of the Russians, why would you do business with them in the first place?"

"What's my other option? I'm supposed to trust you? Because I don't trust you. You steal from your betters."

Moscatelli spoke in circles, around and around, and no one could reason with him or Aris.

I had very little left in my repertoire to distract him.

The gunshots up front slowed down more.

It would end soon.

Val wouldn't meet my gaze, her head down, her breath

shallow and fast, in full panic mode, likely thinking about our son.

I wished for a way to tell her that he would be okay without revealing how in front of her father and brother. Tony planned to take care of Enzo, raise him right, and protect him from her family. I couldn't make her see that if she wouldn't look at me.

"Can we just kill them already?" Aris whined. "This is boring me, and my high is wearing off. I need another bump."

"No, you fucking idiot," I snarled. "You can't kill her. Killing her is as bad as not delivering her to the Russians. You need her alive. And killing me starts a different kind of war that you're not equipped to handle."

"The Russians don't need you," Aris sneered. "And I'm not afraid of anyone who would align with you."

"That's right," Moscatelli said behind me, and I could hear the smile in his voice. "No one needs you, Vignali."

Finally, Val looked at me, her eyes wide and glassy.

Saul cocked back the hammer on his gun.

'*I love you,*' I mouthed to her.

My last words to her.

I braced myself for the bullet's impact, waiting for the pain or darkness or whatever the fuck dying brought with it.

The shot fired.

Blood covered my back, the side of my face.

The metallic scent of death filled the air.

I looked at my hands, still gripping my weapon.

The blood didn't belong to me.

THIRTY

VAL

My heart stopped as Saul's head exploded, time moving in slow motion as his body fell, and fell, and fell until finally hitting the wooden floorboards behind Stefano.

Marco appeared then, standing less than thirty feet away, his gun raised, a small plume of smoke rising and dissipating, his hands still wrapped around the grip.

For a long moment, no one said anything. All gunfire and shouting in the front of the house stopped, the complete silence broken only by the ringing in my ears.

Nausea overwhelmed me. Bile filled my mouth.

Stefano turned his head to see who had taken out Saul while keeping his pistol aimed in my direction. He'd never lowered his arms once, refusing to miss any clear shot at Aris he might get.

Stefano jerked his chin forward, directing Marco to move, then he quickly locked on to my gaze again.

"Marco, lower your weapon and walk over to me slowly."

My legs grew weak. The room spun around me.

Aris screamed, and the situation erupted into chaos.

"What the fuck did you do!"

He lurched forward, crashing against my backside, his hand dropping from my hair. His full attention shifted to Marco, so I took the only chance I might get.

'*Drop in three,*' Stefano mouthed, and I nodded.

One... two...

I jammed an elbow into Aris's stomach and dropped to the floor at his feet, ducking my face between my legs, protecting my head with both arms.

Marco might've planned to kill Aris next—I didn't know—but given the situation and Stefano's position, my older brother wouldn't have the chance. And I was glad for it. If not me, it should've been my son's father who made sure Aris didn't live through the night.

Stefano took the shot.

My ears rang louder.

Hot liquid rained down over me.

My twin's blood.

His body crumpled onto the floor next to me.

I lifted my face. Aris's dead eyes stared at me, accusing me, making sure I would never forget my part in his death.

The world went quiet again, kind of like someone hit a mute button. People spoke all around me, but I couldn't hear their voices. Stefano. Bruce. Marco. Santo.

I couldn't look away from my dead twin, the other half of me, the person who grew inside the same womb as me. Even in death, he wanted to control me, manipulate me.

I shook my head. *No, I won't let you.*

A bond had never existed between us, regardless of what others might have said. We only ever shared two things. A birth date and a last name.

Not anymore. I planned to change my name immediately,

and my birthday now belonged to me alone. We would share nothing. He was nothing. And I wouldn't let his eyes haunt me.

As I looked around me, everything seemed surreal.

What had we done? Was it really over? Aris finally gone?

Still, he stared at me, his eyes open but unmoving, like a sick Halloween prop. Blood pooled on the floor around his head, coloring the white rug beneath us. None of it seemed real.

How could it be?

My hands shook and my lips trembled as reality filtered back into my brain. So much blood. And the bodies.

Aris and our father. Dead.

Overcome with relief and sadness and dread and other emotions I couldn't even name, I began sobbing.

Stefano dipped down and wrapped his warm arms around me, my security blanket, then and always, and as he lifted me, he pressed a soft kiss on my temple.

"I've got you now, Angel," he whispered. "You're safe. He can't ever hurt you again or come for our son. You don't have to be afraid anymore."

He looked across the room at Santo.

"I'm sure you have a family doctor. Get him here now."

"H-her," I said.

I didn't know why I cried so much, so uncontrollably, but I just couldn't stop. It felt as if I had lanced a boil to get all the infection out of my soul.

Santo nodded and tossed over a wet washcloth.

Stefano pressed his lips to my forehead.

"I'm so sorry, Val. Sorry you had to see this. I'm sorry I couldn't stop him from hurting you sooner."

He carried me to the couch and held me, washing the blood off my mouth, dabbing at my lips ever so gently, while

Bruce and my brothers moved Aris and Saul's bodies to the cellar.

I pressed my face against Stefano's chest, listening to his strong heart beating, and watched them go, not looking away until they were gone. Part of me still feared Aris would get up, let out his maniacal laugh, and attack me again.

"He's gone now. He's never coming back," Stefano whispered, addressing my fear like he'd read my mind. "They'll throw his body into the incinerator tonight."

"Good idea," I whispered.

Adrenaline coated my nerves. God, when it wore off, the pain in my body and my face would roar back with a vengeance.

We stayed on the couch, just holding on to each other.

After brushing my fingertips over his cheek and scraping my nails through his beard stubble, I dropped my hand onto the cushion. My nonna had upholstered the couch herself. Dark green velvet. It was where she'd read bedtime stories to me.

"The doctor's here," Stefano said. "Let her tend to you. Then, if she says you can travel, we'll go home."

He shifted me, stood, bent to kiss my blood-stained lips.

"I'll just be in the kitchen with your brothers."

I grabbed his hand as he went to walk away. "Enzo?"

Stefano smiled, and then, without letting go of my hand, he pulled out his phone and got his underboss on speaker.

"The boy's sound asleep in his bed," Tony said. "I have the estate locked down like a fortress. Still, I posted a guard outside his room. Everything's quiet here, boss."

I nodded, so relieved, tears welling in my eyes again.

Stefano let my hand fall away from his as he headed to the kitchen to meet with Marco and Santo.

"I love you, Ace," I blurted.

He glanced over his shoulder. "I know, my angel."

"When did you last eat, Valentina?" the doctor asked.

I couldn't think. "Um, I don't know. I can't remember."

"Santo said it's probably been days. Is that right?"

Yes, of course she knew Santo. She'd been the one who treated the injuries that left scars all over him.

I stared at my feet and shrugged.

She understood this life. I didn't have to explain it to her.

Dr. De Rosa patted my knee. "It's okay not to remember everything right now. You're in shock, and it's masking your physical and emotional discomfort. I'm going to start an IV to hydrate you and get nutrients into your bloodstream. You'll have some euphoric effects... I'm going to include morphine."

She pulled on gloves and went right to work on my arm.

"Next, we'll clean up the wounds, and I suspect we'll need to address multiple broken ribs. Your brother's men are on their way in with my portable X-ray machine. But please, all that said, I want most for you to allow yourself the time you need to process what you've been through, okay?"

"I'll try," I croaked.

I murdered my twin. Stefano might have been the one to shoot him, but he'd done it for me. And it hadn't been a crime of passion. We planned to do it. A premeditated murder.

Neither of us would be punished for it, though. No one would report Aris's death, and his body would no longer exist.

Marco would circulate rumors.

Saul and Aris had traveled to the old country to visit relatives and conduct some business. Maybe the Sicilians or the Calabrians murdered them. Maybe Saul simply abdicated to Marco because he chose to retire in Italy. And everyone knew Aris would never leave his father's side.

Marco would set up a paper trail corroborating his story.

But leaders in a few of the right families would know the truth. Saul Moscatelli's heir had murdered him.

Marco had taken the family in name and by force, making his claim to the empire irrefutable.

The other person who could've but wouldn't make a claim on our family legacy was Santo since Santo had aided Marco.

As the doctor moved me this way and that, snapping images and giving me instructions, so many thoughts and questions blasted through my mind.

What did all this really mean?

What happened next for my brothers?

Would Marco disown me?

Would he honor the Moscatelli deal with the Russians?

Did any of it even fucking matter?

No. It totally didn't matter.

Stefano would see that I went home with him to our son, and without a doubt, he would kill Marco to do it if necessary.

I wanted my son to know his uncles, the men I'd loved my entire life, the only family I had left. Wait—I was a Vignali now. Stefano had said so himself. And I wanted my husband and my brother to unite our families amicably through our marriage.

As the morphine hit my system, nausea struck me, and I covered my mouth with both hands.

My head spun faster. My pulse pounded harder.

Dr. De Rosa handed me a vomit tray, then reached into her medical bag for a syringe and vial. She injected the liquid directly into my vein.

"It's to be expected. This will help ease the nausea."

Santo came into the room, his expression empty, a glass of water in one hand, a shot of whiskey in the other.

"Here, sister. I wasn't sure which one you needed most."

The doctor squinted and pushed her glasses higher on the bridge of her nose.

"No alcohol, please. Your sister can sip on the water." She turned back to me. "Three fractures, no organ damage. Use ice. Don't hold your breath, although breathing will hurt for a while, kiddo. Follow up with your regular doctor right away. We'll want you to start breathing exercises immediately."

I nodded and accepted the water from Santo. My stomach rebelled at the thought of drinking it. I sipped anyway, mostly just wetting my dry mouth and lips, while Santo sat on the couch next to me and shot the whiskey himself.

"What happens next, Santo?" I asked.

"What do you mean?"

"I mean, I'm assuming Marco's taking over?"

My little brother nodded. "Yeah. He's with Stefano. They're talking to the men and seeing to the injuries."

"Will Marco let the Russians take me?"

Santo shifted uncomfortably and scratched the back of his inked neck before making eye contact with me.

"No, he won't. He's making a deal with Vignali as we sit here now. I don't know the specifics, but we'll handle the fine print later. You'll go home with your man tonight."

I blinked at him slowly, like in a dream. "Why?"

"Why what?" Santo asked.

"Why did Marco kill our father?"

Santo sighed. "I don't know if I should tell you this, so keep it to yourself, but Marco had it planned for quite some time. Father's actions were becoming reckless.

"Marco didn't like the direction the old man was taking the family. The bad business deals, the old-school cruelty, the

Russians. Marco has his eyes set on the future, and Father just... didn't care."

"So this was a business decision?"

"Yes—I mean, no. Marco was planning to make a move in two years. He wanted more influence and other arrangements made first, but we couldn't just stand by and let Father destroy you or Klimov kill you. The deal was shit anyway, so Marco pulled the trigger early."

"Pun intended," he added with a snort.

With a small smile, I fake punched his arm.

What he'd said made perfect sense, especially after learning Marco had arranged my escape and the details of my life in Brooklyn. He'd always taken care of me.

And now? He was forging a bond between the Moscatellis and Vignalis through my marriage to Stefano.

My big brother. My hero.

"What about you, Santo?" I asked.

He flashed his boyish grin.

"Well, I'm Marco's second, which means I'm now forced to live a life listening to him preach about dividends and returns while staring at him blankly and pretending to know what the fuck he's talking about."

That made me feel a bit better, for Santo's sake, like maybe he had a chance at something normal. As far as that went in this kind of life anyway.

Marco walked in with a glass of bourbon.

"We've dealt with the bodies."

Stefano came in after him carrying a similar glass.

I squinted at his hand, at the gauze and medical tape. Was he missing part of his finger?

"What the fuck happened to you?" I demanded.

Everyone stared at me like I'd lost my damn mind. I spoke more slowly, so the boys could catch up.

"Your hand. You only have four and a half fingers. There should be five."

"Oh shit, when did that happen?" Santo asked.

"Four and three quarters," Stefano corrected, his tone so casual. "Long story. I'll tell you later."

Marco stared at him. "The fuck you will."

He sat on the chair opposite Santo and me, but Stefano remained standing as he turned his sharp gaze on Marco.

"We had a deal," Stefano snapped. "I'm taking her home, Moscatelli, by force if necessary. Do you mean to operate in bad faith already?"

Marco held up a hand, then canted his head my way.

"Our deal stands, and my sister can leave with you—if that's what she wants. Just because I won't send her with the Russians doesn't mean she automatically goes home with you. She goes back to New York only if she wants to. If not, you're leaving empty-handed and shipping the kid here."

Stefano rolled his eyes and then shifted his attention to me.

I had a choice, something no one had ever given me before. The choice to refuse freely, without consequences.

And like he'd read my mind, Stefano smiled, but doubt seemed to tighten it at the corners. Was he afraid of my answer?

Then, sweet mother of Christ, the man straightened his back, and that smile became a cocky smirk. So fucking hot.

"Would you please tell your brother that you want to come home with me and marry me and live the rest of your life on my massive New York estate with our son?"

As the doctor removed the IV, I glanced over at Marco.

"Well, it is a tempting offer. I mean, he has a really nice kitchen. Huge ovens."

Stefano rolled his eyes again, and Santo laughed.

"What are your terms, Ace? What are you offering?"

This felt different—so easy. I could tease him and vice versa.

An enormous weight had been lifted from our shoulders, and we could just be ourselves now. We could be like the kids we pretended to be when we first met.

Stefano shrugged. "Everything. But it's a forever commitment. There's no backing out for either of us. No second guessing, no decade-long breaks. And this does not end at death."

He held out his hand, his beautiful blue eyes warm despite the blood splatters on his face. Despite all the lies I'd told him.

"You're mine forever, Valentina Vignali."

Taking his hand, I let him ease me up onto my feet.

"You have a deal, Stefano Vignali. Now take me home to our son."

I turned to Santo and hugged him.

A sharp pain shot through me, and I couldn't help but shut my eyes for a moment before getting my voice back.

"You have to call me, okay? All the time, and I mean it."

My little brother nodded and gently hugged me.

Then I went to Marco. Tears burned my eyes. I needed to say so much to him, so much I needed to thank him for, but I didn't have the fucking words.

He eased me into an embrace and kissed the top of my head.

"It'll all be okay, sorellina. When everything settles down, I want to see you again and meet my nephew. Tell him I'm sorry if I scared him."

"I'll tell him all about you. I know he'll want to meet you. You better call me. God, I've missed you so much."

I let go of my brother and put my hand in Stefano's. We headed for the front door, and I didn't even care that I only had on a nightgown. I needed to breathe in my newfound freedom.

As we hit the doorstep, Marco called after us.

"A heads up, Vignali. I need to get my house in order. I can't do that while dealing with the Russians. I'll be telling Klimov that you took her. You need to be prepared to handle that."

Stefano didn't turn around.

His jaw flexed, and he nodded once.

"What does that mean?" I asked.

"We'll talk on the plane."

I already knew, though.

One fight had ended, and a new one waited for us at home.

But why the fuck was he was missing that finger?

THIRTY-ONE
STEFANO

Valentina's bare feet hit the sidewalk in front of the Moscatelli house, and her body trembled in the frigid night air from both the cold and shock.

She'd insisted on walking rather than letting me carry her.

This woman inspired me. I would never get enough of her. She was brave, strong, underestimated—not to mention created by God himself to be a Vignali, to be mine.

My queen.

Mia bellissima piccola regina.

I shrugged out of my jacket and wrapped it around her shoulders, and she tucked into the fabric.

"Thank you, Ace."

I grinned. "You're welcome, Angel."

Ace. The nickname she'd given me on our first and last real date. I received an invitation to a high-stakes poker game during our dinner at my father's casino, and she insisted we attend.

"I've always wanted to learn. Let's go," she'd said. "It'll be fun to see you play. Please, I don't want the night to end."

The beautiful girl who had turned every head in the room watched me turn my twenty-five grand buy-in into two hundred and seventy grand.

The memory made a wicked sense of pleasure erupt inside me and rush straight to my cock.

With a grin still plastered on my face, I squeezed her hand, then signaled to my men to get to the SUVs and Medico's plane.

Marco's car pulled up, and I opened the door for Val to slide onto the back seat.

"Why aren't we going with the men?"

"Your brother offered us your family's private jet, so we can have privacy on our way home. We have things to discuss, Val, and I need to take care of you. Apparently, your father had a shower installed, and I could really use that right now."

She laughed when I made a disgusted face.

We didn't talk on the drive to the airfield. We had so much to talk about, sure, but first we needed to hold each other. To feel the other. To know that nothing could rip us apart again.

Even after boarding the plane, we stayed that way, quiet and clinging. I pulled a blanket around us and wrapped my arms around her beneath it. She cuddled against me, her head on my chest, her arms around my waist.

Once the plane reached cruising altitude, I used the lavatory at the back of the cabin to wash away her father's blood.

The limited water supply meant it wouldn't be the long, luxurious shower I needed, but it would be good enough.

As I stood under the water, my craving for Val intensified.

I wanted her with me. I needed to be inside her. But she was hurting, and the small shower didn't offer enough space for her to be comfortable. She needed time to recover from her injuries, the physical and the emotional wounds.

I didn't want to push her too quickly.

After scrubbing all the blood, sweat, and gore off, I stepped out of the lavatory with a towel wrapped around my hips, expecting to find some clothing in a small closet.

Instead, I found my girl lying naked on the bed.

I stared at the bruising covering so much of her body.

Rage reignited in my gut, burning up my fucking soul.

I'd killed the sick motherfucker who hurt her, but it didn't seem to be enough. I'd taken too long to get her away from him.

After moving my ass around to her side of the bed, I sat down and pulled the sheet over her, then I traced her curves with my fingertips. Using my left hand, of course.

Odd timing, maybe, but I thought for a minute about how I had planned to die if she didn't survive.

"How about a nap before we land?" I asked. "The pilot rerouted around some weather, so there's plenty of time."

She shook her head, threw off the sheet, and spread her legs wide to show me her sweet little pussy.

Fuck.

"I don't want to take a nap," she whined. "I want you to use your tongue and show me how much you missed me."

I grabbed for the sheet, and she kicked it out of my reach.

"It's the morphine, Angel. You don't know what you're saying. Your body needs time to heal. I won't push you."

Even as the words left my mouth, I stroked my cock.

She flashed a devilish little smile, the one she knew made me throb with want. Full of innocence, yet not innocent at all.

"You're not. I'm pushing you."

She pulled herself onto her knees with a grimace and put her arms around my neck to whisper in my ear.

"I need you to erase every trace of their touches, their stares, and replace them with yours. Make me forget them. I want you to own every mark he left on me, make it all belong to you."

I should have been dead tired or maybe even just dead.

My weary bones ached, and I should have wanted only to crawl onto the bed and hold the woman I loved while we slept.

Exactly what I would do.

After filling her with my cum.

I got up from the bed, went to the swiveling captain's chair bolted to the floor, and sank into it.

"Come here, Valentina."

She stood and made a show of turning slowly in a tight circle to expose every bruise on her body. Some I'd seen at the ball, and some I hadn't. Others were only days old, some just a few fucking hours old.

Never again. She would never endure that again.

As she came over to me, I forced the monster back into its cage in the darkest part of my soul. She needed me.

Deal with the rage later.

I grabbed on to her waist, pulling her in close while moving my towel to the side to stroke myself.

"Tell me what hurts, Angel."

"Everything hurts. But I'll show you what hurts the most."

She took my left hand and placed it above her breast—over her heart—and pressed her hand on top of mine.

"This broke when they took me away from you."

"Then let me make it better."

I moved our hands away and put mine on her back, gently pressing her body down, so I could place a kiss over her heart. I trailed more kisses down to her nipples, kissing them, pulling them between my lips.

She gasped and pushed her fingers into my hair, dug her nails into my scalp, then climbed onto my lap, lining up the entrance of her wet cunt with my hard cock.

Jesus, she was perfect, but the pain came through loud and clear in her eyes.

Once her fractured ribs healed, I would let her bounce on my cock all she wanted. I would give her the rough ride she craved. But in that moment, I needed to make love to the woman who would soon be my wife. Needed to feel her, to love her, and taste her.

"Get back on the bed, Val."

She pushed out her lip to pout. "But—"

Absolutely the morphine.

"Now," I commanded.

I gave my cock a few more strokes as she lay on the bed, then I prowled up between her legs, parting her soft thighs and gently positioning them on my shoulders.

She giggled. "What are you doing?"

"Praying."

I placed gentle kisses on her thighs, dragging my mouth over her skin until I got to her hot little pussy.

Just as sweet as ever.

"Stefano, please. I need—"

"I've got you, Angel. Relax and let me take care of you."

Slowly, I licked and sucked, building her climax minute by minute without allowing her to orgasm.

When her thighs went lax on my shoulders, I focused on her clit, swirling my tongue, increasing the pressure until her thighs began to shake and her breathing became rapid huffs.

Val looked so beautiful spread out for me.

When she let everything go and gave over to me completely, nothing made me prouder as a man than making my woman come when I commanded it.

Once she arched her back and let a cry of pleasure escape from her lips, I moved down to lap at her juices and fuck her with my tongue.

She reached for me, so I offered my left hand.

"Stefano, please. I need you. Please," she breathed.

So fucking delicious when she begged.

She'd been through so much pain, and all I wanted to do was make her forget it all and give her whatever she wanted.

Another part of me wanted to take her hard, claim what belonged to me, and punish her for her lies. And I would after she had time to heal. She would get her punishment when I believed the time was right for it.

And when I punished her for the lies, I would leave marks. I would make it hurt—and she would beg for more. Once healed, she would have some very long nights ahead.

I could be angry at her later. I could be vengeful later.

Until then, I just wanted to be grateful she'd survived, grateful to have her back where she belonged.

Still, in her condition, I doubted I could lay her out and make love to her without hurting her under my weight.

I could think of only one way to make it work. I kissed her thighs again, then pulled away to stand up.

"Did you miss me, my angel?"

"Yes, sir," she whined.

"Do you want to show me how much?"

She crawled to the edge of the bed and sat back on her heels while trying to school her face to hide the pain.

"Not like that, Angel. I don't want you to hurt."

I took her hand, helped her off the bed, and led her back to the chair, where I sat and took her onto my lap.

"Be my good girl and show me how much you missed me."

I kept my hands on the outside of her thighs, where the bruises weren't as dark. I guided her down as she took my entire shaft in one smooth but slow motion.

Fuck, she was so wet, so tight, so fucking hot.

Seated on my cock, she made slow circles with her hips.

"Like this?" she asked.

"God, yes."

Panting, I pushed my fingers into her hair and pulled her lips down on mine. She apologized for her deceit and made promises with a long passionate kiss.

And I let her.

She owed me more, but that kiss would do for now.

Caught up in her, in the sensation of our connected bodies, I moved my hands to her hips and supported her weight as she rode me up and down. I slipped my thumb between us to put pressure on her clit.

"Oh god," she cried. "That's literally so good."

She grabbed the back of the chair to hold on.

Her inner walls contracted around my cock.

Not another goddamn thing better existed than when her tight little cunt gripped me and begged me to come.

"Just like that, Angel. Don't stop. Take all of me."

She threw her head back, so I latched on to her nipple, sucking and biting as she cried out my name and came in a hot wave of pleasure.

"Stefano, yes, oh god, yessss."

I followed with a roar of satisfaction and kept her moving

up and down on me, supporting her weight, guiding her through her orgasm while prolonging mine.

Finally wrung out, we clung to each other, working to slow our heartbeats and catch our breath.

As carefully as I could, I lifted her and moved to the bed. I tucked her into a fluffy white comforter and kissed her forehead before going to the lavatory to clean up.

Before climbing in to hold her, I sent Tony a message to let him know we were on the way home.

Then I wrapped my arms around Val's delicate body, careful not to put pressure on her ribs. Having her in my arms was all I could ask for and more than I deserved.

We slept for a little more than an hour, until the plane hit turbulence.

The pilot came on the intercom indicating we shouldn't worry, but it did make sleeping difficult.

Val bit into her bottom lip.

"Is this where we start talking about all the things?"

After a long, thoughtful moment, I decided against it.

"No. We need to sleep, eat a proper meal, and hug our son before we talk about everything that's happened, but there is something I want to tell you while we're alone."

She squirmed, but I held her more tightly against my chest.

"I want to send our son away."

Harsh words to hear, but it had to be said.

Every syllable weighed like a ton of bricks on my heart while the sentence lingered in the air between us.

"What?" Val asked, her voice cracking.

"Not forever. I want him to attend a private boarding school where he'll be safe."

"What?" she repeated. "No. He'll be safe with us. We're his parents. No one could possibly keep him safer than you."

"Something happened while you were gone."

"Does this have to do with your finger?"

I nodded. "What do you know about the Commission?"

She blinked up at me. "Why?"

"Because I took my father's seat."

"Why, Stefano? That's not at all what you wanted."

"I didn't have a better option. The finger was punishment for breaking the treaty when I came to see you at the ball. Their pound of flesh for me going to Chicago."

"Apparently flesh has increased in value since the treaty was written," she snarked.

I kissed her forehead and moved my lips to her temple.

"Yeah, I was about to do it again, and they knew it, so they made me an offer. If I joined the Commission, they would sanction any further actions I took in Chicago."

"Meaning?"

"Meaning I could come get you without losing a limb. And they promised me an army. The council's CEO wants the treaty abolished. He believes Chicago should be taken under New York's control."

Val shook her head, her hair brushing my chest.

"If he thinks that's possible, he hasn't been to Chicago."

I ran my hand down along her spine.

"You might be right, Angel. Either way, I signed the papers, and I'm now a member of the Commission's leadership. Then Edgardo Lordi told me it would take weeks to plan the mission, but you would have been gone by then.

"I did make that point very clear, but it didn't matter. He still put me in a position where if I came to Chicago on my own and lost, he could wipe his hands clean of it and probably even punish me again. But if I succeeded—"

"It would give him an opening to take the city."

"Yes."

"So what are we going to do about it, Stefano?"

"I'm going to kill him. I've been planning it for years. He's the man who murdered my father and brother. But he's cunning. And not only smart, but also strategic. Going after him is going to be very dangerous."

Val sighed. "I guess if he wasn't dangerous, he wouldn't be head of the Commission."

"I'm concerned he'll use my love for you and Enzo as a weakness. He won't hesitate to come after my heir."

Val sat up. I wanted to drag her back down to lie next to me again, but she wriggled away and turned to face me.

"I tried for nine years to protect my son from the world you and I were born into. But it didn't work, Stefano, it just made him more vulnerable. He didn't know what to expect, where to turn, or how to fight if he needed to.

"It's become very clear that I cannot run from my past. I cannot run from who I am or from you, and forcing Enzo to do the same is indistinguishable from being a negligent parent."

I sat up. "So what the fuck are you saying?"

"I'm asking you to teach our son about this life. It's his life too. Teach him how to defend himself and how to thrive, not just survive. That can't happen if you send him away. He needs to learn who we are and what it means."

She took my hands in hers, her eyes hardening with resolve.

"It won't be easy for either of us, Ace, but the only way to keep him safe is to make sure he's prepared. I know we can do this. And you know why? Because one day you'll be king of kings. You weren't supposed to be, but you're the only Vignali who ever could be. And you must prepare our son for what that means."

I fucking loved this woman, the faith she had in me.

She had a point, one I couldn't argue.

Enzo was my heir.

And at only nine, he had the makings of a fearsome prince.

THIRTY-TWO

STEFANO

Val and I walked through the front door of our home in New York just after 6:00 a.m.

With an elated cry that ripped out my heart, Enzo ran past me to his mother. I hesitated to extend my arm and stop him.

"Careful, son, your mother's in a lot of pain."

It didn't matter. She still dropped to her knees and caught him in a full hug with tears streaming down her face.

Tony stood a short distance away. As he greeted me with a clipped nod, a tense smile curved his tight lips.

My soon-to-be wife and our son deserved a few minutes alone, so I gestured for my second to follow me to the operations room. I wanted to check in to be sure everything was in hand, and then I could go to bed and sleep for a fucking week.

Grim lines formed across Tony's forehead after we entered the ops room. He gripped my shoulder.

"Thank Christ you're here, Stef. I worried they would get to you. I don't know how to say this, but when the Medico plane hit the tarmac, motherfuckers were there waiting."

"What? Who was waiting, Tony?"

He didn't answer my question.

Instead, he handed me his phone with an image displayed.

A photo of my soldiers.

Bruce.

Good Vignali men. Slaughtered.

The eight who fought for me only a few hours earlier.

Severed hands. Limbs. Heads. All in one massive pile.

My men had been taken apart piece by fucking piece.

More photos followed—mass mutilation documented methodically, like some sick accounting ledger.

Body parts stacked. Gasoline poured.

Heat surged through me so violently my body rejected it. I gagged, barely turning in time as bile scorched my throat.

Not weakness. Fury.

Tony thrust a trash can into my hands, but I never looked away from the screen. I watched every fucking frame.

I would remember every detail.

Next, a video played...

A struck match.

An inferno.

Then a heavily accented voice spoke over crackling flames.

"Bratva does not honor your treaty. Send Klimov's whore back to Chicago or we'll come to your doorstep next."

Silence settled over the room.

Something inside me went still.

He'd said the one thing that could never be unsaid.

"Never," I said quietly. "She's mine."

And the city would be reminded what happened to men who touched what belonged to me.

READ THIS BOOK NEXT

The war is no longer contained.

Every threat against Stefano's family is answered
without mercy. The Russians circle. The Commission
watches. And the woman he claimed as his own remains
at the center of it all.

Stefano does not retreat.
He eradicates.

The dynasty is sealed in Cruel King.
Get it here: **geni.us/cruel-king**

ALSO BY KELLIANN NELSON

CRUEL KINGS

Book 1 – Wicked Villain

Book 2 – Savage Enemy

Book 3 – Cruel King

DYNASTY OF OBSESSION

Book 1 – You Belong Here

Book 2 – Never Let You Go

ABOUT THE AUTHOR

Kelliann Nelson writes dark romance defined by obsession, power, and unwavering devotion. Her stories follow sovereign men, dangerous dynasties, and heroines claimed at the heart of empires built by men who will burn the world to protect what is theirs. Her novels deliver emotionally intense arcs, calculated dominance, and loyalty that does not bend.

For reading order, exclusive newsletter updates, and content notes, visit **kelliannnelson.com**.

instagram.com/kelliannnelsonbooks
facebook.com/kelliannnelsonbooks
pinterest.com/kelliannnelsonbooks
tiktok.com/@kelliannnelsonbooks

DOMESTIC VIOLENCE HELP

Partner abuse, sibling abuse, and child abuse are forms of domestic violence. These themes may appear in Kelliann Nelson's work as part of a character's history or as narrative conflict, but they are never romanticized.

If you or someone you know is experiencing domestic violence, help is available.

National Domestic Violence Hotline
📞 1-800-799-7233
🌐 thehotline.org

www.ingramcontent.com/pod-product-compliance
Lightning Source LLC
Chambersburg PA
CBHW061631190726
48289CB00006B/1568